"*Bloodsuckers* is a delicious blend of mainstream [...] biting social commentary. Sink your teeth into this [...] *New York Times* bestselling author of *Code Zero* a[...]

"*Bloodsuckers* takes modern politics and adds va[...] already know all the jokes you're making!) to make it actually new and exciting. Washed-up reporter Steve Edwards can't believe what he sees when a Presidential candidate is gunned down by a man who then disappears before his eyes, apparently transformed to a bat. But that's just the beginning as Steve finds he's been framed for the crime and what he's seen is just the very tip of a blood-drinking iceberg. Ventrella's quick, bright dialogue punctuates the adventure with dry humor even as he ratchets the tension up towards an ending that might just surprise even the jaded reader. Highly recommended!" —Ryk E. Spoor, author of *Grand Central Arena* and *Phoenix Rising*

"*Bloodsuckers* draws back the curtain of politics and confirms the fear we've all suspected about our leaders for decades. A cutting expose of the—what, this is fiction? Naw... Well then. Funny, quick, too smart for its own good. Had me viewing politicians with new suspicion." —Mur Lafferty, Campbell-Award-winning author of *Ghost Train to New Orleans* and *The Shambling Guide to New York City*

"Sharp as a stake through the heart, *Bloodsuckers* works both as an entertaining thriller and as satire of our current out-for-blood political landscape. I loved the characters, the political insight and the final revelation!" —Dennis Tafoya, author of *The Poor Boy's Game* and *The Wolves of Fairmont Park*

"What could be more horrifying than vampires with a taste for blood? Vampires with a taste for politics, as well. Mike Ventrella gives us both, plus action, adventure, laughs and chills, in *Bloodsuckers*, a political satire with bite." – Jon McGoran, author of *Drift* and *Deadout*

"Politics, intrigue and vampires—a match made in Washington, D.C. A bloody good political thriller that sucks you in from the start and gets its teeth into your imagination." – Gail Z. Martin, author of *Reign of Ash* and *Deadly Curiosities*

"The book is a lot of fun. It manages to be many things at once. It's both thrilling and humorous. Both politically charged and poignant without being preachy." – Lucas Mangum, author of *Flesh and Fire*

Bloodsuckers
A Vampire Runs for President
by Michael A. Ventrella

FANTASTIC
BOOKS

© 2014

First published by Double Dragon Press.

Cover art by Thomas Nackid, https://tomnackidart.blogspot.com

This novel is a work of fiction. All the characters, organizations, and events portrayed in it are likewise fictional, and any resemblance to real people, organizations, or events is purely coincidental.

All rights reserved. Printed in the United States of America. No part of this publication may be reproduced, stored in a retrieval system, or transmitted in any form or by any means, digital, electronic, mechanical, photocopying, recording, or otherwise, or conveyed via the internet or a website without prior written permission of the publisher, except in the case of brief quotations embodied in critical articles and reviews.

Fantastic Books
1380 East 17 Street, Suite 2233
Brooklyn, New York 11230
www.FantasticBooks.biz

ISBN: 978-1-5154-5828-9

First Fantastic Books Edition, 2024

Acknowledgments.

Many thanks go to the writers, editors and friends who gave insightful comments to early drafts of this book.

Special thanks go to Jonathan Maberry and the gang at the Liars Club, especially Marie Lamba, Jon McGoran, and Dennis Tafoya.

Early readers assisted, including Melinda Berkman and of course my wife Heidi Hooper.

Other friends made certain plot suggestions and they might discover certain characters named after them in this book—but these characters are not based on the real people, so don't go around thinking that the real Zachary Oak believes in vampires. And finally, thanks to my editor J. Thomas Ross.

Bloodsuckers is dedicated to the real John Finnegan and the real Marty Gear. I wish they were both still here to read this.

BLOODSUCKERS

Cool water rolled slowly down her neck, curving between perfect breasts, caressing her stomach. Slowly, her skin absorbed the moisture.

She opened another plastic bottle, but this time swallowed its contents. Energy flowed through her, renewing her. Placing the empty container in the sink, she gave herself the once-over in the full-length mirror next to the tub. She twisted to admire her naked body, then parted full red lips and tossed herself a kiss.

She looked good as a blonde.

Everything was going as planned. This would be one of her easiest assignments ever.

Maybe she'd buy a boat with the payment. She liked boats.

Shaking her head to give her long hair a bed-tousled look, she stepped from the bathroom. Her toes rubbed sensuously against the plush hotel rug as she silently slunk across the deserted sitting room.

The full moon cast a bright rectangle of light in the dark room. The balcony curtains danced in the cool summer breeze wafting from the Charles River through the open sliding glass door. The only artificial illumination came from a small office off the main room of the suite.

"The time of divisiveness is over," she heard Randolph Brunswick say quietly. "America needs to come together!"

She peeked into the office to find the Governor staring at a laptop screen. He grabbed a handful of M&Ms and popped them into his mouth. He then began typing methodically, hunting for each letter. She shook her head. You'd think a man who might be President soon would know how to use a computer.

"As I accept your nomination, it is with the understanding that it is far better to work across the aisle to get things accomplished than to seek unrealistic goals that… that…"

He paused, let out a heavy sigh, and rubbed his eyes. "Still time…"

She glided into the room, circled to the other side of the table, and silently stood before him, waiting.

Brunswick closed the laptop and looked up. His eyes narrowed as he stared, as if his mind couldn't decide whether she actually existed.

"Good evening, Governor," she purred with a deep Southern accent.

Brunswick reared back. His mouth opened and closed but no sound emerged. His gaze covered her trim body.

She smiled.

"What… what the hell is this?" he finally managed. "How did you get in my room?"

"Now, now, sugar. We have other things to discuss." She edged closer and locked her eyes with his.

"We do not!" he replied. "The Secret Service is just outside my door, young lady…" He stopped talking and licked his lips.

She slinked forward. "Come, Governor. Let's look at the moonlight and discuss this."

Brunswick rubbed his eyes, shook his head, and stared back. "No!" He reached for the desk phone. "I don't know what sort of game you think you're playing—"

She dived for the phone and slapped it off the table before the Governor could react.

He jumped up and his chair fell to the side. "How did you—"

"Here, look at me," she said. "Just calm down, it will be all right."

Brunswick dashed toward the door.

Shit. This was supposed to be an easy assignment. She should have known that someone with an ego big enough to want to be President would be difficult. She swooped before him and he reared back.

"You can't get away, honey. I'm much faster than you can ever be." She held out a hand and concentrated on his eyes. Brunswick blinked. His mouth opened and he backed away. Making sure his gaze remained fastened to hers, she stepped forward and grabbed his wrist. "You'll think much clearer if we step out onto the balcony."

Beads of sweat gathered on his forehead. "I will?"

"Yes. You need some air."

"Yes," he replied in a breathy monotone. "Yes. I need some air…"

She slipped her arm through his and leaned close to whisper in his ear as they walked together toward the sliding glass door. He nodded slowly in response.

She opened the door wider for him.

He stepped onto the balcony. The summer breeze blew his few remaining hairs across his forehead, destroying his inadequate comb-over.

Late night traffic rumbled below the balcony on Memorial Drive. The ever-present protesters chanted and shouted below, demanding the governor's attention. A few bored cameramen, stationed at the hotel in case the governor decided to go out for a late night snack, slouched against trees or streetlamp posts, keeping silent watch. Behind her, a tinny voice came through the phone headset, which lay across the floor. "Hello? Governor? Are you there?"

"Now would be the best time," she said.

Brunswick nodded with a smile, oblivious to the phone. He dragged a chair toward the small stone wall, climbed on it, and then took another step onto the wall itself.

"This is a wonderful idea!" he said. He raised his arms, waved to the crowd below, and stepped off.

As sirens blared and people screamed, she congratulated herself on a job well done. "Norman Mark for President," she mumbled.

The door to the suite burst open just as she flew away.

ONE

Karl Weaver adjusted his tie and gave an exaggerated yawn in an attempt to hide his fear.

The secretary continued to ignore him. She clicked away at her computer and typed periodically. Karl didn't imagine she was really working—probably playing Farmville or tweeting about what she had for lunch.

Karl shook his head. He wondered where literacy in America was headed with more and more people seemingly unable to maintain an attention span longer than a hundred and forty characters.

Still, since nothing else in that office was worth looking at, Karl kept his gaze on the secretary. A black girl, mid-twenties, well-dressed. Gold necklace around a soft neck. Hired for her looks, no doubt.

His nervousness prevented a full appreciation of the girl.

Nick had wanted to see him. *Nick.*

And no one says no to Nick.

Karl shifted in his seat. He glanced at the clock, clasped his hands together, unclasped them, and scratched at his nose.

The door finally opened. The secretary waved him in but had otherwise served no function except to look pretty in the waiting room.

Karl stood, needlessly adjusted his tie again, took a deep breath, and walked in.

In a few seconds, his eyes adjusted to Nick's dim office. One of those green banker lights illuminated the papers on Nick's desk while leaving the face of the man behind in shadows.

His host pointed to the comfortable chair facing the large mahogany desk.

Karl walked to the chair and sat, taking in the office.

Bookshelves lined the walls, full to overflowing with nonfiction—American history mostly, along with popular political and sociological treatises from both the right and the left. The absence of photographs or other personal items gave the office the generic look of a catalog display.

"Nice to see you again, Karl," Nick said, leaning back in his chair. "Not really, but that's the right thing to say."

Karl nodded. Apparently, after all this time, Nick was still angry with him. Perhaps rightly so.

Nick clasped his hands on top of the desk. "I have a task for you."

Karl resisted squirming in the chair. He coughed slightly. "Yes, well. Right to the point, I see. We haven't spoken in years, and now you have something you need me for? What can I offer you that one of your employees cannot?"

"I can't trust my employees with this. This is about Norman Mark."

Karl nodded slowly. "I thought it might be, given the urgency of your call."

Nick leaned back, clearly enjoying this. "Tell me what you think of Norman Mark."

Karl lifted his head and gazed at Nick through slitted eyes. What was he getting at? Did he want the truth? "Mark," he said slowly, "is a dangerous liberal who, if elected, will close down my fracking operation and put me out of business. He's practically said as much on the campaign trail."

Nick pressed his fingers together. "What if I told you I could prevent that from happening?"

Karl smiled. "Well, I'd believe you, of course."

"As you should. So you concede that my payment would be sufficient?"

Karl shook his head. "Finnegan's still ahead in the polls. If he wins, what good is your promise then?" He tried to keep his voice calm, but the thought that he was negotiating with Nick chilled him.

Nick nodded. "True enough. You have me there. Very well, then. I can stop the protesters now. Before the election. Surely that is worth something."

Karl considered. "Yes. Yes, I think you could. And the lawsuits?"

"Consider them gone."

Karl smiled, but it was a forced smile. Getting those goddamn hippies off his back would be wonderful, not to mention the lawyers—but what did Nick want in return?

Nick stood and held out a hand. Karl jumped up and accepted, hoping Nick would not notice his sweaty palms. They shook once, let go, and sat back down in unison.

"Now that's settled," Nick said, "let's discuss the details. I need you to… perform."

"Perform. It's been years since I last performed."

Nick tapped a finger on his desk. "Are you refusing?"

Karl swallowed. "No, not at all. I'm sure I can do this for you. And who is the target audience for my performance?"

"Norman Mark."

Karl burst out laughing. It was spontaneous; he couldn't stop it.

Nick waited patiently.

Karl collected himself, crossed his arms, uncrossed them, and gave Nick a long look. "When you said this involved Norman Mark, I didn't think you wanted me to assassinate him."

Nick smiled.

Karl stared at Nick for a very long time before speaking again. "May I ask why?"

Nick shook his head sadly and pursed his lips.

"You know he's a vampire, right?"

This time it was Nick's turn to laugh—but it was short, dismissive, and disappeared immediately. His face once more became unreadable. "This is not your usual assassination; I'll give you more details later. I have a specific time and place where I want this done. Very public."

"I'll need a way to sneak a weapon in."

"I am certain you will find some method," Nick said. "This is your area of expertise, after all—not mine."

"Yes."

"There's a big Democratic rally coming up in mid October," Nick said. "Norman Mark will be there. It's in a baseball park. One of those enclosed box seats at the top should give you a good vantage point overlooking the stage."

Karl found himself getting excited over the possibility—the *challenge*. The assassination of a presidential candidate would surpass his other accomplishments. "Excellent. We also need a scapegoat to distract the police and the press. It should be one of those conspiracy nuts shouting that Mark is a vampire."

"The Batties."

"Is that what they're calling them these days? As in 'you'd have to be batty to believe that'?"

Nick tilted his head. "Blame Jon Stewart for that one. We need more than just a Batty, though. We need a loner, a loser—the kind of person who has been beaten down and shit on by life. Someone who might snap and do something like this. Someone without a family."

"Why without a family?"

Nick spread his hands. "I'm not completely heartless."

Karl paused, and then spoke before Nick could read something into it. "We also need someone who conceivably could have access to the assassination spot. A person who'd have a reason to be up there."

Nick nodded. "I have already thought of all that." He reached for his keyboard, typed a few words, and clicked the mouse. After a few seconds, he smiled and spun the screen to face Karl.

Karl leaned forward and read the highlighted by-line on a newspaper article.

"By Steven Edwards."

TWO

Richmond Times-Dispatch,
September 25
VIRGINIA GROUP CLAIMS NORMAN MARK IS A VAMPIRE
By Steven Edwards

Conspiracy theories in politics are nothing new. There are those who believe that certain politicians belong to the Illuminati or other secret organizations bent on world domination. There are those who think the world is controlled by the Elders of Zion or the Trilateral Commission.

But never in American history has a group seriously suggested that a politician is, in fact, a real, honest-to-goodness vampire.

Zachary Oak leads one such group, inconveniently headquartered in the tiny town of Spring Grove on the outskirts of Richmond. They believe that Democratic Presidential candidate Norman Mark is one of the "children of the night."

He has a room set aside in his home specifically to hold his collection of vampire documentation. A large poster of Norman Mark hangs over his desk, emblazoned with large red letters that say "BLOODSUCKER."

Oak laughs when asked about the poster. "I was holding that sign at a rally recently, and people thought I was objecting to his tax policies."

He makes it clear that this is not just about Norman Mark. "Vampires have been around forever, controlling us behind the scenes. Mark is just one of the most prominent ones in recent history."

Oak says he knows most people won't believe him, but that won't stop him from spreading the word. "They usually work behind the scenes so nobody realizes their power. It's kind of unusual for one of them to be so public."

Oak, a retired truck driver, stated that he learned about the vampire conspiracy from pamphlets and books he has bought over the years. "Now that people can self-publish, there are more of them," he said. "Because before, the vampires made sure the big publishers didn't print nothing."

Oak started the group Virginians Against Vampires about ten years ago. The dozen or so local members occasionally get together, review their materials, and discuss who might be a vampire. The group claims that learning about vampires has become easier thanks to the rise of the internet.

Oak is not afraid of reprisal from the vampires. "If they did attack me or other vampire believers, that would make it obvious that they are out there," he explains. "Someone would investigate and find out. But they ignore us and laugh at us, so they can remain hidden."

When reminded that such an ironic conundrum is pretty convenient for Oak's cause, he shrugs. "They're clever. And since they have the power to control minds, they ain't too worried. Look how long they've gone so far without being exposed."

As evidence of Mark's vampirism, Oak checks off a list of suspicious items. "Ask yourself why you never see Mark out in the daytime. Or why he looks so pale. Better yet, find out where he was born, or if there's any evidence of him existing before he took over his business from his father. Find out why the school he supposedly attended in Switzerland burned down, taking all the proof he had ever gone there."

He also discusses the candidate's obvious charisma. "He's handsome and very likeable," Oak says. "They're all like that. That's part of their vampire powers."

Then Oak drops the bombshell.

"That's how he killed Brunswick, you see."

Governor Randolph Brunswick's suicide, accomplished by jumping off a balcony at the Hyatt in Cambridge, Massachusetts on the opening night of the convention, threw the process into chaos and led to businessman Norman Mark's nomination two days later.

Oak dismisses the fact that Mark was miles away attending a Democratic Party function with hundreds of witnesses when Brunswick died. "There's more than one vampire, you know," he contends. "I'm sure he had someone else do that for him."

He states that the power of vampires to control the minds of others explains everything, including the admittedly unusual suicide of Brunswick. "Fortunately, they cannot do this charming thing without personal contact," he explains. "Otherwise, Mark would just go on TV and control us all."

Oak goes on to discuss the myths about vampires. "Fiction writers have added all kinds of crazy things that just ain't true," he said. "Some of them might've been started by the vampires to keep people from believing that they really exist. Like the 'no reflection in a mirror' thing or the 'turn to dust in sunlight' thing. They don't like sunlight, but it don't kill them or nothing. And of course you can take pictures of them, because just look at all the pictures of Mark." He clarifies one rumor: "The bat thing is true, though."

Virginia Commonwealth University Psychology Professor Dr. Miles Lizak studies fringe groups such as these. "Conspiracy theories provide people with explanations as to why the world is not how we would want it to be," he says. "They provide meaning where real meaning often is difficult to find. And once entrenched, they are resilient and resistant to logic and fact."

Dr. Lizak went on to say, "People who believe these theories thus have a way to morally blame a specific group for all the world's evils, and, most importantly, separate themselves from that group in such a way as to function as that group's nemesis and, in doing so, absolve themselves from responsibility for those evils."

According to anthropologists Todd Sanders and Harry G. West, "Evidence suggests that a broad cross section of Americans today gives credence to at least some conspiracy theories."

"People who believe in conspiracies tend to also believe in more than one," Dr. Lizak states.

Oak, however, makes it clear that this does not apply to his group. "We don't believe in Bigfoot or a faked moon landing or Area 51 aliens or any of that crap," he insists. "We're not conspiracy fools. The difference is this: *vampires are real*."

THREE

"Why did you put a damned vampire story in my paper?"

Steven Edwards grinned and held up his coffee cup in a mock toast. "Come on, boss. Have you been to our web page? My article has more comments than anything else in today's paper."

Gary crossed his arms as if to restrain himself from throwing one of his precious signed baseballs at Steve's head. That is, if he could have found one under all the clutter. Assuming there was indeed a desk under there.

"It's embarrassing," he bellowed. "I don't want to be known as the 'crazy vampire paper.' I wanted to avoid that ridiculousness completely. I've been ignoring all those idiots for months, as you very well are aware."

Using his free hand, Steve removed a stack of old newspapers from the closest chair. He sat, holding his hot coffee away from his body, but the plastic lid kept it secure.

Gary's office met the exacting standards of Gary's image of the ideal editor's office. A maze of comfortless chairs and a couple tables, all covered with paper, faced the desk. Awards, commendations, and framed copies of screaming headlines crowded the walls and the lone bookcase. Since his promotion to the job, Gary had created a space that emulated the offices of the two he believed to be the world's greatest newspaper editors—J. Jonah Jamison and Perry White. Steve just couldn't wait until Gary started saying "Great Caesar's Ghost!"

"I didn't make the paper look bad at all," he said. "It was a human-interest story I assumed you'd like."

"You slipped it past me!"

"Patty approved it."

"When I wasn't here! And yes, I will have a word with her too."

"Come on, boss," he said, using the generic title Gary preferred to his real name. "It's not like I gave their story any credence. It *is* news, you know."

Gary made an inarticulate growl as he stared at the ceiling for a second, holding his hands above his head, fingers curled in. Always dramatic. "You're doing it again, aren't you? You haven't learned your lesson?"

Steve took a deep breath. "Everything is sourced. Nothing is made up. There's been no harm done. And I hardly spent any time on it. A few minutes with the loony, a quick call to the VCU Prof, and the rest were cut from Wikipedia. It's no big deal—"

"It is to me," Gary interrupted. He growled and threw himself into his seat. After a few seconds, he appeared to calm. "Look, Steve, I know you want to cover the national stories, so here's what we can do. There's a Mark rally coming in a few weeks at the Diamond. The AP will be there, but you can go and write something from a local angle, okay?"

Steve smiled. "Thanks, boss!" He stood to leave.

"Remember, I did you a favor by hiring you when no one else would," Gary said. "You can be replaced easily enough, and cheaper."

Gary's final words tempered Steve's mood as he left the office. He knew if he fucked up this job, he had nowhere else to go.

FOUR

Sousa's "Liberty Bell" blasted through the room.
Steve reached over to put his arm around his wife. She wasn't there.

Slowly, his eyes opened as consciousness snuck in. That's right, she hadn't been there for years. Suddenly the tinny Monty Python theme music blasting from the phone didn't seem like such a good idea after all.

He pounded the phone's snooze alarm and then patted the side table until he found his glasses. He put them on and stared angrily at the clock.

Half an hour and one hot shower later, Steve shut the door and locked the deadbolt. The corridor already sweltered. As he ambled down the wood-floored hallway, his sleepiness transformed to aggravation. He stopped beside the black bag of garbage outside Apartment 31. *Those lazy bastards won't even take it downstairs. Damn college kids.*

Steve glared at the bag. No matter how many times he complained to the landlord, nothing ever changed. They'd put their trash out in the hallway, where the heat would slow-roast its contents until every apartment on the third floor smelled like stale beer and rotting pizza. Maybe, after a few days, the kids might notice or remember—or, god forbid, smell it—and then someone from the accursed flat actually might decide to haul it downstairs and throw it in the dumpster.

Or, as usual, Steve could carry it down himself in order to avoid returning home to its rancid scent.

Muttering under his breath, he grabbed the bag, lifted it, and trudged to the staircase. Months ago he had dragged the bulky bag, only to have it burst open and spew its contents all over the hall. After that, he made sure he carried it high enough to avoid contact with the stairs.

At the bottom of the two flights, a glass door led to the small alcove where the mailboxes for the apartments lined one wall. Steve gently placed the bag on the floor, opened the door and propped his back against it to keep it open, retrieved the bag, and took a step.

Chinese menus, drenched from the previous night's rain, slid under his feet. His back slammed against the floor. The garbage bag flew across the small room and burst against the mailboxes. Beer cans careened off the walls, like cartoon atoms in an educational film.

Steve lay there for a minute, breathing heavily. His head pounded and his back sent him nasty messages about its condition.

"Fuck it," he said.

He slowly pulled himself to his feet. He held his hands from his side and stared down at his now wet, stain-covered shirt and pants. With a shake of his head, he pulled out his keys, opened the door, and trudged back to his apartment.

Emerging five minutes later in clean clothes, he made his way back down to the foyer, which remained a smelly mess. Walking tenderly around the garbage to avoid contact, he emerged into the morning light and headed to his car.

He slid into the beat-up Saturn, started the engine, and sighed with relief when the engine kicked in. It wouldn't be long before the old thing would need to be replaced. He pulled out and headed straight for the Broad Street 7-11, a routine so entrenched he often found himself there without remembering the trip.

He entered the 7-11 with his shoulders slumped.

A few minutes later, two coffees in hand, Steve slid back into the Saturn. The smell of fresh coffee filled the car and lifted his spirits slightly. He placed his cup in the plastic cupholder stuck into the driver's side window and the other on the passenger side and then started the engine.

Richmond is a beautiful city, even if Hell exports its weather there every summer. The smell of tobacco that used to permeate the streets had vanished many years ago, but on certain Tuesdays, a waft of fresh vanilla still drifted over the Fan from the spice factory on Broad Street.

Stonewall Jackson stared straight ahead as Steve drove by, and Steve, as usual, paid him no mind. Wide Monument Avenue, with its ancient brick paving, required constant attention (and constant shock absorber replacement). The cavalcade of Southern Civil War heroes that lined the broad median provided the road with another moniker among the local college students, who referred to it mockingly as "The Avenue of Losers" —a constant reminder that Richmond remained a city sprinting to the future while being heavily anchored in its past.

Steve used his driving time to mull over ideas. The book he planned to write about politics had bubbled in the back of his mind for years. *How Politics Has Been Ruined by Politicians.* A treatise discussing how the media had transformed government by weeding out anyone original and presenting the voters only with an array of terrible leaders. One day he'd get around to starting it…

As Steve pulled into the *Times Dispatch* lot and grabbed his usual parking spot, he shelved the book plans in the back of his mind. Back to covering the idiots in the House of Delegates and the morons in the State Senate.

Like many newspapers, the *Times Dispatch* had seen better days. Once thick and thriving with local news, it was now scrawny and filled with articles culled from syndicates, releasing the paper from having to pay and give benefits to its own reporters. The few remaining reporters concentrated on local sports and politics. "Investigative journalism" had practically disappeared.

The building seemed cold and uninviting from the outside. The parking lot needed paving, and overgrown and unattended bushes partially blocked the sidewalk.

Steve grabbed the coffees and exited his car, slamming the door with a push of his ass. The back door facing the lot was always locked, so Steve headed toward the alleyway.

"Here you go, Red."

A dirty man in a cardboard box wedged between a chain-link fence and the mottled walls of the neighboring building flashed a toothless smile. He reached for the offered coffee. "Thanks, Steve."

Steve nodded, then trudged through the glass doors. He headed to his cubicle, ignoring his coworkers.

Situated in the middle of a row of similar boxes, his spot contained a coffee-stained table, a standard-issue office chair, a computer, a small lamp that looked too tacky for even K-Mart to sell, and a black desk phone with a hold button that didn't work.

Today's first task would involve an impossible effort to make a city council meeting about a new parking garage interesting to readers.

Steve tossed his bag in the corner, placed his coffee on the desk, and threw himself into his chair, which swiveled under him like a tilt-a-whirl. He slowed it with his feet and stared at nothing. In the back of his mind, he imagined Terry Gilliam's animations.

He blinked and stared at his bag. He then reached in and grabbed his greenphone. He checked the screen.

Linda. Just what he needed.

"Hello."

"Steve, you never got back to me about the trip."

With his free hand, Steve pulled at the white plastic top covering his coffee cup, which slid slightly across the desk—but the lid remained stubbornly closed. "Whatever. Do what you want. I'm sure Gabby won't miss me."

"Your vacation time with her can be changed. We've been planning this trip for months, and she really wants to go to Paris."

"She thinks she'll see Belle and the talking teacup there."

"Don't be ridiculous; she's a smart girl and you know it."

"Can I talk to her?"

"No, she's at school."

The cup wobbled in his hand. He placed his palm over the top and tried to pick open the white plastic with his forefingers.

"Well, ask her to call me when she gets home."

"You know you're late with your child support again."

"And of course, Gabby is starving because of it. Good thing you married a doctor who can treat that."

"She's still your daughter and you're still—"

"I know, I know. I don't need a lecture. But I'm not earning what I used to."

"That's your fault, not mine."

Steve grabbed at the coffee cup as it shifted under his grip. He didn't reply.

"You could have had your lawyer file to have your payments reduced—"

"I can't afford a lawyer."

"You always were stupid. It'll cost you more in the long run."

"You didn't used to think I was stupid."

"That was before you got stupid and did stupid things. Look, we're taking Gabby to Paris, and if you want to object, you'll just have to get a lawyer to do something about it."

"Good thing you called, then, to let me know."

"Steve, do something with your life! You're stuck at that rag of a paper and you're going nowhere—"

"Hey, I've got big plans! You'll see!"

Steve heard a huge sigh and then Linda said, "I gotta go."

The phone went dead. Steve reared back as hot coffee spurted over his shirt.

"Son of a bitch!" Steve jumped up, dropped the crumpled cup in the trash can under his desk with one hand, and lifted his shirt away from his chest with the other. He ripped off his shirt and tossed it to the floor, cursing Linda's name. Rubbing his burned chest, he walked to the storage closet and retrieved one of the promotional tee-shirts the paper had given out at a recent ball game. The fit was tight, but at least the shirt was clean and dry. He then grabbed some paper towels from the break area, marched back to his desk, and began mopping up. Moving papers, CDs, pens and keys off his desk, he slowly wiped the area, glad that the splattering coffee had spared his computer and keyboard. He dropped to his knees and dabbed at the thin carpeting.

After tossing the paper towels into the trash bucket, he stood and inspected the cubicle walls surrounding his desk to make sure no coffee had splashed there. Old campaign posters shared space with favorite political cartoons and comics—Doonesbury and Candorville especially. Pictures pinned over his computer smiled down at him—his red-haired daughter Gabrielle beaming while riding a merry-go-round; an old friend from political campaigns long gone; his old punk band from college; him at his desk at the *New York Times*....

Twenty minutes later, he realized that he was still standing.

FIVE

Associated Press, October 5
POLICE FIND NO EVIDENCE OF
FOUL PLAY IN BRUNSWICK DEATH

A spokesperson for the Cambridge Police, working in conjunction with the FBI, stated today that they have uncovered no evidence to indicate that the death of Governor Brunswick was anything more than an unexplained suicide.

"The investigation is not complete," stated Cambridge Chief of Police Scott Gillespie, "but so far we have discovered nothing to suggest that foul play was involved."

The FBI has interviewed witnesses, analyzed videos, and thoroughly examined the scene. Witness testimony corroborates the physical evidence, which shows that after meeting with his staff, the governor remained alone in the suite.

Surveillance video confirms the Secret Service testimony that no one entered or left the room during that time. Amateur video taken from outside the Hynes show the Governor stepping out onto the balcony, standing on a chair, waving to the crowd, and then diving to his death.

The governor's wife of twenty-seven years, who had planned to join her husband at the convention for his acceptance speech, received the news at home from a staff member. Kathryn Brunswick has remained in private mourning with her children and family since that time.

The autopsy report names blunt force trauma as the cause of death. Investigators found no evidence of alcohol or drugs in the governor's bloodstream which could explain his strange behavior.

None of this has prevented bloggers from presenting any number of theories to explain the incident. The more mundane range from an unusual brain aneurism which caused spasms or some other unknown family or personal health problem to political corruption which has yet to be disclosed. On the more fanciful side, some have proposed terrorist hypno-rays, alien mind control, or even vampiric charming powers.

SIX

Two months of the most exciting political news in modern American history had passed without any real input from Steve. He snorted. He had his regular blog posts where he commented on the national race, but he was lucky if fifty people a week would read it.

Still, enthusiasm filled him that night. He would get to see Norman Mark live, and maybe even be lucky enough to ask him a question with the rest of the press corps.

He shuffled along with the thousands who trickled into The Diamond—the ridiculous name for the baseball stadium which had replaced Richmond's Parker Field many years ago. Stoic protesters holding crosses posed for the cameras while standing to one side. A few attendees pointed at the occasional "Mark is a vampire" sign and laughed, but most ignored the demonstrators.

Behind a barricade on the opposite side of the ingoing crowd, a few drunken college students, dressed in their best Halloween gear with fangs dripping red and black capes swirling, jeered at the protestors.

One by one, people stepped through the scanners to get their bags the once-over from the guards. Security seemed very tight. Obvious Secret Service agents—still wearing their sunglasses even though the sun had set—stood alone or in pairs in every direction Steve looked.

Steve had submitted the required picture and ID days earlier in order to obtain permission to enter the press area. With the press pass dangling around his neck, security quickly passed him through.

Steve dodged people walking in every direction to cross the promenade to where he could look out at the field. Bright night lamps lit the scene, obscuring the stars above. The hoard of American flags flapping in the cool autumn breeze added to the festive feel of the evening.

Center field now contained a wide stage, canopied in case of rain, and a perfectly centered stark podium. Behind and flanking the podium, two groups of seats had been positioned on a tiered platform to offer local politicians superior camera coverage. They'd sit dutifully, listen attentively and clap in the right places, leading the audience like human "applause" signs at a sitcom taping.

The first speaker was scheduled to appear on the stage within the hour, and by that time, the place would be packed. Mark's charm and youthful appearance appealed to the many college students in Richmond, and liberal Democrats—who weren't always appreciated outside of the city itself—poured in for that rare opportunity to gawk at a politician they actually liked.

Steve walked through the crowd with ease, the pass dangling around his neck. He felt invigorated—finally, the chance to write a story with national implications. Perhaps Mark would even take questions from the media afterwards.

He headed toward the press section, trying to think of a way to "keep it local" to please Gary.

"Hey, you're Steve Edwards," came a voice from behind.

Steve turned to find a smiling middle-aged man with dark hair and brown eyes. The man, who wore a deep blue business suit and red tie hung loosely around his neck, held out his hand.

"Yes, I am," Steve said, warming to the man instantly. "And you are?"

"Collin Babcock, manager of The Diamond." He held Steve's hand in a strong grip. "Pleased to meet you. Don't suppose you know me, but I recognize you from the paper, and that story about the vampire believers was quite interesting."

"I'm happy you liked it," Steve replied sincerely.

"You don't believe the Suckers, do you?"

Steve laughed. "They don't like being called that, you know. Others call them 'Batties,' but they call themselves 'the Illuminators,' like the light they think will expose the vampires."

Collin shook his head. "Just when you think politics can't get any crazier." He nodded toward a refreshment stand and indicated that Steve should follow. "I stay out of politics myself, but I do read your blog every now and then, even though I disagree with you a lot. Especially the one you wrote about taxes. I don't know how you—two waters, please—I don't know how you expect a businessman like me to hire people and run a business with even a slight profit if you're going to tax the hell out of me."

Steve graciously accepted the water from Collin, who waved away Steve's offer to pay. "Well, it's more of the huge corporations that are the problem, not the small businesses..."

Collin snorted. "That's what they always say… and then my taxes go up so the government can pay bums with food stamps. But you don't want to talk about that, I can tell. You're here for Mark. You think he's going to win? Wouldn't that be something?"

"It's possible," Steve said. "He has the advantage of being something new. People often project their hopes and desires on the new guy, and it takes a few months before they start getting disillusioned. Fortunately for Mark, by that time, the election will be over."

"He's still behind in the polls, though."

"Well, his very liberal views are not going over too well with much of America," Steve conceded. "Thanks for the water. I've enjoyed talking to you, but I need to get to the press area before all the good seats are gone."

"Listen, would you like to see this thing from the box seats?" Collin asked. "You can watch from my box, if you're interested."

Steve glanced around the park. He didn't need to be near the stage to write his story. He could easily grab quotes from the prominent notables after the speeches had ended and the crowd thinned—no politician leaves until the last TV camera is turned off. In fact, watching the crowd from a high angle would give him a perspective on the gathering that no other reporter could claim.

"Sure, that would be great."

"Here," Collin said, pulling the string over his head and handing Steve his pass. "We'll switch passes and turn the pictures face down. With this green one, my people will let you by. They're not checking passes on people once they're inside. I'll stick yours under my tie. Everybody knows me. No one will ask to see it."

Steve accepted Collin's pass and looked at it. A color picture of Collin with his name beneath in boldface was set against a green background with the word "Staff" in an oversized font.

"I don't know," Steve said. "We're dealing with the Secret Service here. If they challenge us…"

"No one's going to question you while I'm with you. Look, in the unlikely case that any of the Secret Service should stop us, I'll explain that we dropped them accidentally and then put on the wrong ones. They're not going to arrest you because of that—after all, you really do have a badge and are allowed here. The worst they'll do is not let you up in the box seats. No big deal."

Steve pulled his pass off and handed it to Collin and then placed Collin's around his neck.

Collin motioned for Steve to follow. "Walk this way."

Steve grinned as he imagined John Cleese saying those words, but wasn't sure if Collin would get the reference if he replied with "If I could walk that way…" Instead, he followed silently.

The guards didn't give them a second look.

SEVEN

By the time Mark took the stage, the crowd had grown restless. The previous speakers must have felt as invisible as the bands who opened for the Beatles—sure, they were competent, but they weren't *the Beatles*. They weren't who everyone had come to see.

Mark's appearance certainly reminded Steve of a rock star's performance. The crowd cheered and clapped as he waved his hands and pretended to recognize people in the audience. Large screens on either side of the stage amplified his image to the farthest reaches of the stadium.

"See?" Collin said. "This is much better than being down there in that mob."

Steve couldn't disagree. The two of them, cans of cold Coors in hand, perched comfortably above the din in a private booth above the bleachers. A large refrigerator in the back held more beer and other refreshments. The cool night breeze wafted through the open booth, which gave them an unobstructed view of the stage and the field. Even so, a large flat-screen TV hung over their heads, providing the same feed as the amplified versions on the sides of the stage.

"*Are you ready to take your country back?*" Mark cried to the crowd, who roared back their assent.

Steve leaned forward and cupped his hands around his mouth. "Free Bird!" he yelled.

"*It's time we, the people, ran our country—not the banks, not the insurance industry, not the lobbyists, and not the same old politicians who got us into this mess!*"

Collin took a long swig of his beer as the crowd cheered again. "He sure knows how to get the crowd cheering."

"I'm enjoying this campaign," Steve said. "Mark is a dynamic candidate, and I hope he wins. The problem is that all he is doing is exciting the liberals. He needs to get the moderates if he wants to win. The polls show he's not doing that yet."

"Well, neither is Finnegan. His VP choice is a loon. Did you read what he said about gays? And Muslims?"

Steve nodded. "Had Brunswick not died, it would be a fairly reasonable debate between two moderates, but instead, with Proctor pulling the Republicans to the right and Mark pulling the Democrats to the left, we're getting a battle between extremes."

"That makes it a lot more interesting though," Collin commented. "And now Proctor is getting press because of what Mark said about religion."

"They're blowing that all out of proportion. All he said was that religion didn't belong in politics. It's not like he said he was an atheist."

"The atheists think so, though... Silverman and his gang are supporting him now. I even saw some 'Atheists for Mark' buttons out there."

Steve snorted. "Atheists aren't organized. That's why they're atheists. I doubt it will make much of a difference. There'll be more liberal Christians who will now refuse to vote for him because of those comments than atheists who will."

They paused to hear what Mark was saying. "*Are you happy knowing that your taxes keep going up so that rich people like me don't have to pay our share? Do you sleep well at night despite the fact that your child may get an inferior education because a huge farm conglomerate is getting your tax money to not grow anything? Do you feel confident in your government when you hear that lobbyists invested billions of dollars last year to get laws passed that allow them to sell you inferior products with no oversight? Is there anyone in Washington on your side?*"

Collin let out a low whistle. "Class warfare! He doesn't play around."

"*Right now, the oil companies in America receive tax breaks and subsidies to encourage them to drill. Last year, they took in four billion dollars of your money—four billion! And what was their annual profit? Forty-five point six billion, which includes the four billion you gave them!*"

Mark, who evidently had a small microphone attached to his lapel, left the podium to speak directly to the crowd. He made eye contact, jabbed his finger at them to emphasize key points, and made sure to stay within camera range. He spoke like a revival preacher raging against the sins of the flesh, stirring the faithful. The crowd ate it up.

"They don't need your money. Do you really think they will stop drilling if we don't pay them their extortion? Of course not! It's profitable! Instead, they take your money and give it to their CEOs in the form of million-dollar bonuses because we let them! Because no one tells them no! That's a welfare program that needs to be cut now!"

"You've got to admit, he has charisma," Steve said.

"Actually, I have to take a second to apologize," Mark intoned seriously, and the crowd grew quiet. *"I wasn't completely honest when I said that the oil companies earned forty-five point six billion in profits last year."*

He lifted his eyes slowly to the camera, paused for effect, and then said, *"That was just Exxon's share."*

Once more, the crowd cheered.

"...And that's just the oil companies," Mark was saying. *"You add in the tax breaks and subsidies all the other corporations in America get—including my own—and now we're talking real money!"*

"That's ridiculous," scoffed Collin. "His policies will cause the stock market to plummet. Businesses will panic. These tax breaks mean jobs for Americans. Companies will move overseas if he keeps this up."

"No, they won't..."

"And he's simplifying everything to the point of absurdity. This is just a drop in the bucket when you look at the total budget."

Steve laughed. "It's symbolic and meaningful, and it's getting a great response. I'm very impressed. He's doing pretty well for someone who has never run for office before."

"And especially for a vampire," Collin added with a wink.

"What are you, a bigot?" Steve taunted. "This is America, where all persons are entitled to equal rights, living or undead. That's in the thirty-seventh-and-a-half Amendment."

"Oh, so you're the spokesman for Undead Americans now, are you?"

Steve grinned and reached for some potato chips Collin had poured out into a large wooden bowl.

"And why should you trust me to bring our country out of this mess, when every other politician has not? Because I... can't... be... bought." Mark stretched each word out dramatically and received the expected explosion of support. *"What could someone possibly offer me that I don't already have? I will not accept lobbyist money for my campaign. No*

special interests will have a say in my policies. My only concern will be the well-being of the American people."

Collin finished his beer. On the stage, Mark stressed all the great things that the money America would get from cutting tax breaks and loopholes would provide: better and cheaper education, clean energy, aid to small businesses—all the Democratic buzzwords to pump up the audience.

"A lot of Christians aren't going to vote for him because they think he's a vampire," said Collin.

Steve shrugged. "They already believe in magic and devils, so to them, vampires are a real possibility."

"You don't think vampires can exist?"

Steve paused, embarrassed at his comment since he did not know his host's views. He hoped he had not touched a sore spot. "Um, no, I don't believe in vampires. I mean, look at him—you can see him in a mirror, he's been doused with holy water, and recently some people handed him crosses and he accepted them without a problem. He's no undead."

"But what about all that stuff about the bat in the video?"

"You mean the clip showing Brunswick's balcony right after he jumped? Yeah, that's all over the web. It might show a bat, but it might be a bird, too."

"At midnight?"

"Some birds fly at night. And even if it was a bat, it could have just flown by right then. It's not a good video, and doesn't clearly show the creature coming from his window."

Collin's mouth stretched. "Still, it's a coincidence you can't overlook."

"Well," Steve said. "If I have to choose between a coincidence and something that defies the laws of nature, I'll choose the coincidence."

They sat in silence for a few minutes while Mark launched into his traditional "many different cultures and ideas forming America's greatness" speech. The diverse crowd loved it.

"I'm going to get another beer," Collin said, rising. "Want one?"

"Sure."

Soft thuds, clinks and clanks sounded behind him, but Steve's attention centered wholly on Mark, who had become very serious, and the crowd very silent.

"*This is a dangerous quest we are on,*" Mark said in a hushed voice. "*Many powerful people do not want us to succeed. They don't want* change. They know that if I'm elected they won't be able to take advantage of the American citizen anymore. They know that I'll shut down their tax shelters in the Cayman Islands and cut off their tax breaks when they ship our jobs overseas. They know that they will not have someone in the White House they can buy. And they will do everything they can to—"

The shots echoed across the stadium. Mark's eyes grew large on the giant screens and then he fell backwards, clutching his chest.

Screams filled the air. Steve jumped up, unable to hear over the ringing in his ears.

Below him, politicians dove off the tiered platform and scrambled for cover. Mayor Ross clamped her hand over her leg, blood spurting through the gaps between her fingers. Another victim lay still in a pool of blood. Secret Service agents stormed the stage with weapons drawn. Two knelt at Mark's side; the others turned in all directions. People in the audience tripped and fell over each other in a mad dash to the closest exits.

Steve noticed all this in the brief, stunned moments before he turned to Collin, who cursed, dropped the high-powered rifle, then turned to Steve and winked.

In a matter of seconds, Collin's transformation into a bat was complete. His clothes fell to the floor and the bat disappeared into the night.

Someone threw open the door.

EIGHT

"I didn't do it!" Steve shouted, raising his hands above his head.

A short woman with curly hair barely confined by a Yankees baseball cap stared at him for a second. "Come with me!" she said, her hand still on the doorknob.

Half-deaf from the rifle shots, Steve furrowed his brow and tried to read her lips. She certainly didn't look like Security...

She rolled her eyes, whipped off her cap and tossed it to him. Somehow his hands rose to catch it.

"Put it on!" she ordered.

As he pulled the cap as low over his face as possible, she ran forward, grabbed his wrist, and dragged him from the room and into the uproar.

The screams of terrified patrons nearly drowned out the amplified voice of someone begging everyone to remain calm. Sirens echoed through the stadium.

"What if they—"

"Shut up!" she hissed. "Look scared and act like you've come from the crowd."

Steve had no problem looking scared.

The woman drew Steve into the mayhem. People shouted and screamed and jammed the exit routes. A few idiots held up cell phones and cameras to record the insanity. One stood atop a bleacher screaming about the need for gun control.

Stadium security, not trained to deal with such a melee, ineffectively yelled for calm. Though ill-equipped and insufficient in numbers, the police did their best to bring order to the exodus. Groups of Secret Service agents scanned the crowd, while others stormed up the stairs Steve and the woman had just come down.

Steve gulped, lowered his head, and pushed after the woman. The crowd shoved them back and forth. The woman painfully tightened her grip on his wrist. Elbows poked him. Feet stomped on his.

The mob propelled them into a trash receptacle. Steve used his bulk to ram their way back into the stream of bodies. Somehow, they thrust their way through the exit bottleneck and out of the stadium.

The wire fence that separated the inner area from the ticket counter collapsed under the weight of the crowd, which poured into the parking lot and onto Belvidere Road. No longer concerned with merely getting away, the crowd seemed angry, scared, and hostile.

"Over there!" came a voice from behind.

Steve started to turn, but the woman jerked hard on his wrist and dragged him into the midst of the crowd.

She ripped off his baseball cap and tossed it aside. "Stay low!"

They pushed forward like determined linebackers. Shouts and curses surrounded them as they forged ahead.

Sirens grew louder as ambulances and more police converged at the scene. A loud crash that announced the collapse of another wire fence added to the chaos. Instantly, half the crowd moved in that direction, trampling anyone in their way. Steve grimaced as the woman tugged him after them.

"Do you have a cell phone?" she asked suddenly.

"What?"

She shouted her question in his ear.

"Yes…" he replied. He reached into his pocket and pulled out his greenphone.

The woman grabbed the phone, hurled it into the crowd, and yanked him in a different direction.

"Hey!" Steve yelled. "Are you crazy? Do you know how much—"

Ignoring his protests, the woman dragged him to the downed fence. As they climbed the angled chain links with hands and feet, Steve's ID lanyard caught on a damaged link. The string tightened into a choke-hold before snapping.

His neck stinging, Steve scuttled the rest of the way over the fence. He wouldn't need that ID now anyway.

That ID.

Steve's eyes widened. In all the craziness, it hadn't occurred to him before. He had handed his ID to Collin. It now was back in the booth, with the pile of clothes, next to the smoking gun.

Sweet Jesus.

Steve wrenched from the woman's grasp, spun around, and fought his way back to the fence. He jumped onto the fallen chain link barrier and elbowed aside a couple college kids as he bucked the tide.

When he came to the tangled lanyard, he knelt and grasped Collin's ID tag. A huge foot stomped on his hands. Screaming, he shouldered the legs aside. Yells and curses erupted as he tore the tag free.

The curly-haired woman grabbed his arm and pulled him to his feet. "Come on!"

Steve stuffed the ID in his pocket as they dashed into the parking lot. They darted around cars and scattering groups of people, each attempting their own escape.

The night took on a surreal quality. Steve felt as if he stepped into an unending loop of one of those terrifying dreams where some nightmarish creature chased him and he ran and ran and could not get away.

The woman stopped before an ugly orange Honda Element and opened the back door. "Inside!" she ordered when Steve stood in momentary confusion.

Steve climbed into the back. The woman slammed the door behind him, circled the front of the car, and got behind the wheel. As she started the van, Steve lay flat on the floor and drew blankets over him, leaving only a small opening for his eyes and nose.

The back seats of the vehicle had been strapped against the sides, just like Steve had done in the van he had owned in college when he needed to carry the band, the roadies, and all their equipment. Sometimes they'd have three or four people riding on top of everything. And there was that time they had to go back to Club Kozmo's because they realized they had forgotten one of the roadies who had come with them...

A sharp turn rolled Steve to the side of the Element and jolted the past from his mind.

He readjusted the blankets stared at the roof, watching the stars through the skylight. *This is weird*, he thought. *I don't feel anything. I'm not afraid, and I'm not angry—is this what shock is like? Shouldn't I be in a blind panic?*

"Where are we going?" he asked the woman.

"Disneyland," she said. "You look like you need a vacation."

"Who are you?"

"The person who rescued you."

Steve stared at the sky. Nothing made sense. Vampire assassins. Strange women in baseball caps throwing phones. He should have a million questions. Why didn't he?

My brain has shut down, he convinced himself, *to prevent me from going absolutely insane.*

NINE

NBC Nightly News, *October 21*

WILLIAMS: An assassination attempt has been made on Democratic Presidential candidate Norman Mark. He has been rushed to a hospital, but his personal doctors assure the public that his wounds are superficial and that he will be back on his feet within a few weeks, assuming there are no complications.

The candidate was speaking at a rally in Richmond, Virginia, earlier this evening when a shot rang out. A single bullet pierced the candidate's upper left chest, missing his heart. Two more shots hit guests on the podium with the candidate, and their condition, for now, is uncertain.

For more on this story, we go to Lisa Myers.

MYERS: Brian, I am standing outside of The Diamond—the baseball park where the assassination attempt occurred. As you can see, the Secret Service has blocked the entire area off and is not allowing the press entry. We have been told that the attempt on Norman Mark's life apparently came from a private viewing booth high above the field that is only accessible to the owners and caretakers of the park, none of whom were present at the time.

Sources report that inside the booth, the Secret Service found the weapon that may have been used in the attack as well as an ID belonging to a local newspaper reporter named Steven Edwards. Edwards' press pass did not give him permission to be in this area. At the moment, there is no verification of his actual presence in the booth, but sources claim he could not have entered without an accomplice. The Secret Service has made no accusations and states that Edwards, who has not been seen since this incident, is merely a "person of interest."

WILLIAMS: Lisa, do they believe Edwards was the shooter?

MEYERS: Brian, no one is willing to state what they believe at the moment.

WILLIAMS: What do we know about Edwards?

MEYERS: Edwards is thirty-three years old. He covers local politics for the *Richmond Times Dispatch*. He once worked for the *New York Times* but was fired after it was revealed that he had fabricated some of his sources. According to opinions expressed in his weekly blog, he clearly shared the views of most liberal Democrats and seemed to be a Mark supporter. However, he recently wrote an article where he interviewed a group that believes Mark is a vampire. Some police officials now suggest that the group converted Edwards, who decided to become a "vampire hunter."

WILLIAMS: And what of the security breach? How did anyone sneak a high-powered rifle into a rally like this?

MEYERS: Brian, that is certainly going to be a major focus of the investigation. Sources speculate that the gun had been hidden prior to the start of the rally. The owners and caretakers of The Diamond are being heavily questioned about that very issue.

WILLIAMS: And the subsequent riot?

MEYERS: While Mark's campaign officials praise the Secret Service for their quick response in protecting the candidate, many people blame both the Secret Service and the local police for insufficient preparation —that the delay in reacting not only allowed the, uh, 'person of interest' to escape, but exacerbated the riot that followed. The Diamond suffered over a million dollars' worth of damage and at least fifty people had to be hospitalized from the injuries they sustained while trying to get out.

WILLIAMS: Thank you, Lisa. We now turn to Dr. Michelle Stagnitta from the National Institute on Mental Health. Dr. Stagnitta, can we expect more more of these kinds of attacks from those who believe the tales about vampires?

STAGNITTA: It is possible, of course. While most believers in conspiracies would never become dangerous, all groups have more radical adherents. Some of the radicals become convinced that such an action is the only way to prove to everyone that they are right. They feel that once the 'truth' is exposed they will free themselves from the thoughts that haunt them. I wouldn't be surprised, in this instance, if Edwards—or rather, whoever the shooter turns out to be—used a silver bullet to make that point.

Do I think there may be further attacks? Well, that is always a possibility. Various radical individuals may set their sights on prominent political figures, which is why we have the Secret Service protect all major candidates....

TEN

Steve stared through the skylight at the dark sky. From the movements of the Element and the lack of traffic noise, he surmised they had left 95 a while ago. Bumping along back roads was a bruiseworthy method of travel, but Steve had no complaints.

Instead, he marveled at his continued lack of emotion.

He felt oddly detached from reality, as if the Steve who rattled along in the back of the orange van bore no connection to the reporter who had sat in the stadium booth.

The woman had the news on the radio. Although he could barely hear it, he knew they were discussing the assassination.

How many hours had passed? It felt like he had been lying in the back of the van for days.

At length, the Element slowed noticeably, made a series of turns, and entered a road so rough it shook Steve like a seed in a maraca. The van slowed to a halt. The keys jingled, the seat belt clicked, and the front door squeaked open.

The ceiling light made Steve blink, and he sat up, groaning with discomfort.

The woman opened the back door.

Steve slid to the side and stepped onto the hard-packed dirt. The scent of lush, green growth came to him on the chill night breeze. He shivered.

"Where are we?" he asked.

"At Mr. Hillman's home."

"Hillman? Who's Hillman? Who are you? Are you—are you vampires, too?"

She sighed and said in a condescending tone, as if lecturing a child, "No, we're the *good guys*. Now come inside."

She began walking around the building.

Steve followed. In the darkness, he kept tripping over ruts and holes in the dirt driveway.

A car—an old model, by its bulky lines—was parked at an angle in front of the Honda. Beyond that, they walked on grass, though the crunch of gravel beneath his feet told Steve that this was an overgrown part of the driveway.

A light shone softly from around the corner. When they came to the front of the house, Steve blinked at the brightness of the double spotlight beside a screened-in porch.

The place was an old, two-story farmhouse with peeling paint and sagging shutters. Closed curtains blocked every window, but yellowing light escaped through their central slits.

Steve halted on the edge of the driveway and surveyed the dilapidated home. "This is your secret hideout?"

"Right, but only the chosen one may enter by incanting the magical password."

"I don't know…"

"You want to go back? We can split the reward I'll get for turning you in."

"No. Lead the way."

Squinting at the light, Steve followed the woman to the front of the house. The two followed a path of slate stepping stones barely visible through the weeds and tall grass. They mounted the creaking wooden steps of the front porch, and the woman opened the rickety screen door.

Several tables and chairs, all covered with piles of musty-smelling newspapers, furnished the porch. Insects flew in and out between gaping holes in the screens.

The woman knocked and then stood silently.

"What does Mr. Hillman do?" Steve asked.

"Take a long time to answer the door."

"No, I mean—"

The door swung open. A short man with gray hair poking out above his ears—and from his ears—squinted at the two on the porch. His white skin hadn't seen much sun, and his dark grey sweater had seen too many moths. He appeared to be in his late sixties, and his face held a kind of serene acceptance of his current position in life.

"Hannah? What are you doing here?"

"I'm sorry, Mr. Hillman, but we have a bit of an emergency. Can we come in?"

Hillman's expression changed and he scowled at Steve with sudden suspicion. "No," he replied. "No, I do not give you permission to enter my home."

Steve furrowed his brow and stared at the man. Hannah, however, walked right past her host into the house. She turned back to Steve, rolled her eyes, and gave him a signal to enter.

Steve shrugged and, keeping an eye on Hillman, followed her in.

They stood in a wood-paneled foyer with a doorway to each side. A flight of stairs along the right-hand wall led to the second floor. More newspapers overspread the two chairs and small table beneath a dusty mirror.

Arms crossed over his chest, Hillman looked Steve up and down. He gave a short harrumph. "Right, then, who are you?" he asked as he headed into the room to the left.

"I'm, uh, Steven Edwards, a reporter..." His voice died as he followed Hillman into the room.

Bookshelves packed every spare inch of wall space. Books, piled sideways and more than one row deep, filled not only the shelves but every table in the room. Classics such as *Oliver Twist* stood next to encyclopedias, old textbooks, numerous biographies, and Reader's Digest collections. One shelf seemed dedicated to old comic strip collections from the '50s, and another area held piles of magazines. And every bit of reading material looked like it had been read. More than once.

In one corner at the far side of the room, an old-fashioned TV set with buttons and knobs on the front sat atop one of those gaudy entertainment centers that they flog at Walmart. The opposite corner held a small desk with a massive, out-of-date computer monitor. Between the two, a soot-darkened stone fireplace dominated the room. About twenty pictures of Mr. Hillman standing with various people stood at attention in small frames upon the mantelpiece. Quite a few featured the younger version of the man in a pressed army uniform. Scattered among those, an impressive array of children and grandchildren smiled down from their frames.

No matter which direction Steve looked he saw a cross, a picture of Jesus, or other Christian imagery. Between the books, and at various spots on the walls where room permitted, were mirrors. Lots of them.

As Hillman settled himself in the comfortable La-Z-Boy recliner to the right of the sofa that faced the fireplace, Hannah removed the wool blankets, oozing clumps of cat hair, from the sofa, methodically folded each one, and set them atop the paperbacks on a table. Steve didn't like the looks of the lumpy sofa, but a two-foot stack of newspapers occupied the small kitchen chair to the sofa's left.

"The blankets keep the davenport clean from cat hair in case guests arrive," Hillman explained. "You're not allergic, are you?"

"No, not to cat hair," Steve answered. "I'm allergic to oak pollen, but I didn't find that out until I…" He shook his head. "No, not cat hair."

Hannah sat and motioned Steve to join her on the sofa. "But don't step on the rug."

Steve didn't move. He stared down at the small throw rug indicated. Its circular design suddenly reminded Steve of a target.

"Trap," Hillman said.

"More than one in here," Hannah added. "Mr. Hillman's protection in case they find him."

"More outside, too," Hillman said. "So, just be careful."

Gulping audibly, Steve sidled to the sofa, making sure to stay as far from the rug as possible. "Listen, can I have a glass of water?"

Without a word, Hannah rose, trotted off toward a small alcove, switched on a light, and disappeared behind the wall.

As Steve gingerly lowered himself into the sofa, he listened to the familiar sound of shuffling, clinking of glasses, and running water in the adjoining kitchen. He looked at Hillman and they stared at each other uncomfortably until Hannah returned. Steve thanked her, took the glass, gulped down the water, and held the empty glass out to her. Hannah rolled her eyes, and with a quick tilt of her head, indicated the table behind the sofa. Steve reached back and wedged the glass in between two piles of paperbacks. When he turned back to his hosts, he started at the sight of a huge calico cat sitting at his feet, looking at him inquisitively.

"That's Mina," Hillman said. "She's not afraid of no one. The others are hiding until they're sure you're okay."

Steve leaned forward and held his fingers out for the cat's inspection. When Mina rubbed against his leg, he scratched the top of her head, grateful for the distraction. He still felt nonplussed and detached, like he was a visitor in his own body. *Usually, I'm not this quiet*, he thought. *I wonder why I am not saying anything?*

Hillman harrumphed again. "What's wrong with him?"

Steve straightened and glared at Hillman.

"He's been through a lot today," Hanna replied. "The vampires tricked him."

"Oho!" Hillman said, suddenly interested. "They did? What happened?"

"They framed him for assassinating Sal."

"What? Is he dead?"

"Doesn't look like it."

"Wait!" Steve yelled, jumping to his feet. He stood there a moment, surprised to find himself standing. He took a few deep breaths while his two hosts waited patiently for him. "I think someone needs to explain everything to me, right now. I've just been kidnapped—"

"Rescued," corrected Hannah.

"—and brought to who-knows-where with who-knows-who talking about vampires—which, as far as I know, don't exist. And assassinating Sal? What are you talking about? I demand to know what's going on!"

"Oh, sorry," Hannah said with a pout. "Gee, we didn't mean to upset you. The phone is over there. Why don't you go call the police and let them know about your problem?"

"Some rescue," Steve groused. "Just tell me what is going on, will you?"

"Sit down first," Hillman said. "You need to sit."

"I need a drink, is what I need," Steve mumbled.

"We just gave you—"

"A drink!" Steve said as he plopped himself back onto the sofa, which puffed up clouds of dust and cat hair in protest. "You know. A *drink*."

Hillman gave another harrumph. "Don't have any alcohol here. It dulls the senses. Trust me, you need all your senses right now."

"Fine." Steve sighed. "Just tell me already."

"You realize that vampires exist, I take it." Hillman unwrapped a small butterscotch candy and popped it into his mouth.

Steve grimaced. "I've tried very hard not to realize that. I mean, I keep thinking that there must be another explanation. Vampires are fictional, like ghosts and Santa Claus. I could have been fooled by some fancy magician's trick there. Occam's Razor and all that."

Hillman stared at Steve, tumbled the candy around in his mouth nosily, and then turned to Hannah. "Maybe you had better tell me what happened first."

"I went to the rally to see what Sal was up to," Hannah said. "I noticed a few potential vampires, including some Secret Service guys, and then I saw Karl."

"Karl? Karl Weaver? What was he doing there? He hates Sal."

"Exactly." Hannah pointed at Hillman using her thumb and forefinger like a gun. "He's the assassin, you see, but at the time I had no idea what he planned. I followed him around, and he seemed to be searching for someone. Then he saw you—"

"Me?" Steve said, pressing himself against the sofa arm as if Hannah's finger was loaded.

Hannah slitted her eyes. "No, not *you*. I was pointing to the *cat*." She turned back to Hillman. "Anyway, Karl zoomed right to Steve and began talking. They exchanged IDs and then walked off together. That aroused my suspicions, so I followed. When they entered a restricted area and headed up some stairs toward a booth, I stayed nearby. When I heard the shot, I knew where it came from. The security guards took off toward the stage and I ran up the stairs, found Steve alone in the booth, and dragged him here."

"So Karl shot Sal. Interesting." Hillman rattled the candy around in his mouth again.

"Yeah, but the news said it wasn't that bad. He'll survive."

Steve leaned forward. "*Now* can you explain it all to me? Who is Karl? Who is Sal?"

Hillman gave a heavy sigh and regarded Steve with an expression that indicated both sadness and exhaustion. "This could take some time. How about coffee? I don't have alcohol, but I do have some very good coffee."

Steve smiled and nodded. Anyone who offered coffee couldn't be too bad.

ELEVEN

Steve felt as shaky inside as if he had already consumed enough caffeine for an army, but he riveted his attention on the special TV coverage of the assassination attempt. One of those blonde and busty Fox News reporters—hired for looks and not brains, Steve felt certain—read an uncharacteristically objective report from the teleprompter, though she ruined the effect by repeatedly pointing out that the main suspect was a "liberal."

Steve's eyes strayed from the TV screen just long enough to acknowledge Hannah's return with three steaming cups on a small tray.

"Hey, that's a very flattering photo of you," Hannah commented as she handed Steve his cup. "I assume it was taken at a Halloween party?"

"It's the photo that runs above my blog," Steve answered absently, missing Hannah's sarcasm for once. His eyes never leaving the screen, he took a sip of the coffee. Bland and tasteless. Probably instant. Still, better than nothing.

"Edward's ex-wife stated that she has not heard from him since this incident," continued the Fox blonde, "but added that the last thing he told her was that he 'had big plans.'"

Steve groaned and lowered his head. "That's not what I meant!"

"You have a blog?" Hannah asked.

Steve slowly raised his head. He looked at Hannah for a few moments before replying. "I'm a reporter. I have a weekly blog that discusses politics. I even did a story on the Batties."

Hannah walked over and turned off the television. "Oh, of course! The Batties. Those crazy people who believe that there are such things as vampires."

Steve blinked. "Sorry. I didn't mean to be insulting." He remembered the coffee in his hands and took a sip.

"Our organization is just one of many that keep an eye on them," Hillman said as he took his coffee from Hannah with a polite smile. "We call ourselves the Van Helsing Society. We have members all over the world. We're *not* batty."

"And you lead the society?"

Hillman shook his head. "No, but I do write the newsletter. I've authored a few of our books too—although, I guess, they're really more like pamphlets—and they sell okay whenever something in the news stirs up interest. And I use my home to get mail for the organization, when we get any. But this is just my house, not our headquarters. Hannah knew to bring you here because I'm the closest, see?"

"All right," Steve said. "I appreciate you taking me in. I'm, just... well, I've been through a lot today. I've seen something I can't explain, and I've suddenly become a treasonous assassin."

"Then let me tell you about vampires..."

"The short version, please," Hannah begged.

"Yes, all right, the short version," Hillman said with a frown. He stared down at Mina, who had crawled into his lap and was purring contentedly. Hillman absently rubbed her neck.

"Vampires," he finally said, "have existed as long as humankind, and have lived secretly among humans during that entire time. Usually, they work behind the scenes, running things so that the results turn out their way. Once in a while one of them will step forward and try controlling things more publicly, like Mark is doing."

Steve nodded. So far this sounded like the same old conspiracy shit that constantly amused the paranoid.

"You see, they can be very persuasive when they want to be, and this allows them to manipulate governments and businesses. It's kind of a mind-affecting thing where you do what they want while thinking all the time it was your idea, see?"

As he listened to Hillman's assertions, Steve had serious second thoughts about taking refuge with these people. Did the old man realize how crazy he sounded?

He stared into his coffee cup. In the hours since the shooting, he had begun to believe that he had been deluded, affected by all the vampire talk. There had to be a logical explanation for the assassin's quick escape, some gimmick or illusion that a magician could explain. Collin had tricked him somehow, that's all. And Steve had surely misidentified some night bird as a bat. Or maybe a real bat, hiding up on the ceiling, had flown out at just that moment, and his own shocked mind had put the two together....

"Are you paying attention?" Hillman asked.

Steve flinched, almost spilling his coffee. "Yes, of course," he lied. "There's just so much to assimilate, that's all."

Hillman studied Steve for a few seconds, harrumphed, and continued his tale. "Anyway, the vampires don't all get along. There's not a lot of them, but they compete for power all over the world. And now this guy Mark wants to be President, so it's no wonder that other vampires want to kill him, I guess."

"So Mark really is a vampire, then?" Steve asked with false but convincing sincerity in his voice.

"Oh, yes," Hillman said, eyes wide. "We've been watching him a long time."

Steve frowned. "But I thought all vampires were evil…"

"Are you kidding?" Hillman replied, taken aback. "Of course Mark is evil! He wants to ruin the American economy! He wants fags to get married and illegal immigrants to steal our jobs! He's a Godless communist who is trying to destroy our country and our way of life, and sell us out to our enemies! He's a bloodsucking spawn of Satan, here to bring about the apocalypse! How can you not see that?"

Hannah smiled broadly. "Fox News says Steve here is a liberal, Mr. Hillman."

Hillman stared at Steve as if the devil himself were sitting on his cat-hair sofa. For many long seconds, no one spoke, but Steve noted that Hannah seemed quite happy with herself.

Never taking his eyes off Steve, Hillman took a sip of coffee, placed the cup gingerly on a side table, and said, "See what I mean about them being able to charm people into believing their evil?"

"You have yet to give me any evidence that vampires even exist," Steve countered. He paused, trying to figure out a way to say what he felt without being insulting. "I… can't just take it on faith like you do."

Hillman glared. "And what is that supposed to mean? Because I put my faith in the Lord, I therefore believe in impossible things?" He picked Mina up, placed her on the floor, stood, and pointed to the door. "The Good Lord has led you here and protected you so far, but maybe you think you'd be better off on your own."

Hannah jumped up and held out her hands. "Now, Mr. Hillman, the Society would be very upset if you don't help Steve," she said in a soothing voice Steve had not previously heard from her. "Think about it. Karl wanted to frame him for some reason. Steve must know something that he doesn't realize. We have to protect him until we can take him to Asia."

Steve furrowed his brow and stared at Hannah's back. *Asia?*

Scowling, Hillman took a few heavy breaths. When he had lowered himself back into his chair, Hannah resumed her seat beside Steve.

"I'll help," he said, glaring at Steve. "But in my house, we do not disparage The Lord Our Savior. Is that clear?"

Steve nodded.

"Look, Steve, consider your situation," Hannah said in the same voice. "You don't have much negotiating power here. We're taking a big risk in hiding you. The police are surely trying to track you down right now, but we can keep you hidden. You give us a hard time, we can just turn you over, you know."

"But I must have something you want," Steve countered, "or else you wouldn't have saved me."

"Right," Hannah replied, sounding like herself once again. "It is impossible for me to do a good deed or help someone in trouble without having an ulterior motive."

Steve blanched. "That's not what I meant—"

"Oh, of course not. It's just what you said."

Steve stared into his coffee again. Mina padded up and rubbed against his leg, but he ignored her.

"Are you ready to learn about vampires now?" Hannah asked.

"Yes."

"About time," sneered Hillman. "Now listen, because I don't want to have to go through this twice."

Keeping his expression neutral, Steve sat still and gave the old man his attention—a skill he had perfected years ago. After all, his job required him to listen, without showing his true feelings, to the repetitive bullshit politicians spouted all day.

"Every culture in the world, no matter how separated, has a vampire tale," Hillman began. "Do you know how unlikely that is? That totally unconnected cultures, time after time, would have similar tales? It's darned impossible—unless the tales are based on truth. Oh, now, I admit the stories aren't all exactly the same, but you know, that's what you'd expect in an oral tradition. People exaggerate and embellish when retelling a story. 'Course, the vampires themselves spread false, far-fetched tales so no one will believe the truth, see?"

Hillman paused and gave Steve an appraising glance. "Most of the stories involve the undead in some way, but not all do. Nearly every culture says that they can shape shift into animal forms—and bats are not the most common. Wolves are mentioned a lot. It is our belief that they can change into many shapes, and use the bat form mostly because it allows them an easy escape, see?"

"But how do they do that?"

"They are Satan spawn, that's how! But I know you won't believe that."

Steve took a sip of his coffee and then tilted his head slightly towards Hillman. "You do know that Mark has been handed crucifixes and doused with holy water without any ill effects?"

"That just shows how powerful he is," Hillman replied.

"Interviewers have asked him outright if he's a vampire and each time he denied it completely."

"Oh, well, that settles it!" said Hannah. "After all, he might drink blood and ruthlessly kill those who stand in his way, but lying? He'd never do that."

Hillman gave Hannah a stern look and turned back to Steve. "Let me get back to explaining about vampires, will you?"

Steve frowned but nodded Hillman on.

"As I said before, vampires mostly work behind the scenes. When they do come to the public's attention, it's usually disastrous. You've heard of Vlad the Impaler, of course?"

"Sure," Steve replied. "The inspiration for Dracula."

"Yes, that's right," Hillman said, obviously pleased. "Vlad Draculea III, Prince of Wallachia. He went too far and was killed by the peasants. And then there was Countess Elizabeth Bathory—'The Blood Countess,' they called her. She'd take actual blood baths."

"I've heard of her," Steve acknowledged. "But naming those obvious choices doesn't prove anything. You're not going to tell me that every evil person in history was a vampire, are you?" Steve glanced from Hillman to Hannah. Typical conspiracy rubbish always placed the bad guys on one side and the heroes on the other.

"No, we humans do a good job of being evil all by ourselves," Hillman answered, to Steve's surprise. "There aren't a lot of vampires. They live a long time, and they avoid public notice, because then people would go, 'Hey, this guy's not getting old' and boom! Their cover's blown. Most of them just use their abilities to get rich and then they live nice, see?"

Hillman sipped at his coffee. "And they got plenty of time to do that in, so they're patient. They live about ten times longer than we do, so a vampire that looks fifty—like Mark—is really about five hundred. He's been around."

"That's why reporters can't find information about Norman Mark before the early '60s," Hannah added. "Because he didn't exist before then."

"What do you mean?" Steve asked.

"Well," Hillman replied as he scratched his nose, "we can't trace him back no further than when he came to America and took the name Salvatore Mark after World War II. He kept himself real private while he built up his electronics business. You've heard of Mark Electronics, of course?"

"How could I not? They make almost every phone and computer in the country these days."

"Right. Well, he used to make record players and musical instruments and stuff, too, back then. Anyway, in the '70s, he faked his own death and pretended to be his son."

"Wait. You mean—no, that's not possible."

"I'm not saying it's easy. It takes a lot of planning, a lot of laying the groundwork ahead of time, but it can be done. He makes up a story about the kid being away at school in Switzerland, and then the school burns down, taking all its records with it. So, no one ever sees the son till he's grown. That's why they can't find no more than one or two pictures of Mark from his school days, and those are doctored. Not hard to do these days with all those fancy computer programs on the market."

Steve started to speak but paused. As much as he hated to admit it, this could explain a few things.

"Getting false documents is even easier," Hillman continued. "'Cause they got the power to control people, they can easily get fake birth certificates and driver's licenses and stuff like that, see? So, making a new identity for yourself every now and then is not hard."

"Right," Steve said, "but why does that make them evil? I mean, Dracula and Blood Countess I understand, but has Mark really done anything evil? And I don't mean just taking political views you don't like, because there are plenty of non-vampires who have those views and, believe it or not, we're not all evil."

"They kill people and drink their blood! That's pretty darn evil, right? And Mark, well, he killed that Senator, what's-his-name!"

"Brunswick," Hannah said. "Governor."

"Right!" Hillman nodded, leaning forward in his seat. "You saw the video. He just headed to the edge and jumped off without the slightest hesitation, smiling like he was going out for a Sunday walk—just like someone being controlled by a vampire would do. And then, if you watch that one video someone took where they kept the camera focused on the balcony, you can see the bat flying out of the room."

"That doesn't mean Mark killed him. When that happened, Mark was miles away, with hundreds of witnesses."

"He didn't do it himself," Hillman replied, waving his hand before him dismissively. "One of his vampire buddies did it for him. Think about it, Steve; you're a reporter. It makes sense. Once Brunswick is out of the way, who do the Democrats pick?"

"Remember, vampires can't charm you through the television," Hannah added. "They have to meet you personally. Once Brunswick died, Mark and his vampire campaign workers had an excuse to meet with the delegates personally within a short period of time. The delegates' grief and emotional state made it even easier for Mark and his cronies to 'convince' them to throw their support to Mark."

Steve shook his head. Dammit! This was all making too much sense. "But if all that's true—if vampires exist and they've survived all this time by staying out of the limelight—why is he running for President? There's nothing more public than that."

"Well, that's the mystery," Hillman said. "Obviously, some of the other vampires don't want him to run, because they tried to kill him."

"I thought you had to use a wooden stake," Steve replied.

"Yep, everything you see in the movies and on TV is absolutely true," Hannah remarked. "There's no way to get rid of a vampire without a Mr. Pointy. Unless, of course, the vampire sparkles. That's different."

"Now, Hannah," Hillman chided gently, "you didn't know any of this either when we first met."

Hannah looked down but said nothing. Hillman took a couple of sips of his coffee and then returned his attention to Steve.

"A wooden stake could work, but so can anything else that could kill a human," Hillman continued. "Killing a vampire is next to impossible because they heal so quickly. They got some kind of power to control their bodies on a cellular level. Probably connected to their ability to change shapes or something. So you have to kill them instantly before they can heal themselves, see?"

"So a gunshot could kill one?"

"Yeah, if it's a killing shot. If you hit them in the brain or something."

"Like a zombie?"

"Like anything that gets a bullet in the brain. It's hard to heal head damage."

"Don't you need a silver bullet?"

"No, that's werewolves."

"Werewolves exist, too?"

"Don't be silly."

Steve slitted his eyes and pressed his lips into a tight line.

Hillman tapped on his coffee cup and stared into the distance for a few moments. "You know, you bring up a good point. If Karl really wanted to kill Sal, you'd think he would have aimed for the head. Or put a few more shots into him."

"There were more shots," Hannah said, "but they hit other people. Maybe he just missed."

"He seemed mad that he didn't do better," Steve said. "He was cursing, like he was upset, just before he turned into a bat. And who is this Karl guy, anyway? He told me his name was Collin."

"Karl Weaver runs an energy company—natural gas mostly. He's one of the guys we keep watch on, but he's never been connected in any way to Mark until now. Given Mark's views on the environment, I can see why Karl wants him dead."

"It could also be because Mark's too public," Hannah added. "Some of the vampires have to be worried that Mark will slip up and then people will realize they exist."

Hillman nodded. "Could be. Two birds, so to speak. But you'd think they'd have done a better job of it, wouldn't you?"

"Perhaps they just want to send him a message," Steve said. "You know, not kill him, but make him reconsider running for President. If these guys are anything like the Mafia, a kill would result in retaliation, and that would bring even more public attention." He nodded his head as he reflected on the ramifications and then froze when he realized he was seriously considering the possibility that vampires existed. He glanced at each of his hosts, who smiled at him.

"A good theory," Hillman said. "You could be right."

"Okay, but won't it be obvious to the doctors? One blood test and they'll know he's not human. A DNA test would give it all away."

"That's why Mark was rushed to a private hospital with his own personal doctor," Hannah replied.

"Still, Karl took a big risk there," Hillman said. "This crazy scheme of his could've made the situation worse."

Hannah shrugged.

Steve frowned, then took a long sip of his cooling coffee. "We were talking about how to kill a vampire, and you implied that it wasn't that hard—that you didn't need wooden stakes or anything special."

"Well, the hard part is getting to them," Hillman replied. "They know how to protect themselves, see? And even if you manage get to one, they're very strong. And fast. They can tear you apart before you take a breath. And if they're outnumbered or outmatched, they just change into a bat and fly away." He sighed. "So we can't really do much except watch them."

"Well, what good is that? If they really are evil, you're not going to defeat them by *watching* them."

"Look, Mr. Liberal, I'm an old man," Hillman snapped. "I'm not about to go vampire hunting. That's for the younger folk. What I do is gather and coordinate the information from our members and report my findings on the message board so we can keep track of the ones we know. What is done with this information… well, they don't tell me about it—"

"How do you know they do anything, then?" Steve interrupted.

"Because sometimes one of the vampires disappears," Hillman replied.

"Well, they've just gone into hiding, then."

"Sometimes. But if anyone in the Society *did* kill a vampire, you think they're going to announce it? Everyone thinks these are *people*, so killing one is murder. You don't go telling people you murdered someone."

Steve opened and shut his mouth a few times, considered his words, and then emptied the last of his coffee.

Hillman pointed a quavering finger at Steve. "I know what you're thinking. But we make sure we're right before we act. These aren't innocent people we're talking about; they're murderers, see? They kill people to drink their blood, and they murder anyone who gets in their way, like that Governor. Trust me, he won't be the only one. You watch; someone else who opposes Mark will 'mysteriously die' soon."

Steve winced as Hillman's fingers did air quotes while he said, "mysteriously die."

"And here I am, the most wanted man in America right now."

"Because of *them*, Steve," Hillman said. "They don't care about you. They do what they want and don't care who gets hurt because of it."

Steve took a deep breath and stared into his empty coffee cup.

TWELVE

Associated Press, October 22
MARK RECOVERING; Finnegan Suspends Campaign Activity

According to his campaign staff, Democratic candidate Norman Mark is recovering well and plans to resume campaigning within the next week. "The injury is superficial," stated Mark's personal physician Dr. Rahul Sethi. "Fortunately, his metal American flag lapel pin and the greenphone in Mr. Mark's pocket deflected the bullet, or the injury would have been much worse. He tells me he's keeping the now-inoperable phone with the bits of the flag imbedded in it as a memento."

Dr. Sethi stated that he would not allow Mark to see reporters during his recovery but assured the media that Mark should be well enough to attend the debate scheduled for October twenty-seventh.

Meanwhile, the assassination attempt has the political world in a panic. While Constitutional scholars discuss what would happen if a candidate died just before an election and political strategists argue over whether this will help or hurt the Mark campaign, news reporters tiptoe around controversial issues they would normally cover so as not to show disrespect for the hospitalized candidate.

John Finnegan's campaign has suspended all commercials for a few days at least, and although public appearances are being rescheduled, Finnegan still attends fundraisers. "With all due respect, there is no way we can compete against Mark's attempt to buy this election otherwise," said Finnegan campaign strategist Donald Lantz.

Unlike the Finnegan campaign's temporary shutdown, the many political action groups that formed after the unexpected nomination of Mark have not stopped their constant attacks. Thanks to recent Supreme Court rulings, these groups can spend unlimited amounts of money without having to reveal where the money originated, so they are running pro-Finnegan ads at a pace to match the funds Mark is pouring into his campaign.

Liberal blogs have complained that these new attack ads are backed primarily by huge business interests and overseas financing, but without the evidence to support these allegations, the complaints have not taken hold with the public.

The Finnegan campaign, for its part, appreciates the help but is frustrated that they cannot control what these groups say.

One specific ad is getting a lot of attention. In it, the announcer questions Mark's background, asking why no one has found his school records, pictures of him as a child, or original birth certificate. To accentuate its point, the ad features dark tones and eerie music, and at one point, a European castle as a background.

"These kinds of ads are a common political tactic," states political analyst Howard Fineman. "A controversial ad not only gets people talking, but the ad gets shown over and over again on TV talk shows and as people repost it all over the web."

Of course, what makes this one different is the unspoken accusation that Mark is a vampire—the latest and most absurd conspiracy theory to make the rounds.

"What's most amazing about this is that *Weekly World News* fiction is now being treated by a small percentage of Americans as fact," Fineman said with a laugh. "They apparently believe that Mark will get into the White House, drink the blood of his opponents, and appoint a space alien from Area 51 as his Chief of Staff."

Still, no matter how unbelievable, the ads are having a result. Although only a small minority actually believes Mark is a vampire, even a few voters can have an effect on the election.

THIRTEEN

Steve gasped for air. He couldn't breathe. A heavy pressure crushed down on his chest.

He forced open his eyes. A large striped cat stared back. And grinned. Steve wondered if he had fallen down the rabbit hole.

The feeling of disorientation lasted but a few seconds, and then Steve leaned to the side, causing the cat to jump to the floor. Freed of the weight, he found breathing easier. He tossed off the blanket Hillman had dug from an old cedar chest and sat up. His head felt stuffy and his eyes watered. Dust and cat hair had never been a friend to his sinuses.

The sunlight shafted into the room through spaces between venetian blinds, throwing a design across Steve's chest that reminded him of prison stripes. In that dim, yellowish light, the stacks and shelves of books, magazines and newspapers appeared older and more worn, like relics of an ancient library frozen in time.

Steve glanced at the clock partially buried under magazines on the end table beside Hillman's recliner. He shifted to see it better. Did it really say 4:45? In the afternoon? Had he slept that long?

Steve rubbed his eyes. What time had they arrived last night? Had to have been long after midnight. And they must have talked at least an hour. Then he had spent hours tossing and turning before finally falling asleep. With all the worries racing through his head, he marveled that he had gotten any sleep at all on the cramped sofa amid a sea of cat fur.

Probably shouldn't have had that coffee, either.

Steve scratched at his face. He needed a shave. As he pushed himself to his feet and ambled toward the bathroom, he wondered where Hillman and Hannah were.

Hillman had a collection of used razors in his medicine cabinet. After taking a close look at them, Steve decided it probably wasn't polite—or sanitary—to use another man's blades. He would just have to make do with a shower.

As Steve took off his shirt, he looked out the bathroom window. The small side yard badly in need of mowing extended about twenty feet from the house. Beyond that grew a stand of trees, thin at first but deep and dark in the distance. The yellows, golds, and reds of the turning leaves glittered in the sunshine with a reassuring warmth that made Steve smile.

He carefully folded each piece of his clothing and created a neat pile atop the toilet tank—the only uncluttered surface in the room. Steve took a clean, rolled towel—Hannah's handiwork, he felt sure—from a wall rack and hung it on the towel bar near the tub.

Twenty minutes later, he stepped from the shower to a rapid hammering at the bathroom door.

"Hurry up in there!" Hillman said. "I only got one bathroom, you know."

Steve wrapped himself in a towel quickly and grabbed his clothes. As soon as he exited, Hillman rushed in and slammed the door.

Enjoying the after-shower clean feeling, Steve walked to the sofa, set the towel aside, and dressed quickly. Putting on clothes he had sweated in profusely the previous day banished the good feeling of cleanliness.

He folded up the towel, looked around, and set it on the arm of the sofa. After deciding against turning on the TV, he grabbed a random magazine and leafed through it.

A few minutes later, Hillman stepped out of the bathroom.

"You want a snack before dinner?"

The question awakened Steve's hunger. "Sure. Thanks."

After Hillman disappeared into the kitchen, Mina jumped onto the sofa and demanded attention. Steve obliged, scratching her around the ears.

Mina jumped down when Hillman returned to the room with a tray containing two bologna sandwiches on white bread. He set the tray on the chair Hannah had used the night before and handed Steve a plate.

Hillman took a plate and a sandwich and settled in his recliner. "I don't keep soda," Hillman said. "And the coffee's gone. If you want something to drink, you can get some water from the sink. Glasses are in the cupboard above it."

Steve smiled appreciatively and took his advice, and a few minutes later the two were sitting in the living room, eating their sandwiches in silence.

"Where's Hannah?" Steve finally asked.

"She went to Wal-Mart to get some stuff," Hillman responded. "She should be back soon."

"So what happens now?"

"Now we sneak you into Brooklyn to see Asia."

"Asia?"

"Anastasia. She leads the Van Helsing Society, as far as I know."

"What do you mean, 'as far as you know'?"

Hillman shrugged. "The Society is just a group of people, see? It's not like we elect leaders or nothing. There could be someone above her."

Steve took another bite of the sandwich; which Hillman had gobbed so thick with mayonnaise that Steve could barely taste the bologna. He hated mayonnaise but wasn't about to complain to his host. He chewed silently for a few moments before speaking again. "This isn't a very organized group, is it?"

Hillman grinned. "Nah. It's not like we have meetings. We just all share an interest and give comments on the website's bulletin board and post links and stuff. People can join and then we send them the newsletter I write. I am helping in my own way by keeping Asia informed of things I find."

"What kinds of things do you find?"

"Oh, you know. Stuff."

"No, seriously, I don't know. Remember, I'm still new at all this."

Hillman gave Steve a glance. "Stuff like newspaper reports about people who disappear or who die in mysterious ways that the police can't explain. Articles about bat attacks on people. Strange blood losses that doctors can't treat. You know—*stuff*."

Steve placed his empty plate back on the tray. "And other than keeping track of them, you don't do anything else?"

"Nah, I'm retired. I let Asia and the others do any follow-ups."

Steve cracked his knuckles. His mind conjured the image of an overweight elderly gypsy lady in Brooklyn wearing a tinfoil hat, surrounded by crystals and blogging about the vampire menace. "So you think Asia will be able to help me?"

Hillman pursed his lips and stared at the floor. "I don't know."

"I can't hide forever."

"Yeah. But maybe she can think of something I can't. Honestly, I'm more worried about Hannah at this moment. What if the vampires have figured out that Hannah is involved?" He fidgeted. "I probably shouldn't have let her go out by herself."

"How do you know her?"

"Met her on the bulletin board. She just started posting one day, maybe a few years ago now. She came up one time and we shared a ride into Brooklyn for a meeting with Asia." He gave Steve a considering look. "You owe her a lot, you know. She really did save you there."

"I know, but I'm not too sure I'm better off."

Hillman raised an eyebrow.

"It took me a long time to fall asleep last night, and I did a lot of thinking. If I had stayed there, they'd have arrested me, and I could then describe Collin—I mean Karl—and tell them that he got away. After all, my fingerprints aren't on the weapon. I could've offered to take a lie detector test and everything. But now I've run and that automatically makes me appear guilty."

"You underestimate the vampires," Hillman said. "If you had stayed, you'd be dead. The vampires have infiltrated the Secret Service. One of their own would have run upstairs and gotten you while you were alone. He'd have shot you down and then told everyone it was in self-defense. Who would doubt his word? Nobody'd think to check the rifle for fingerprints then. He'd be the hero who stopped the assassin, and you'd be the dead crazy guy. I'm sure that was the plan."

Steve furrowed his brow and scratched at his stubbled chin. That made sense. "Still… I know some cops in Richmond I trust. I could call them and let them know. I'm sure they'd believe I didn't do it."

"And then what?" Hillman said. "Then they turn you over to their superiors who give you to the FBI. Somewhere along that line, there will be either a vampire or someone controlled by the vampires who will be given orders to silence you in the most violent way possible, like they did to Lee Harvey Oswald."

Steve looked at Hillman askance.

Hillman took another bite of his sandwich. "There's no one you can trust right now," he said between bites, "except the Van Helsing Society."

Steve stared at his sandwich, unable to even think about eating. He tried to change the subject to get the image of a violent silencing out of his mind. "So… what's with these traps?"

Hillman shrugged. "Doesn't hurt to be prepared. Learned the trick in Vietnam. Got the whole place trapped, but some of them only work if I hit a switch, see? More outside, too."

"How can a trap stop a vampire?"

"Well, you got to use garlic and crosses and holy water and stuff, too," Hillman replied. "The trap won't hold them long, but the other stuff might slow them down enough to give you a chance."

Steve jumped at the sound of a car approaching.

"That's probably Hannah," Hillman remarked.

"Not risking it," Steve said, as he dashed for the closet. He stuffed himself into the back, pulled the door closed, and pushed dusty old coats in front of his face.

A car door slammed. Steve tried not to sneeze.

Three quick knocks.

Hearing Hannah's voice reassured Steve and he emerged.

Hannah walked to the long table behind the sofa, carrying four plastic bags tightly in her fists. "Ah, finally came out of the closet, I see."

"Did you bring me some candy?" Steve asked.

She placed the bags on the table, dropped her keys into a dish, and started pulling items from the bags as if she hadn't heard him. "Some new clothes, hair dye, sunglasses, and a cheap coat because it's getting chilly. Plus some underwear. I hope it's what you like."

"Is it clean?"

"Yes."

"Then I like it. I owe you."

"You think?"

He moved closer. "Hair dye?"

Hannah held up a box and a gorgeous blonde model smiled back at him. "Hair dye," she repeated. "I was going to buy you a pirate disguise, but the inflatable parrot looked too sad."

"Pining for the fjords," Steve mumbled.

Steve caught Hannah's quick look of recognition before she removed the remaining items from the bag and continued on. "We have to get you to New York while avoiding as many people as possible. Don't say it, I know—we're heading to the most populated city in America when we really need to avoid people."

"Can't Asia come here?"

"I don't know, Steve. Continental drift doesn't usually work that fast—"

"We can't contact her, Steve," Hillman interrupted as he walked in the front door with two more bags of groceries and supplies. "We have to assume that the FBI is now monitoring the phones and emails of everyone connected with the group. At the moment, they probably consider the Van Helsing Society and others like us to be home-grown terrorists."

"They might be watching the house, too," Hannah added as she opened the hair dye box.

"Did you feel like someone was following you?" Steve asked.

"Well, no," she replied.

"I don't think they suspect me in particular," Hillman said. "Or Hannah. I mean, there are lots of people on our bulletin board, even more since the Mark campaign began. They can't suspect us all."

"Still, it's possible that eventually they'll see some video or picture and realize Hannah was at the speech and put two and two together," Steve said.

"That's why we have to get out of here as soon as possible," she replied. "Mr. Hillman, I'll need your help. Can I borrow your car?"

Hillman shook his head. "It's a piece of junk. It's been sitting in the driveway for months. I can't even start the darn thing. Peg from the church takes me to ShopRite every week, and to CVS when I need my medicine."

Hannah sighed. "All right. I guess we'll have to take my car then and hope no one is looking for it. I don't want to abandon it, though."

Hillman frowned. "Well now, how about if I give you Peg's number? You call her from a phone booth somewhere and tell her where your car is. Tell her she has to give me the message in person, not by phone. When I know where it is, I'll pay a couple local boys to fetch it and leave it at your house. That okay?"

"That's great. Thanks."

"Do you need money?"

"I'm afraid so. It's not like we can use Steve's debit card anywhere."

"All right. I can spare some."

"Thank you," Steve said through a tightening of his throat as the import of their words sunk in. From now on, his life depended totally on the generosity of other people—people he hardly even knew.

"When you see Peg, could you ask her to go to the post office for you?" Hannah said as she pulled a pair of disposable gloves from the hair dye box.

Hillman looked confused. "Letter to mail?"

"I want to leave my phone on and mail it to my sister in Colorado. In case they're using it to track me."

"Good idea," Steve said.

"Of course it's a good idea!" Hannah replied, using the voice of God from *Monty Python and the Holy Grail*. She slid clear plastic gloves over her hands. "Now let's find out if blondes have more fun."

FOURTEEN

Associated Press, October 22
DEMOCRATIC NOMINEE MARK
A MAN OF CONTRADICTIONS

While Democratic nominee Norman Mark recovers from the assassination attempt, many people are beginning to realize that they know very little about the secretive billionaire.

Mark is a man of contradictions—a successful businessman who treats his competitors aggressively while giving millions to charities. A public speaker who uses his charisma to promote his products while keeping his private life completely hidden.

What we do know about Mark comes primarily from his own website and promotional materials.

Mark's father Salvatore emigrated here from Italy in the 1930s, but little is known of his family before that. Like many immigrants, Salvatore Americanized his name. Norman Mark will not say what his original family name was, stating only, "My last name has been Mark from the day I was born, so that's all that matters."

Unlike many immigrants of the time, however, Salvatore came here with great wealth, which he used to start Mark Electric. Originally concentrating on household items like refrigerators and small appliances, Salvatore switched to war supplies during World War II and created targeting products for the military. After the war, the company's emphasis changed to constructing military computers of the type that filled a room with vacuum tubes and fans.

Salvatore Mark never offered his company for public sale and never had stockholders. He claimed this gave him the freedom to take great risks that stockholders would have prevented.

Some risks—like his stereo system when no one made stereo records—were too far ahead of their time, but others—such as the earliest calculators and later, the inexpensive remote control television—hit the market just when the public wanted them.

The younger Mark was born in the late fifties and kept from the public eye "for his own protection." During the tumultuous sixties, his family shipped him off to Switzerland to be educated in the prestigious Appenzell Academy, where he studied business, music, languages and politics.

Norman Mark's mother died in a plane crash when he was twelve. His father died of a heart attack just as the younger Mark was graduating from the Academy. As Salvatore Mark's only heir, he took over the business.

It soon became apparent that Norman had the same business savvy as his father, and perhaps with a younger man's enthusiasm and viewpoint, broadened the business in the '70s to include one of the first personal computers and some of the first wireless telephones.

As a lifelong music lover, Norman Mark expanded the company into developing electronic instruments and equipment, working to bring the new synthesizers to rock bands everywhere. He marketed one of the first relatively inexpensive four-track home recorders, and soon garage bands all over put out cassettes of passing quality.

His inspired creation of GreenTech had a huge impact. He understood the impression of purity and cleanliness that Earth Day and the environmental movement inspired. Long before other businesses adopted a 'green' profile, Mark grabbed the concept and used it to sell his products to young people. At a time when most advertisers feared using rock music in their ads, Mark cultivated an unheard of youthful image. His ads were also among the first to feature minorities in prominent roles.

Even though Mark promoted his products with the promise that two percent of all sales would go to environmental causes, many cynics saw the promotion of Greentech as no more than a shrewd marketing move, especially since electronics have very little 'green' about them. Mark, however, has not only followed through on this promise, but he has also donated much more of his own personal wealth to various charities, primarily to fight poverty, hunger, and disease.

Gay rights groups tout Mark's early involvement in the fight against AIDS and his donations to hospitals for testing blood donations for the disease. He quietly funds projects to free political prisoners, primarily through Amnesty International. Rumors have him supporting freedom movements in places like Egypt and Iraq, but detractors point out that his aid principally consists of providing fax machines, computers, and later cell phones to the rebels.

In fact, Mark's creation of the social networking site Bridge transformed the internet in ways even he did not predict. Bridge made it easier for people to connect based on their shared interests (or "bridge" as the terminology now holds), but it also allowed for the sharing of information which aided democratic rebels and insurgents who could communicate without government interference. Some analysts claim that Bridge helped to bring about the "Arab Spring," ousting many dictators.

Throughout these early years of his business career, Norman Mark kept a low profile, which earned him the nickname of "Howard," after the reclusive Howard Hughes. Pictures of him during this era are rare.

"This was on purpose," he explained during an interview at the start of the campaign. "I saw how celebrities were treated by the press and I wanted no part of that. Moreover, as an ordinary person without a famous face, I was able to travel through my factories and go to trade shows and watch, *Prince and the Pauper*-like. I could get honest feedback from the people who actually use my products without the spin added by my advertising people and without those ridiculous focus groups, which only give us crap like 'New Coke.'"

All that changed for Mark about ten years ago. He shifted course and began to appear at trade shows to promote his latest gizmos, and later, on television interviews and talk programs. His attendance at prominent New York social events—usually accompanied by a beautiful starlet or model or, on occasion, two—became common. He used his newfound fame to promote his charities, holding lavish fundraisers with some of his favorite musical acts: Bruce Springsteen, Elvis Costello, and Paul McCartney, to name but three of the biggest.

Once he had established himself as a prominent supporter of charities, Mark moved on to making his political views known and speaking out against unfair taxes, among other things. "Why is it that I pay a lower tax rate than my secretary?" he asked in one YouTube commercial posted by the liberal group Tax Equity.

Mark backed up his political opinions by supporting various Democratic candidates around the country. In some cases, his financial assistance helped long-shot candidates win elections.

The announcement of Mark's candidacy in the Presidential race generated a swarm of media attention and a league of young campaign volunteers weaned on his electronic devices. However, while money can help a campaign, it does not guarantee success. Most analysts agree that Mark ran a poor campaign in the primaries because he concentrated on TV and radio and hardly made any public appearances. He was seen as just another rich politician, trying to buy his way into office. Aloofness is not a winning strategy in New Hampshire and Iowa, where voters expect to personally meet the candidates before going to vote. Mark's support fell dramatically after his losses there, and he spent the rest of the primary season as an afterthought.

Worse yet, he became the target of the late-night jokers. Jay Leno, for instance, had a running gag in which a purported film clip of Mark at a rally showed a limousine zooming along a road with money flying out its windows.

Despite his long-shot candidacy, Mark refused to drop out or endorse anyone. "I want to make sure that the issues that matter to Americans are not ignored," he stated.

With the implicit threat that he would refuse to fund or assist the winning candidate if treated with disrespect, prominent Democrats everywhere avoided criticizing him—a decision which seems very wise in retrospect, now that Mark is the Democratic candidate for President.

FIFTEEN

Steve stepped out of the shower for the second time that day and rubbed a towel over his newly blonde hair. At least this time, he would be able to put on clean clothes.

He walked to the sink and slid the towel over the fogged mirror, but this only made the image blurrier. His hair didn't look any lighter, but then again, perhaps it had to dry more first.

"Oh shit!"

Hannah's comment from the other room came through the door loud and clear, bringing Steve to a full stop. He stepped to the bathroom door and put his ear to the crack. Hannah's footsteps raced from the front of the living room and she scurried around, shuffling bags and papers and growling like a berserk wild animal.

Curious, Steve wrapped the towel around his waist and grasped the doorknob.

A loud knocking hammered the front door.

Steve tossed down the towel and began dressing quickly.

Not until the pounded sounded a second time did Hannah's light footsteps cross the room to the front door. And she waited for the third bombardment before she opened it.

"Yeah?" said Hannah.

"Good morning, ma'am. I'm Special Agent Anderson and this is Special Agent Galanti. We're from the FBI. Is this the home of Oliver Hillman?"

The announcement sent Steve's already tight nerves jangling. Trying to keep as quiet as he could, he stuffed his legs into his new pants and yanked the zipper up.

"Yeah."

"We would like to speak to him."

"Why?"

There was a short pause. Steve held the pants up with one hand and reached for the belt. Apparently Hannah thought he was larger.

"Are you related to Mr. Hillman, ma'am?"

"No. He's just a family friend. And wipe that look off your face. He's an old man, and I help him out sometimes. I've been sleeping on the couch, as you can plainly see. It's still a mess."

"Yes, ma'am. We need to speak with him."

"What about?"

A hundred possibilities ran through Steve's mind. Had they noticed something? Three cups of coffee left on the table, perhaps? His wallet by the sofa? Would they ask to search the house?

"Ma'am, no one is in any trouble. We'd just like him to look at this picture and see if he knows this person."

"Hey, that's the assassin! I've seen his picture on television."

Another slight pause. "Yes, ma'am. Do you know him?"

"Is there a reward?"

Steve's heart pounded so loudly he thought for sure the agents would hear it echoing through the bathroom. He pulled the dark blue turtleneck over his head in one motion and sat on the toilet seat to tug on his socks and shoes.

"Possibly," the agent said with a noticeable interest in his voice. "Do you know him?"

"No. I was just curious. This is kind of exciting, isn't it?"

Slow footsteps padded from the kitchen. Hillman. His gait sounded uneven, like he had a limp. Steve didn't remember Hillman limping, but maybe he'd been too overwrought to notice.

"What's all the noise?" Hillman grumbled. "Who are these people, Hannah?"

"Mr. Hillman?" the FBI agent said. "Could we speak with you, please?"

"What's this all about? Who are you?"

"Sir, we're from the FBI. We're just doing a routine check of all those who may have been acquainted with this man."

"What man? That guy with you?" Hillman's steps dragged toward the door. "Never seen him before."

"No, Mr. Hillman. I'm Special Agent Anderson and this is my associate, Special Agent Galanti. We want you to take a look at this photograph."

"I'll look at it, but I ain't inviting you in, you understand?"

"Yes, sir. Are you acquainted with this man, sir?"

"The assassin? Why would I be… Oh wait, I get it now!" Hillman's voice rose. "I know why you're here. You got my address from our newsletters, didn't you? You think that we're part of some great conspiracy to have Mark assassinated, is that it? Well, we're onto you and your government cover-ups!"

"Sir, we—"

"We know all about you. We know you're keeping the truth from honest, God-fearing Americans—you're hiding the fact that vampires run the world, and how they have infiltrated all parts of American society."

"Sir, we just need to know—"

"Oh, it all makes sense now! In order to quiet us down, you fake an assassination and then try to claim we're behind it! You probably already have this guy, whatever-his-name-is, and are just trying to arrest us to shut us up! Well, it won't work! The whole world will find out what you're doing here today! This time we'll—"

"Ma'am, would you please stay here?"

"I'll be back in a minute. I have to go to the bathroom," Hannah said in a very innocent voice, just loud enough to be heard over Hillman's continued ranting. "Women stuff."

Although no one could see into the bathroom from the front door, Steve took no chances. He ducked into the tub and pulled the shower curtain as quietly as he could. The door opened and Hannah came in. She glanced toward him but gave no indication that she had seen him, and then closed the door again.

Hillman had not even taken a breath. "Look, buster, I know my rights! I'm a loyal, patriotic citizen. I love this country! I fought in Nam for this country! You go right back to your Trilateral Commission masters and tell them and whatever vampire lords you obey: we're not giving in. The truth will be found out. No matter how much the Illuminati may be helping you, you can't stop the truth."

The closing of the bathroom door muted Hillman's words. Hannah turned water on in the sink before whisking open the shower curtain. As Steve climbed out of the tub, she scanned him and then the room.

Hannah opened the bathroom window and nodded her head toward the opening. Frowning, Steve climbed onto the toilet seat and glanced out.

"Wait!" Hannah whispered. She gathered his discarded clothes and squeezed onto the toilet seat beside him and pointed out the window.

"There's a flagstone path into the woods. Keep about a yard to the left of it."

"What?"

"Hide nearby and I'll come get you when it's safe."

"But—"

"Go!"

Steve nodded and heaved himself out the window. He rolled as he came to rest in the tall grass. His dirty clothes scattered around him.

Steve gathered his clothes and darted for the woods, careful to keep about a yard to the left of the stepping stones. When he reached the tree line, he slowed as he shouldered his way between bushes and young trees.

The air smelled of pine and mint. A brisk autumn breeze whipped through Steve's still-wet hair, chilling him. Leaves blocked out most of the sky as he hurried toward shadowed woods. Eyes wide, his gaze bounced between the pathway and the treetops.

The FBI had no idea of his whereabouts. How could they? They had come to Hillman's house to question him because of his connection with the Van Helsing Society, and for no other reason.

A large, thick bush sat at the edge of the forest. Steve stooped and placed his dirty clothes beneath him to protect his new clothes from the dirt. Kneeling on these provided him with cover from the house, but allowed him a good view in case anything happened.

The muffled tones of Hillman's raised voice drifted from the front of the house. Steve smiled, wishing he could witness the old man in full spate. Hopefully, the agents would judge Hillman harmless and leave.

Steve held his breath, but he could hear no better. The woods, the building, and the distance dispersed the sound. When he grew light-headed with the effort, he let out a huge exhalation.

A few minutes went by. Or at least it felt like a few minutes.

Then a light appeared.

A flashlight. Coming from around the house. Scanning the ground from left to right and back again. Methodical. Searching.

Steve held his breath again. He considered stooping lower, but thought the movement might make things worse.

When the light wasn't pointing toward him, Steve barely made out a clean-cut man in a suit. He walked up the driveway, pointed the flashlight around the backyard a bit, but didn't move any farther. His gun remained strapped to his side, but his hand rested on his belt next to it. His movements telegraphed precision in use.

Steve blinked nervously.

The agent paused, and then aimed the flashlight directly at Steve.

Steve shut his eyes to prevent them reflecting in the light. He scrunched up his face and listened as hard as he could.

"This is the FBI," a voice said. "Come out with your hands raised."

This was it. They had him now. And he's hiding with a bunch of Batties. Even if they he told them someone else did it, they'd hear from Hannah and Hillman that it was because of vampires.

Steve opened his eyes. Hiding behind the blackberry bush seemed foolish now. What looked to be opaque in the haze of twilight revealed its secrets in the glare of the powerful flashlight.

The agent held his weapon before him but didn't point it at Steve.

Steve began to stand, and then paused. For all he knew, these agents worked for the vampires. Or were controlled by them.

They might even be the ones who were supposed to kill him at the Diamond, if Hillman's theory was right.

It would be much harder to shoot someone moving.

Steve made up his mind in a split second. He jumped up and dashed into the darkness.

"Stop!" he heard.

He didn't look back.

Keeping his arms before him, Steve crashed through the underbrush. He lifted his legs high to avoid obstructions and bounced between trees like a pinball. He tried to hear the sounds of the officer chasing him but could not overcome his own noise and his extremely loud heartbeat.

He blew into a clearing canopied by large trees and hanging ivy. His foot locked against a misshapen root. He tumbled forward, arms outstretched.

Behind him, the agent radioed for help.

Rolling over in pain, Steve threw himself back to his feet. The clearing would provide an open view for the agent.

Steve instead ran around the perimeter, staying close to the trees and brush.

"That's enough!" he heard from behind.

And then a shot rang out.

Steve threw himself to the ground. His glasses flew off into the fallen leaves. He spun himself over and looked back.

The agent approached as a bright light. He breathed heavily from the unexpected exercise. "That was a warning shot."

Steve didn't reply.

"Don't move, and keep your hands where I can see them." The agent walked across the clearing toward Steve. "If you're who I think you are, then we—"

Leaves danced around Steve like an autumn ballet. Dirt blew across his face. The light flew up in the air. A scream from the agent echoed through the still night. A powerful smell blasted through Steve's nostrils. Above him, the trees swayed and arched as if possessed.

The agent gave a loud incoherent cry.

Steve stumbled for the flashlight, which lay unmoving on the ground, obscured by leaves, pointing its beam on a strange angle to nowhere. He swayed it around the clearing until the agent's head came into view. Moving the beam revealed the agent's predicament.

The agent hung upside down, waving his arms to steady his movement. His right leg wailed about helplessly while his left anchored him to the strong rope that hung down from the darkness. He helplessly tried to knock away the many garlic cloves that dangled down from the rope at various locations, but they bounced right back to him.

The agent cursed and warned Steve of various laws that were being broken, but Steve ignored him and spun the light around on the ground. He grabbed his glasses and put them on. Nearby, coins, keys, a wallet, and a gun arranged themselves like a store display of things the excited escapee would desire. Steve kicked the gun out of reach and grabbed the keys.

He dashed back to the house, ignoring the agent's screams.

Hannah ran around the corner, by the parked cars, eyes wide at his approach. She visibly took a deep breath upon seeing him.

"Come on," he said, and ran to the cars.

Her Honda was blocked in the driveway between Hillman's Oldsmobile and a dark blue Ford Escort.

"Shit!" Hannah said. "Keys are on the table."

Steve dashed to the Escort. He opened the door and jumped into the driver seat.

He turned the agent's key and the car started. Hannah opened the passenger door and slid in as Steve put the car into reverse and backed down the driveway.

Hannah stared at him, fear in her eyes. "Are you sure this is a good idea?"

"No."

He spun the wheel and the Escort slid back into an opening between the trees. Shouts came from the house. Shifting gears into drive, he revved the engine and pulled out from the driveway onto a road that hadn't been paved since the Truman administration. He turned left.

"No, right!" Hannah said.

"It doesn't matter," Steve replied. "We just need to get away!"

They drove into the darkness, hearts pounding. The yelling behind them faded away.

SIXTEEN

After a few minutes jolting along the pothole-pocked road, Steve reached around and fastened his seat belt. He never felt comfortable in a car without a seat belt. In the back of his mind, the incongruity struck him. Here he was, chased by vampires and the FBI, and he was worried about seat belts.

Hannah looked to Steve and then fastened her belt.

"We had to run," Steve said, as much for himself as her. "They would never have believed our story. And now they have your vehicle, so they'll know who you are, too."

"I know."

"And for all I know, those two had been controlled by the vampires and just wanted to kill me."

"Did he try?"

Steve furrowed his brow. "He took one shot, but he claimed it was a warning shot. He didn't shoot me when he could have, though. Then again, maybe the other agent would have if given the opportunity."

"And even if they weren't controlled, they might have taken you back to someone who was."

They drove in silence for a few minutes.

"I'm worried about Mr. Hillman," Steve said. "They've probably already arrested him."

"He volunteered for that."

Steve glanced in her direction. "What do you mean?"

"Before he began that rant, he looked to me and I knew what he wanted me to do. He did all that ranting to distract them so you could hide."

"Really?"

"Yes… He doesn't believe any of that bullshit about the Illuminati and the Elders of Zion or anything else he was saying. He deliberately risked himself for you."

Steve swallowed. "What happened after I climbed out the window?"

"I stayed in the bathroom and listened. One agent told the other to go around and check on me. I guess they thought I might be trying to escape."

"What did you do?"

"I stayed there, of course. I hoped he'd look outside, find nothing, and come back inside—and then I'd just walk out of the bathroom like nothing had happened." She twirled her hair around her finger and stared ahead. "When I heard a shot, I opened the bathroom door. Hillman took off toward the fireplace and the agent chased him."

"Is Hillman all right?"

"He's fine. Hillman lured him onto the rug, and he fell into the trap."

"Holy shit."

"Well, holy water, anyway. The trap is a slide that leads to a pool of holy water in the basement, and unless you're a bat, you can't get back up without help." She bit at her fingernails. "Hillman told me to get you and run."

"But what about Hillman?"

"Don't worry. He's had escape plans for years. He always expected the vampires to come after him. Probably has some secret underground network of ex-marines or something. And since we moved the agents' car out of the way, he has my car and keys to make his escape."

They drove in silence for miles. Steve took random turns onto empty rural roads with no idea where he was or where he was going. An ever-changing rush of emotion s assaulted him—dread at the new charges that piled up against him, fear that they would be caught, admiration for the old man's nerve, amazement at the effectiveness of the booby traps, and disbelief that the whole mess could be more than a bad dream. And in the middle of it all, a great longing to hear his daughter's laugh again.

He turned onto a major road in much better condition. "Hey. That sign says Maryland Route 210."

"And?"

"When did we get to Maryland?"

"Mr. Hillman lives in Maryland. We've been in Maryland all along."

"Oh." Steve turned onto a side street to avoid the main road. A slight rain began to fall.

"Well," Steve said after a few more minutes. "We need to get to Brooklyn, right? Do you know how to get there without taking the main roads?"

"We need to ditch this car as soon as possible," Hannah replied. "We can catch a bus in D.C."

"A bus? Isn't that too public?"

"Not this bus."

Steve frowned.

"For now, just try to keep heading northwest," Hannah said. "Follow signs for D.C. Avoid the main highways."

A pounding had started in Steve's head, but he ignored it. "What do we have with us?"

"Oh, we're in perfect shape," Hannah replied. "Couldn't be better. I grabbed some money before the FBI agents came to the door, but my ID and credit cards are back in Hillman's house. They'll make great trophies for those agents, along with your wallet."

"Look through the car."

Hannah opened the glove compartment. "Papers, papers… Here's a small flashlight. It's like a cute little baby flashlight compared to the big one you have. A pair of old sunglasses. A map. Ooh, and a Swiss army knife, in case we decide to go camping with the Boy Scouts."

"See if the map helps."

Hannah pulled out the old map and unfolded it.

"You'd think this car would have a GPS," Steve said.

"Be thankful it doesn't. They could probably trace our location with it."

"Oh. Right."

"It doesn't seem to be an official FBI car or anything. Maybe they let the agents use their own cars."

"Or maybe those weren't really FBI agents."

Hannah glanced out the window, studied the map, looked out the window again, and then folded the map smaller. "Well, they weren't vampires, judging by how easily we escaped them."

Steve nodded. "And the garlic on the trap didn't seem to affect him. But then again, if—"

"Police!" Hannah said.

Steve tilted his head forward as far as possible. A police vehicle sat at the intersection. A lone officer was silhouetted in the driver's seat.

Steve glanced at the speedometer. Under the limit.

He passed the police car and kept his eyes low.

"He's coming!" Hannah said.

Steve felt a sudden terrible urge to piss. He tried to ignore it and continued to watch his driving very carefully.

"He's following us," Hannah said.

"Stop looking back. I can see him in the rearview mirror."

"Maybe he's following us because we're not locals. We're in the middle of nowhere, and they're always looking for out-of-towners to give tickets to."

"It's not *that* nowhere," Steve replied. "There are housing developments all over the place."

"I'm so glad my comforting words calmed you."

Steve realized how tightly he was grabbing the steering wheel and tried to relax. "If he stops me, I don't have an ID."

"Yeah, that's the big worry, isn't it? Trying to kill Mark is nothing compared to driving without a license."

Ever conscious of the headlights reflected in the mirror, Steve looked straight ahead. As the windshield wipers beat out a rhythm, he made sure to obey every traffic signal and sign. Despite the October night, he felt very hot, and licked his lips constantly.

"He's turning," Hannah announced.

Her words lifted a huge boulder from Steve's stomach. He found himself shaking as he checked the rearview mirror. "He could still be calling our license plate."

Hannah returned her attention to the map. "Turn left at the next intersection."

Steve turned onto a less-traveled side road.

A quarter mile down the road, the headlights caught the half-lit sign of a building supply center. Steve slowed down as he approached it and turned in when he noticed the black pickup truck in the dark parking lot. Perfect.

Aside from the dim light from the sign, a faint light from the store windows lit the parking lot. However, pallets of stones and lumber locked behind a chain-link fence shadowed one side of the pickup, and Steve pulled the Escort into the shadowed spot and turned off the engine and lights.

Hannah looked at him with one eyebrow raised but said nothing.

Steve reached across Hannah, opened the glove compartment, and pulled out the army knife. After exiting the Escort, he crouched down and crab-walked around the car to the rear of the pickup truck, where the Escort blocked him from view from the road. He crawled to the truck and began to remove the rear license plate. The rain picked up and drenched Steve's hair and clothes.

Loosening the screws didn't take long, but the small Phillips-head screwdriver on the Swiss army knife proved woefully inadequate for prying the plate off. Steve cursed and yanked at the license, and after what seemed too many long minutes, it released so suddenly he fell backwards into a cold puddle.

When he moved to the front of the truck to remove the other plate, Hannah joined him. "This is taking forever," she said.

"You got a better idea?"

"No. But I'm going to drive after this."

Steve cursed as the screwdriver slipped again in the rain but didn't comment. Hannah was right. The police would more likely recognize him, and if she drove, he could recline the passenger seat and lie down unseen.

Hannah went back to the car and climbed in the driver's seat.

The second plate finally came off, and Steve carried the two to the Escort. Fortunately, the Escort's license plates were not as tightly attached, and Steve made the change quickly and slid into the passenger seat.

He threw the old plates into the back, thought twice, and then reached for them again. Jumping out of the vehicle, he dashed to the truck and fastened the Escort tags to the pickup. It took a few extra minutes, but it might slow down an investigation. The truck's owner might not notice the change for a while, and by then, he and Hannah would have ditched the Escort.

Even more thoroughly soaked, Steve hopped into the passenger seat. He pulled off his glasses, pulled his pants pocket inside-out, and wiped them on the relatively dry cloth. Steve flipped the heater to high and adjusted all the vents to point at him. Then he reached under the seat, pulled the release, and lay flat.

Hannah turned the key. As the motor purred, she adjusted the mirror, switched on the lights and windshield wipers, and familiarized herself with the vehicle.

As she eased onto the road, Steve turned his head toward her. "Make sure you don't speed. Use your turn signal and come to complete stops at signs."

"Good advice from a criminal."

"We don't want to give the police any excuses to pull you over."

"I understand as well that a bear shits in the woods. Are there any other completely obvious things you'd like to tell me?"

Steve snorted. Hannah's sarcasm was comforting.

SEVENTEEN

"Karl, this was not supposed to happen."

Karl looked down at his entwined hands. "Unforeseen circumstances arise in any operation." He slowly lifted his eyes to meet Nick's. Nick specialized in hiding his emotions, but this time, Nick let his displeasure show… which did not bode well for Karl's immediate future.

Not the slightest twitch of a muscle in Karl's face revealed his thoughts. He forced himself to meet Nick's gaze.

Nick did not speak.

Karl found himself clutching the armrests. He loosened his grip. He had always prided himself on his speed and skills, but he had known Nick for a long time. Among the strigoi, Nick was unmatched. If Nick attacked now, Karl would not survive.

He surveyed the room. The sole door offered no hope. Every window in the room was closed. No easy escape. No escape at all.

Nick glanced at the TV screen. The sound was off. A CNN reporter outside of Mark's hospital spoke into a microphone as the crawl reported that the candidate was recovering. The reporter was interviewing Mark's personal physician. Nick pointed to the screen without looking at Karl. "This is great publicity for the campaign. Nothing but constant news about the candidate. Brilliant."

Karl remained silent, not wanting to remind Nick of his earlier anger.

"The problem you have now," Nick finally said, returning his attention to his visitor, "is that there isn't a dead scapegoat."

Karl choked on a forced laugh. "Well, you know, it's a funny story…"

"I can't wait."

Karl gulped. "The security guard assigned to take out Edwards missed his cue. The idiot was taking a shit when it happened. By the time he got back, Edwards had vanished and the Secret Service had the weapon."

Nick placed his hands together as if he were about to pray and then pressed his fingers against his mouth. "Hilarious," he said without humor.

Karl remained silent.

"You made no provisions for a backup? How short-sighted of you."

"As you are aware, it has been some time since I last attempted such a task." Karl kept his face expressionless, but a small bead of sweat formed on his forehead, trickled along the top of his brow, and trailed down the side of his face. He hoped Nick had not noticed.

"And where is Edwards now?"

"My contacts haven't dug up anything. We're as much in the dark as the police."

"Surely he's used his credit card somewhere or been caught on a surveillance camera."

"Maybe. But my sources have not found anything yet."

"What if the FBI gets him first?"

Karl squirmed. "I had someone plant incriminating evidence in his apartment. That should convince them. Maybe he'll run and they'll shoot him down."

"If they don't, and if he talks, you are in big trouble."

"I—I know that."

"And your trouble could become my trouble."

The words hung in the air between them like spears aimed directly at Karl's heart. "That…," Karl swallowed. "That won't happen."

Nick shook his head slowly. "There's only one thing left to do."

Karl's mouth went dry. His mind blanked.

A smile twisted Nick's lips. "You'll have to get Edwards."

Karl let out a heavy sigh. "I can do that."

"Hopefully, better than last time."

Fully cognizant of the implicit threat, Karl nodded. This situation had soured quickly—at first, it seemed that Nick would owe Karl a favor for such an enormous task, but now…

Nick turned back to the TV. "And then bring him to me. Unharmed. Understood?"

"Understood," Karl said. He would locate the wayward reporter—and then figure out some way of turning this debacle to his advantage.

EIGHTEEN

Seen on foot in the moonless dark, D.C. didn't look at all familiar. Steve followed Hannah as she walked down H Street. He kept his head low and shivered in the chilly night, wishing he had been able to grab the new jacket she bought him.

He stumbled over an uneven sidewalk. "Dammit! Do I have to wear these sunglasses? It must be almost midnight."

"No, of course not," she responded quietly without looking back. "Here, take this neon sign saying 'I am the assassin' instead."

Steve grumbled but continued on, opening his eyes as wide as he could as if that could let in more light. Their footsteps echoed through the mostly empty streets.

"Is this Chinatown?"

"What there is of it."

Steve frowned. "Not very impressive. I mean, really. Look, there's a Friday's."

"I'll be sure to register your complaint with the proper authorities."

They turned the corner. A few buildings down, a group of a dozen or so tired-looking Asian men and women clustered in the lee of a lighted doorway. Some leaned against the wall of the building, others smoked cigarettes. One graying man stared at the clipboard in his hand. No one talked.

"Wait here," Hannah said.

Steve watched as Hannah strolled up to Clipboard Man and handed him some money. The man took it, nodded, and without a word, made a note on the clipboard.

Hannah walked back.

"What was that all about?" Steve asked.

"Buses run overnight between Chinatowns in D.C., Philly, New York, and Boston," she said as she looked down the road. "They're mostly filled with people who travel to different cities on different days to work in the food shops. The cheap price is augmented by the terrible conditions the buses are in. I used them a lot back when I was a student."

"Oh? What did you study?"

"Lots of things. Art, for a while, but that didn't work out. Then I changed my major to psychology, but I found out that everyone who studies psychology is crazy, so I switched to photography with a minor in architecture. But then I got married and dropped out altogether…"

She paused and then gave Steve a long look.

"It's okay," Steve said. "You can talk to me like a normal human being if you want to."

She studied him for a few seconds but turned away as the approaching bus chugged toward them.

Hannah hadn't exaggerated. The dilapidated bus that lumbered into view had been repainted and labeled with unreadable Chinese script. Clipboard Man waved them over to stand in line behind the regulars who, Steve was pleased to note, extinguished their cigarettes before entering. Many appeared half asleep. A couple carried on a quiet conversation, and several texted or played games on their phones. None of them paid any attention to Hannah and him.

Steve climbed the steps and found seats near the back that were mercifully not ripped. He leaned over to try to close the window but, though he put all his strength into it, the window refused to budge. He sank into the hard seat, grumbling about the chilly night air.

"Do you think anyone recognized me? If they did and they're talking about it, we won't even know," Steve whispered to Hannah as she sat next to him.

"They probably don't even watch the news," she replied. "Besides, look at them."

The other passengers were settling into their uncomfortable seats for the five-hour drive. The talking had quieted. Even the texters had pocketed their phones. Not one person looked in their direction.

Steve forced himself to relax. As the bus rumbled into the minimal traffic, he leaned over to Hannah. "Can I ask you a question?"

"Yes. Do you have a second one?"

"How can Asia help us?"

Hannah sighed. "I don't know, but she has more resources than I do. If nothing else, she may be able to hide you better for a while."

"Where does she live?"

"In DUMBO."

Steve shifted in his seat. "Are you making fun of me?"

"District Under the Manhattan Bridge Overpass," Hannah explained. "Now shut up and get some sleep. People are starting to look at us because we're keeping them awake."

Steve slumped down and stared out the window. He doubted sleep would come.

NINETEEN

(SCENE: A hospital hallway. Two guards in dark glasses and suits stand before a door, looking very serious. A doctor walks up to them)

DOCTOR: Gentlemen, we have a visitor who would like to see the patient.

GUARD #1: I'm afraid that is not allowed, Doctor.

DOCTOR: But this is a very special guest.

(Finnegan enters)

GUARD #1 & GUARD #2: Senator John Finnegan!

FINNEGAN: Hello, fellow patriotic Americans! I am here to see how Mr. Mark is doing, because I care about the health of all Americans, as long as they can afford it.

GUARD #1: I am sorry, Senator, but we Secret Service have strict orders not to let anyone in except medical personnel.

FINNEGAN: But I have my own Secret Service men, too.

(Two other Secret Service agents enter)

GUARD #3: It's fine, sir. We can all stand guard outside. I can't imagine that Senator Finnegan would cause harm to Mr. Mark.

GUARD #1: Yes, sir. (opens door)

(SCENE: Typical hospital room, but the bed is empty. Finnegan enters and looks around.)

FINNEGAN: Norm? Are you here?

(There is a flash of light and a puff of smoke, accompanied by ominous organ music. Mark stands before Finnegan, arms outstretched, wearing a black suit with a black cape, dressed like Bela Lugosi. When he speaks, he has the Lugosi accent)

MARK: John, my good friend! It is a pleasure to welcome you to my room!

FINNEGAN: Norm, you look… different. And what's with that accent?

MARK: Ah, my friend, when I am alone, I can relax in comfortable clothes, and I am afraid that my accent sometimes reverts to the language I heard as a child when I was schooled in… (His eyes widen and shift back and forth for a few seconds)… Switzerland.

FINNEGAN: So that's what the Swiss sound like, huh?

MARK: Yes, of course! Here, have some chocolate.

FINNEGAN: No, thanks. I could use a good drink, though.

MARK: I never drink… wine. (Mark snaps his fingers and a disheveled looking hunchback enters)

RENFIELD: Yes, Master?

MARK: Renfield, please fetch some wine for our guest.

RENFIELD: Yes, Master. (He leaves)

FINNEGAN: Who was that?

MARK: My campaign manager.

FINNEGAN: Ah, I wish all my volunteers would obey me as easily!

MARK: Well, I have to admit, some of my volunteers suck. (They both laugh as Renfield comes back with a glass of wine that he gives to Finnegan)

FINNEGAN: Do you have a napkin?

MARK: Here. (Hands Finnegan a piece of paper)

FINNEGAN: (Looks at paper) This is a birth certificate.

MARK: Don't worry, I have dozens of them.

FINNEGAN: Aren't you having something to drink?

MARK: Of course! Allow me to get it. (He rises and walks over to the side of the bed, reaches up to the blood bag hanging from the I.V. unit, and drinks from the tube coming from the bag. Finnegan doesn't notice, as he is looking out the window. Mark returns to Finnegan's side) So, as you can see, I am doing much better. I should be up and about in no time. I hope you're getting ready for our debate next week.

FINNEGAN: I've been studying up and practicing. You won't get the better of me!

MARK: Are you worried?

FINNEGAN: Not at all! I'm still ahead of you in the polls. And I'm working hard to get those undecided votes. I have a strong stake in this debate.

MARK: You have a what?

FINNEGAN: A strong stake.

MARK: (Angry and scared) Where? Where is it?

FINNEGAN: Ah, you kidder. Anyway, don't worry, it will all be over soon.

MARK: It sure will be! (Mark grabs Finnegan and bites him on the neck. Finnegan screams and goes slightly limp, but does not fall to the floor) So, my friend, what say you now?

FINNEGAN: (in a hypnotized state) I will tell everyone that they should vote for Norman Mark.

MARK: Very good.

FINNEGAN: And I'll say one more thing…

MARK: Yes?

FINNEGAN: (Faces camera) Live from New York! It's Saturday Night!

(Cue music)

TWENTY

By the time Hannah and Steve walked across the Manhattan Bridge, the sun had peeked through the buildings, casting low shadows over New York. Delivery trucks and early commuters spewed their fumes into the air, and morning joggers flashed past, distracted by their headphones. No one took a second look at two ragged-looking walkers.

Steve stopped to take another sip of coffee, needed after a night of restless and often-interrupted sleep on the bumpy bus. He was thankful Hannah had agreed to the indulgence. She glanced back to see where he was and then joined him.

For a few moments, they stood aside from the early morning bustle with their backs pressed against the tiny section of brick between a paint-chipped doorway and a book shop window. Hannah's silence fit his momentary mood. The heat of the coffee helped hold the chill away.

As Steve gazed at the surrounding buildings, he felt a strange nostalgia, even though he could not recall ever having set foot in this neighborhood—or, for that matter, hearing of it. The build-up of DUMBO had apparently occurred after he left the city. New York had teemed with wonder and magic for an up-and-coming reporter. It was here he had met Linda. It was here he made and destroyed his name.

Steve took another sip of coffee and pushed the past into the back of his mind. He glanced around at the neighborhood. "DUMBO, huh? I don't remember them calling this area that when I lived in Park Slope."

Hannah began walking. "I visited here a few years ago with Mr. Hillman. I hope I can remember how to get to Asia's."

Steve took pace beside her.

"Asia told me that this area used to be old warehouses and factories, but then musicians and artists looking for a cheaper place to live in the city started moving in. It's close to the subways, and if you go up on the roofs there's a good view of the Manhattan skyline and the East River." She waved her hand toward a Starbucks. "Of course, as soon as it became clear that this was the new hip spot, the prices increased, forcing most of the artists to look for new places. Now it's full of condominiums selling in the hundreds of thousands of dollars, and there are galleries and book stores and record shops."

This renaissance, however, only lasted a few blocks. As Hannah and Steve walked west on Plymouth Avenue, the area took on a gloomy and dangerous aura. Boarded up or blank windows stared ominously at passers-by. Graffiti defaced empty buildings. Damp, foul-smelling trash mixed with the smell of urine from shadowed doorways.

Rusty trolley tracks ran down the center of cobblestone streets dating back a hundred years. Moisture from the night's rain still glistened on the rough stones. A stop sign, its post twisted and broken, lay on the sidewalk.

"My!" Steve said. "This is pleasant."

"It all used to be like this a few years ago," Hannah said. "It'll get better as the yuppies move this way. And it's the weekend, so there's no one here to work in the warehouses. Makes it look more abandoned."

As they approached Bridge Street ahead, Hannah slowed to stare at a five-story brick building to their right. Patches of brighter brick showed attempts to repair the walls, but many seams lacked mortar. Thick vertical bars stretched from bottom to top of the arching first-floor windows, protecting and imprisoning whatever was inside.

Hannah stopped beside a freight elevator door, which was recessed into the building's wall about three feet off the ground and framed by a fire escape platform, its ladder raised above ground level. To its immediate right, three cement steps led to a thick basement door.

Hannah nodded to herself, walked down the stairs, and knocked at the door.

Steve followed. "You sure no one is watching this place or anything?"

Hannah shrugged. "As far as I know, Asia is pretty good about not advertising her location."

"You thought Hillman's place was safe, too."

"No, I specifically said we should get out of there as soon as possible. Remember, Hillman used his house for the return address on all the Van Helsing newsletters. Asia only lets certain people know where she lives."

The door opened wide. Steve blinked slightly and tried not to stare.

A beautiful Asian woman stood before them, dressed in a blue sweater and jeans. Her dark hair fell across her face and hung to her shoulders in strands as if she had just gotten out of bed fully dressed. She raised an eyebrow.

"Hi. Anastasia?" Hannah said. "It's me, Hannah. We met last year when the Van Helsing Society had that meeting…"

"Oh, yes!" Asia said with a smile. "Now I remember! With Mr. Hillman. Come in, come in!"

Steve followed the two into a cavernous, dark basement. Removing his sunglasses helped. His eyes quickly adjusted to take in the room. He stood on a landing, and three more stairs led down.

Dim fluorescent tube lights hung from the many pipes that ran along the ceiling and did little to brighten the place. Thin sheetrock, broken only by a few featureless doors, walled in the unfurnished entry.

"I know; not the most beautiful place, but it's huge and I can afford it," Asia said. "The landlord owns the cardboard box factory upstairs and he leaves me alone, which I like. He can't afford a watchman, and he likes having someone here at night and on weekends. The building's not zoned for living but no one really cares that I sleep here, although I once had to hide my bed under a bunch of boxes when the fire marshal did an inspection of the factory."

She led them to the left, to an opening opposite a large makeshift door constructed of two plywood boards where the freight elevator would be. A prominent lock secured the boards, preventing anyone upstairs from taking the elevator down and gaining entrance to the basement unapproved.

Beyond that was darkness. From what he had seen of the building's exterior, the basement area had to be massive.

The opening led to a room decorated like a medieval tavern, with a bar at the far end. Not at all what he expected to see. Steve stared at the scene in bemusement.

Four heavy wooden tables and a scattering of chairs lined the side walls beneath a display of fake medieval weaponry divided by unlit, old-fashioned wall sconces. On the wall behind the bar, "The Dragon's Flagon" was painted in ornate lettering in a semicircle above a fanciful, multi-colored dragon. Through the arched opening to the right of the painting, Steve could see cabinets and a sink.

"This used to be a LARP place; you know, where people dress up as knights and play Dungeons and Dragons and stuff," Asia continued without taking a breath. She offered them a seat at one of the tables. "They'd also rent it out to people to play vampire games, isn't that a gas? They'd dress up all goth-like and pretend to be undead. Ironic, huh? Want a drink?"

Steve and Hannah both held up their coffees.

"Good idea," Asia said. "I'll make some up for me. Get comfortable."

As she glided to the kitchen, Steve slid onto an uncomfortable wooden chair. Hannah took the seat next to him.

"Her nickname is 'Asia' and she's Asian?" Steve whispered.

"Don't blame me, talk to her parents."

Steve shrugged and took a sip of coffee. "Seems friendly enough, though." He gazed around the room and imagined Asia dressed like a medieval bar wench. Had she played the LARP games here, or did she just like the medieval atmosphere?

Normally, women with that perky friendliness annoyed him. He wondered if her beauty had blinded him, if she had gone to the kitchen not to make coffee but to call the authorities. But Hannah trusted her.

"There, brewing." Asia said as she returned and grabbed the third seat at the table. She turned to Steve. "Hi, I'm Anastasia, and you are?"

"Steven Edwards. The assassin."

Asia's eyes grew wide and she looked to Hannah.

"He didn't really do it," Hannah explained. "He's just a reporter. He was set up by Karl."

As Hannah related the story to Asia, Steve studied the two women—bright-eyed Asia with her head tilted as she intently listened to Hannah's matter-of-fact recitation of the events that had changed his life.

"So, Steve," Asia said when Hannah had finished. "You didn't believe in vampires before this, I take it?"

Steve sighed. "How can any reasonable person believe in vampires? For all I know, I am sitting in a mental institution at the moment, imagining all of this."

Hannah kicked him under the table and Steve yelped. "You have quite a vivid imagination, Steve," she said with a smirk.

Steve rubbed his ankle. "Anyway, Mr. Hillman told me all about vampires, so I understand what's going on now a little…"

Asia scoffed. "Hillman! He doesn't know anything. He thinks the vampires are all creatures of the devil. He's seen too many bad movies."

She shook her head and then brushed her hair out of her face. "Vampires have been around forever, Steve, and are found in every culture—even those with religions that don't have devils. The stories about vampires don't all match because so much fiction has been added to the mix. And, of course, religious zealots had to write themselves in as the saviors so they could burn the evil vampires and witches and anyone who opposed them. There's something really ironic about that. Or maybe hypocritical. It's all very complicated, and of course I'm skimming over it quickly."

Steve stared at Asia in fascination. If she spoke this fast *before* she had her coffee…

Asia suddenly jumped up and dashed to the kitchen. There was a rattling and then Asia returned with a steaming cup in one hand and a pot in the other. "Anyone want to warm theirs up? Sugar's on the bar and cream is in the fridge. Oh, and there are donuts in the fridge too, but they're a day old."

For a few moments, concerns of the stomach supplanted thoughts of vampires as the three grabbed donuts and hot coffee. As places were once more taken around the table, Asia continued on exactly where she had left off.

"Vampires are like humans, except they live longer, are very powerful, heal quickly, can turn into bats, and need to drink blood to survive. You know, now that I say that, maybe they aren't like humans at all. Except they look human and have human-like emotions."

"Human-like?"

"Well, sure. They can hate and love and be stupid just like everyone else. The key here is that they live such a long time that they have a very different view of the world. They tend to be quite patient and not in a rush."

She popped the remainder of a donut into her mouth and chewed a few times, swallowed, and took a dainty sip of coffee before continuing. "They also tend to look down on humans as lesser beings. Or pets! When you live for a thousand years, the death of a human every now and then doesn't seem like such a big deal, you see?"

"So not all vampires are evil, then, like Hillman thinks?"

"Oh, no. Well, some are evil, sure, just like some humans are evil. But many see themselves as caretakers of humans, in the same way people treat their pets with love and care."

When Asia paused only long enough to sip her coffee, Steve marveled at her ability to talk nonstop without seeming to take a breath.

"A number of vampires feel guilt over the way they have taken advantage of humans over the years," Asia continued. "Some want to right the wrongs of the past. So they're not all bad."

"But where did the vampires come from?" Steve asked.

"They call themselves 'strigoi,' which is from some old language, I guess. Where they came from? I don't know. Some think they just evolved along with humans. I mean, there are some weird creatures in the world, you have to admit—creatures that can camouflage themselves to look like other things—so why can't one of them evolved the ability to turn into a bat?"

"Because it defies the laws of physics? Conversion of mass and all that."

Asia shrugged, unconcerned. "I don't know how they do it, and I don't really care. Maybe they came from another dimension or something, another planet, who knows? They're here now, and we have to watch them to make sure they don't go around killing humans for their blood and stuff."

Steve leaned forward. "Is that what you do? Monitor them?"

"Basically. I have a server in the other room, and I manage the web page and the bulletin board and coordinate things. People donate and I have Google ads, so that keeps me living well, as you can see." She winked and took another sip of coffee.

Steve took a deep breath. "The FBI is looking for me. Seems like you'd be the most likely place they'd visit."

Asia waved her hand dismissively. "Nobody knows I'm here. I'm *really* good with computers. No one has ever traced me down."

Steve wasn't comforted. No one ever had a reason to trace her before. As Hillman said, the vampires left these people alone because they seemed so absurd that no one could take them seriously. The FBI had felt the same, but the FBI in pursuit of an assassin might see things differently.

"Is that what you do for a living, then? Computer stuff?"

Asia shrugged. "Sort of. I used to teach martial arts for a while, but I find computers more interesting now. I get by doing jobs here and there. Temp work."

Steve scratched at his incipient beard. "So, vampires have been around forever, influencing humans?"

"Yes, but not like you think," Asia replied. "They mostly want to be left alone, to build up their fortunes and live nice—well, who wouldn't? They often work as investors or bankers or advisers and stuff like that. They don't want the truth to be discovered, so they try to avoid public attention. Every once in a while, though, one of them will become more public, like Mark is doing, but that's rare. Sometimes one of them becomes infamous, like Vlad the Impaler or Idi Amin, and sometimes they're sincerely trying to do good things. Jesus."

"What?" Steve asked.

"Hm?"

"You said 'Jesus' like you'd just thought of something bad."

"No, I said 'Jesus' to give you an example."

Steve's mouth opened and closed a few times. "Jesus? You said 'Jesus' as in—*Jesus was a vampire*?"

"Well, they like to be called strigoi—"

"This is ridiculous!" Steve said, rising. "Just when I think I might be discovering the truth, you spout off crap like every other conspiracy nut out there. Jesus was a vampire? Give me a break."

"I thought you didn't believe in Jesus," Hannah said.

"I don't, which is why this is so absurd." He paced to the bar and back. "You're telling me that Jesus not only existed, but that he was a goddamn vampire?"

"Well, that's what I've been told," Asia said. "Like I said, not all vampires are evil. Some actually want to do good. Jesus was one of them. He used his vampire powers to do tricks that impressed the uneducated, making them believe they had seen miracles. He used his charm to convince them he was the Messiah so that he could lead them to a better world."

"You expect me to believe—"

"He riled the authorities, and they got to him and crucified him, which wouldn't kill a vampire, you know. And then when they thought he was dead, they stuffed him in a cave and shut him in. Three days later, when they opened the cave, his body was gone. Nobody noticed the bat flying out over their heads, of course—who pays attention to bats flying out of caves?"

Steve stared.

"And so when he appeared before his followers, alive again, they all believed it was another miracle and started spreading the word. Over the years—behind the scenes, of course—he and a number of his strigoi followers formed the basis of the Catholic church."

"So what happened to him?" Hannah asked.

"Some of his strigoi followers eventually took over the church and turned it into the corrupt institution it became in the Middle Ages. I don't know why he didn't stop them. Maybe they killed him. Or maybe he died of old age. Vampires live a lot longer than humans, but they do die, you know."

Steve reached out with his hand, found the back of the chair, and sat in a daze.

"The Church is still dominated by the strigoi today, and they've mostly forgotten the original message of Jesus. Now they're just like other vampires—they just want to collect wealth, live nicely, and have some control over humans."

"*The entire Catholic church is full of vampires?*" Steve yelled.

"Don't be ridiculous. There aren't that many vampires on earth. Maybe only a few thousand. They don't breed too often, you see. And you can't create new ones by biting people on the neck, no matter what Hillman might have told you."

"But the church is still run by them?"

Asia nodded. "Most Catholics, including many higher-ups, have no idea that the church is run by vampires. You'd think they'd get a hint when they do that ritual where the people pretend to be drinking Jesus' blood and eating his flesh, right? But the fact is that the big guys at the top are almost all vampires, and some are not very nice people."

"Next you're going to tell me that the pedophilia scandals are really about vampires biting children and then charming them into thinking it was only sex."

"No, those scandals are real," Asia said with a sigh. "I told you there were some bad people out there. The strigoi are working on that problem —they don't want the Church to be scrutinized too closely, you see—but there just aren't enough strigoi to control everyone."

Steve looked askance at Hannah. "Every day I think I can't be surprised any more…"

"Jesus is ancient history," Asia said, "but his story is important because Mark apparently sees himself as the new Jesus. He thinks he's going to charm his way into the Presidency and then do all this good for humanity. I think he's sincere about all that. The problem is that unlike Jesus, Mark doesn't have any problem killing off those who stand in his way."

Steve shook his head. "Well, he has to win first. He's still behind in all the polls."

"Oh, he's going to win. You don't have to worry about that." Asia crossed her arms and gave a forceful nod.

"What, because he has so much money? That doesn't mean—"

"No," Asia said. "Because he is willing to cheat. Because he's not honest." She leaned forward. "Because most states these days use electronic voting machines that are made by Diehard Industries. And if you do a bit of research and go behind the corporate names and dig through the secret accounts in Switzerland, can you guess who owns one hundred percent of Diehard Industries?"

Steve's eyes grew. "Jesus."

Asia nodded. "Exactly."

TWENTY-ONE

Agent Richard Walker rifled through the glove box of the Honda Element. Tissues, lipstick, registration, some coins... nothing to give any indication that the owner would conspire to assassinate a Presidential candidate.

He climbed out, stretched his neck in just the way the chiropractor had instructed, and shook his leg to loosen it up. The long drive from Richmond had proved painful for his back, despite the support pillow he constantly used.

He lifted the yellow "Police Line" strip and ducked under.

"They're inside," said a young agent taking notes on a clipboard. She didn't look up.

"Thanks," Walker mumbled. He approached the house and climbed the few steps at a snail's pace, eying everything in the vicinity. His sore back, though a definite factor, wasn't the main reason for his slow speed. In his experience, the tiny things other investigators often overlooked could provide the clue that solved the case. He scowled at the cluttered porch and stepped through the open front door.

The two agents in the living room looked up and came to a ragged attention. One had scrapes on the left side of his face. Both had the drawn look of men who had not slept. Walker glared silently at the pair until they fidgeted.

"Anderson, Galanti," he said at last.

"Sir," they responded in unison.

Walker glanced around the room. Books piled everywhere. A sofa that had been slept in recently. Keys in a bowl on the table, wallet nearby. Dirty cups and glasses scattered on every available surface. Signs of cats. Religious symbols. Mirrors.

He sniffed the air. His nose creased. Frowning, he licked his lips. "What *is* that smell?"

"Garlic, sir," said Galanti.

Walker looked him up and down. "Advertising your ethnicity, are you?"

Galanti glanced nervously at Anderson. "No, sir. It's from the Batties. They laced a trap with garlic. It's a vampire thing where—"

"Yes, I've seen the B movies," Walker replied. "You're referring to the trap that yanked you into the air, where you dangled helplessly while the suspects stole your vehicle?"

Galanti nodded once and kept his eyes focused straight ahead. "It was dark, sir…"

"Yes. Well, why don't you tell me what happened? I'm *dying* to hear the tale in your own words."

Anderson and Galanti exchanged glances. Neither wanted to speak first. Walker didn't blame them; they had been outwitted by a crazy old man—not that an experienced agent would have fared better. Walker sympathized, but he had no intention of letting them off lightly.

Galanti straightened. "We were sent to check out this address, which is the mailing address of one anti-vampire group's newsletter.…"

Walker waved his hand. "I know that part."

Galanti stiffened even more and swallowed noisily. "The homeowner, Mr. Hillman, seemed like a harmless old man until we tried to explain why we were there. He started ranting about government conspiracies and vampires, getting louder and making less and less sense. It was obvious we weren't going to get anything from him."

Galanti looked to Anderson, who stepped in. "He had a young woman with him, sir, who said she was a family friend. She went into the bathroom. The old man kept ranting on, and she was gone for a while, so I sent Galanti around back in case the woman had slipped out another exit or tried to climb out the window."

Walker crossed his arms. "Not bad thinking, I suppose."

Both agents shuffled their feet. Anderson looked at Galanti, who took up the story. "I didn't see anyone at first, but as I was turning around I spotted a figure hiding in the bushes. I ordered her to step out, but when she—the figure—fled. I could tell by the height and build that the figure was a male, possibly Edwards. When he refused to halt, I fired a warning shot and gave chase, and ran into… the trap."

Walker stared at Galanti. "A garlic trap."

"For vampires…"

"And you dropped your gun, and your keys." Walker placed just enough dry scorn into his voice to make the rookies squirm.

Galanti's face reddened. "He didn't take the gun," Gilanti said. "Just the keys."

Walker raised his eyebrows. "Interesting." He walked to the worn recliner. "Forensics finished in here?"

Galanti answered. "Yes, sir."

Walker lifted the recliner's cushion, frowned at the cat hair, and after carefully replacing the cushion, settled on the edge of the seat. It felt good to get off his feet. Because of his back problems, he tended to unconsciously clench his butt cheeks to stand without pain, which only caused more pain in the long run.

He studied what he could see of the room, letting the silence drag on. When he felt the two rookies had suffered sufficiently, he let his gaze come to rest on Anderson. "And what were you doing during this time?"

"I remained with Hillman, sir. When I heard the shot, I ordered him not to move, but the old man backed away and then ran through the living room. I gave chase. I was calling for backup when I, um, fell into the other trap. Sir."

"Another garlic trap?"

"No, just water, but at the bottom of a chute. I couldn't climb out."

"We didn't get free until the back-up arrived," Galanti said.

"And neither of you saw whether Hillman and Cohen left with Edwards in your vehicle?"

The two men exchanged glances. Anderson spoke. "No, sir. We assumed—"

"Assumed?" Walker sneered. "You assumed a paranoid war hero who's been a recluse for years—who's booby-trapped his property against vampires—would not have some sort of escape plan of his own? Or some underground hiding spot?"

Anderson and Galanti looked like they had eaten something rotten.

Walker relented. "I have a team combing the woods now, carefully. If he's hiding, they'll find him. And Cohen, too, if she's with him."

Walker shifted his weight. The old man's chair was not as comfortable as it looked. He stared at the mantle, where a photo of Hillman in his army uniform sat beside a framed citation and a purple heart. What could have caused a hero to start believing such nonsense?

"What evidence has your team uncovered?"

Galanti pulled out a small notepad and flipped a few pages. "A collection of the Van Helsing Society's propaganda brochures—which confirms that the old man is involved with the group. Forensics took his computer to see what they can pull off it. He didn't have time to delete anything. Plus he has an old hand-written address book with a number of names and phone numbers from all over the country."

Walker nodded. He would get local police to check out the addresses in the book to see what they could find. "What else?"

"Edward's wallet and the ID of a Collin Babcock from the night of the assassination. The ID could have been forged or stolen and would have allowed Edwards access to the restricted area. We're following up on that."

Collin Babcock might provide a solid lead. Walker scratched at the side of his face, trying to figure out how a reporter like Edwards had become involved with the Batties.

Galanti turned a page. "The woman—Hannah Cohen—left her purse with her wallet and license as well as her vehicle. She claimed she's a friend of the family, sir, but it turns out she's a Van Helsing Society member too. We're trying to track down how she became involved in all this, and whether there are any others." Galanti looked up from his notes. "We also found the remains of a hair dye package in the bathroom trash."

Walker put his hands on the edge of the armrests, leaned forward, and rose carefully. "You two haven't had much rest. Get out of here for now, and report to headquarters tomorrow."

Walker almost laughed at the agents' expressions of relief. They stumbled over their own feet in their rush to the exit.

"And Galanti," Walker added as they reached the door, "for God's sake, take a shower."

TWENTY-TWO

Steve blinked and rubbed his eyes. He hadn't realized how much he'd needed that nap. The old mattress on the floor with its ripped and faded blankets had felt like luxury, although with the gallons of coffee he'd consumed in the past few days, he was surprised he had slept at all.

He yawned, sat up, and scratched at his days-old beard. They'd have to dye that too, he supposed.

After pushing himself off the mattress and locating his crumpled clothes on the floor, he dressed with reluctance. He'd give just about anything for clean clothes. Maybe the place had laundry facilities he could use.

He could hear the voices of the women in another room. As he ambled toward the sound, he still felt groggy but he felt rested too—even though he had dreamed of wolves, bats, and blood-stained vampires chasing him through endless foggy streets of dark, empty cities.

Hannah and Asia sat in a small room to the right of the tavern, perched side by side on chairs facing a long table containing a half dozen monitors and computers. Most showed varying screen savers, but one in the middle displayed the vampiresareamongus.com index page. Asia and Hannah scrolled through a bulletin board on the monitor to its right.

Hannah looked Steve up and down and then turned to Asia. "I didn't think zombies were real, too."

"Oh, ha ha. Such a wit. You put Dorothy Parker to shame. Perhaps if I could borrow the shower, I might appear less undead."

"Sure, no problem," Asia said. "It's to the left of the kitchen, up a few stairs. Hey, I ordered some pizza for us. Should be here soon."

"Great," Steve said. "But no anchovies."

"No anchovies," Asia repeated.

"I don't have any money to help, though," he said.

"It's okay." Asia waved her hand dismissively. "I put some money by the front door. Includes tip."

Steve looked over Asia's shoulder. "That's your page?"

Asia smiled. "Yeah. I take care of it. We have links to other pages, and we post pictures and have a bulletin board and everything. Our hits have gone up a lot since Mark's nomination. Donations are up; ad revenue is up."

Steve slid one of the plastic chairs from under the table and sat. "But do you have any real evidence? Anything that the mainstream media would pay attention to?"

Asia pouted. "Well, we think so. Of course, *they* say it's all speculation and circumstantial."

"What you need is a professional to present it. Someone who has access to the press."

"Who? You, Bernstein?" Hannah laughed. "Everyone thinks you're a loon who tried to kill—"

"I *know* what they think," Steve interrupted. "Enough with the sarcasm, already! We're in this together now, you know, whether you like it or not. I would appreciate a bit more support here."

Hannah kept her face to the monitor but gave him a brief sideways glance.

"Look, I've been thinking." Steve leaned over the table so he could partially see the women's faces. "Vampires exist and are running the world behind the scenes! This is the story I've been waiting for all my life—a Pulitzer Prize story. It's the story of the century. No, it's the story of... well, for*ever*. It's got everything! Violence, conspiracies, politics, mystery..."

Asia crossed her arms. "What are you going to do, tell everyone you saw Karl turn into a bat? No one will believe you."

"I know, I know," Steve said, rising. He paced the room. "But dammit, I used to be an investigative reporter. I used to do stories uncovering corruption in politics all the time. I can find something; I can *do* this."

Asia crossed her arms. "Why did you stop?"

Steve paused. "I got fired."

Neither woman responded. Steve stared at the floor as the weight of the silence filled the room. He took his seat again.

"It got too easy." Steve said to the unasked question. "I had everything—a beautiful wife and daughter, a job at the *New York Times*, a nice apartment in Park Slope—and I was making a name for myself as a serious journalist." He twined his fingers together and his voice lowered. "I was doing a story about a corrupt state representative. I had quotes and evidence about the bribes he had taken from a mob-owned company in order to let them build in an area that…"

Steve raised his eyes. "You don't need all the details. I had everything except the missing link I needed, the smoking gun. I knew it had to be there. All the evidence pointed to it being there."

His hands clenched into fists. "I had to get that bastard! I couldn't let him get away clean. So, I took some of the quotes I had and combined them. I created a source, put the words in his mouth, and wrote what I knew was there but couldn't prove.

"I figured eventually the guy would crack. That somebody would read the stories and come forward with the final piece." His tone pleaded for understanding. "But it never happened."

Steve stared at his tight fists, remembering the waiting, the interminable waiting for the phone to ring, for his email in-box to ping. He relaxed his fingers and splayed them flat on the table. "And that gave the rep's lackeys what they needed to attack me. They got court orders demanding the names of my sources. The court subpoenaed me to testify about what I knew."

When he didn't continue, Asia asked, "So what happened?"

"The *Times* backed me at first. Then I told their lawyers I had condensed multiple sources into one fictitious person who had supposedly witnessed the corruption. They didn't care that everything I had written was true. I had fudged the data because I had no hard evidence. They… they tossed me out. Fired me on the spot. They apologized to the corrupt representative. Nothing ever happened to him. The bastard's still in office."

He looked at Asia and Hannah. "Everything I wrote was true. Just… not exactly the way I presented it. But no one would hire me. I had crossed a line and I ended up broke. I started drinking. And eventually Linda left me."

Asia and Hannah remained silent.

"For five years I took whatever menial jobs I could get: working on political campaigns, serving hamburgers, temp work… until I finally landed another reporting job. Now I cover city council meetings, groundbreaking ceremonies, community affairs, and whatever other trivial shit they throw me."

Asia mumbled, "I'm sorry."

Steve stood and leaned toward them. "I *have* to do this. I *have* to expose this vampire story, if no other reason than to clear my name. To prove that I can expose the truth."

"Don't take this the wrong way," Hannah said, "but the problem is that no one will believe you, given your reputation. You've already burned that bridge, haven't you?"

"That's why I need clear, unimpeachable, and well-corroborated evidence." Steve paced back and forth. "I'll need your help, Asia. Surely you must have some connections."

Asia smiled. "I can make a few calls."

"And don't call me Shirley," Hannah added.

Steve smiled. "Towels?"

"In the bathroom," Asia said. She and Hannah went back to the website and began watching a video about vampire hunters. The background music was ominous.

Steve headed to the bathroom. He had a lot to think about. A thousand possibilities bounced around in his head. Getting a confession out of Mark would be the best, but that wasn't too likely…

In the back of his mind, he heard a faint muffled knocking. Pizza. He walked toward the door, lost in thought.

Some kind of photographic evidence, perhaps? In this day and age with cell phone cameras and recording devices everywhere, there had to be some way of capturing irrefutable evidence…

He opened the door and held out his hands for the pizza. Two police officers stepped back, surprised.

"It's him!" one yelled as he reached for his gun.

TWENTY-THREE

Karl gently set his martini down on the wooden coaster. He crossed his legs and leaned back into the overstuffed sofa. He resisted the urge to drum his fingertips on the side table.

Gregor had arrived precisely on time, and Zoe a minute later. She now sat at the far end of the sofa, thumbs tapping rapidly on her phone, while Gregor stood by the window, staring at the Manhattan skyline with a bored expression.

Karl looked at his watch. "Where's Margaret? She should be here by now."

Gregor shrugged. "I do not know." His Russian accent remained strong after all these years. "I have not spoken to her in a very long time."

That was probably true, Karl reflected.

Gregor had maintained a low profile for over a century, ever since the uproar caused by his notoriety as the mad monk Rasputin. Despite the many attempts on his life—including one by Karl—the man had managed to survive. After promising to never again become involved in politics, Gregor had faked his death in 1916 and taken a new Name. He had kept his promise and had established a number of charitable organizations in Russia and Western Europe from which he embezzled millions.

Karl didn't like Gregor, but he admired his efficiency. After all, he had planted the damning evidence in Edward's apartment without leaving a trace.

"Margaret's on her next Name," Zoe said without looking up. "She wants to be called 'Candy' now."

Gregor gave a loud laugh. "Candy? What kind of name is Candy?"

Zoe typed a few more words and then set her phone on the end table. Her deep green eyes flashed as if a hot fire raged within, yearning to escape. Karl noted that she had straightened her frizzy black hair. The way she wore it pulled back fetchingly emphasized the soft lines of her ebony face. Despite her beauty, Karl could not recall ever having heard of any romantic encounters.

"She recently broke up with Malcolm, you know," Zoe said.

Gregor's eyes brightened. "I had not heard." He walked over and sat in the lounge chair beside Zoe. "Do tell!"

"There was a huge spat involving some girls she found with him one day, and she left. That's when she took her next Name."

"After all those years together." Gregor shook his head. "So, who gets the place on the Riviera?"

"Candy, of course. You didn't think she'd let *him* keep it, did you?"

"But *Candy*?" Karl muttered. "That's a porn star name."

Zoe shrugged. "She's decided that's what men want." She lifted her head, fluttered her eyelashes, and waved a hand to impersonate Margaret's new persona. "Men don't care about intelligence, sugar. They don't want strong partners; they just want beautiful bimbos on their arms."

"What's with the southern accent?" Karl asked.

"Candy is a belle from Atlanta or something," Zoe said.

Karl shook his head. "Oh, that's just perfect. I hope that won't affect her ability to help us. I mean, she's one of the best when it comes to persuasion. She could sell..." He searched for a phrase. "She could sell an elevator to Geronimo!"

"Yeah, I got that album, too," Zoe said. "You're so clever. Anyway, I'm sure Candy can be just as persuasive as Marge, maybe more so. She convinced that governor to jump off that building, you know."

Karl paused, his glass halfway to his mouth. "That was her?"

Zoe nodded. "Probably why Nick recommended her. So, you and Gregor had better humor her if you want her help."

As if on cue, the door opened. A stunning blonde in a low-cut blouse and short skirt struck a pose in the doorway. She smiled with ruby red lips and held out her arms.

"Darlings!" she said. "It is so pleasant to once again see y'all!"

Gregor rose and Karl belatedly followed suit but crossed his arms and remained silent.

"Always a pleasure, Karl. Do forgive my tardiness." She ignored Karl's snub, lightly touched his arm, and breezed past him to offer a hand to Gregor. "You're as handsome as always, darling."

Gregor lifted her hand to his lips.

"Such a ladies' man." She turned and patted Zoe's cheek. "And Zoe! I love what you've done with your hair. Very chic."

Candy deliberately seated herself in Karl's place beside Zoe on the sofa. "So nice to see you all again."

Karl ignored the affront and sat in the vacant chair across from Gregor. "We don't have time for pleasantries. Nick specifically recommended you three because you each have something to offer this endeavor."

Candy crossed her legs. "Which is?"

Karl refused to look at Candy's shapely thighs. No point in gratifying her overlarge vanity. "We have to find Edwards and deliver him to Nick as soon as possible. Nick wants him before Election Day."

Gregor leaned forward, raised a fuzzy eyebrow, and rubbed his fingers together.

Karl shook his head. "You don't need money, Gregor."

Gregor grinned. "Perhaps, though one should never turn down more. To tell the truth, I have a favor I would like to ask Nick—but he has refused to see me for many years. This," he said, pounding his index finger into the end table, "is how I get in the door, no?"

Karl pondered someone wanting to ask Nick for a favor. If Gregor was that foolish... "We've all been promised generous pay once we accomplish the deed," he said. "But we have to find Edwards first. He got away somehow, and he's done a good job staying hidden. I think he's had help."

Gregor scratched at his beard, which was mercifully close-trimmed instead of that hideous thicket he had worn as Rasputin. "From other strigoi?"

"Possibly."

"Why not let the police deal with this?" Gregor asked.

"There's something you should know," Karl said. "Edwards wasn't the shooter. I was."

The three stared at him. Their incredulity gave Karl a moment's satisfaction. He let the news sink in before he continued. "Nick picked Edwards as the fall guy," Karl said. "I charmed all the guards at the ballpark, and none of them will ever mention seeing me. But Edwards..."

"Why didn't you bite him?" Candy asked.

"He would have needed more than I had time to give, and there wasn't the opportunity." Karl said. "That was a mistake. If he turns himself in or gets caught by the police, they'll get a very good description of me. And if other strigoi are helping him..."

"...then he will know your Name," Gregor finished.

"Please!" Zoe said. "The police won't believe him."

"Yes, they will. He won't tell them I turned into a bat. He'll just say I shot Norman Mark and then we both ran. My fingerprints are on the rifle, not his. And if he still has my ID…" Karl winced.

"Ah," Gregor said with a smile. "You really fucked up, no?"

"And now you need us to save your ass," Zoe said. She grabbed her phone off the table. "It seems you and Nick will both owe us favors."

Karl's mouth tightened. "Fuck all of you. This is Nick's game plan, not mine. I won't owe you bastards shit. Admittedly, I—Gregor, use the coaster! What do you think it's there for? —Admittedly, I benefit from finding this guy before the police do, but we go by Nick's plan and follow his rules."

"Dead or alive?" asked Gregor, placing his glass onto the coaster with exaggerated care.

"Alive," Karl said. "Nick wants to talk to him for some reason. After that, I don't know."

Candy leaned forward until her low-cut neckline gaped open. Karl was certain her boobs had not been that large the last time he had seen her. He frowned and redirected his gaze to her face.

"So what do y'all know about this Steve gentleman?" she asked, the southern accent oozing from her lips like honey.

"Nothing you haven't already seen on the news," Karl replied. "He has no family; he hardly ever sees his ex-wife, who moved to Nevada. She's been interviewed and clearly doesn't know where he is. His daughter has made crying pleas for him to turn himself in."

"Is he straight?"

Karl shrugged. "I assume so, given that he's been married and has a child. My gaydar didn't go off when I met him."

Candy waved her hand at Karl dismissively. "You thought Hoover was straight and he was prancing around in women's clothing."

"That was a long time ago," Karl said. "That subject wasn't much talked about back then, even among us."

"Oh, they didn't have gaydar back then?" Candy said with a smirk.

"No, it wasn't invented yet," Gregor said. "They only had gaydio."

"Hilarious. Can we possibly get to the point sometime this century?" Zoe's fingers flicked madly across her phone as she texted who-knows-what to who-knows-whom.

"Right," Karl said. "Well, Marg—*Candy*, I need you to use your wiles to try to trace Edward's path. Check with his friends, neighbors, coworkers—someone in Richmond must have a clue where he went."

"Bor-ring."

"Candy, no one surpasses you at this," Karl said. "You can gain information I'd never be able to get. Hell, you've practically gotten me under your spell now and all you're doing is pouting and letting your tits hang out."

Candy smiled. "Aw, Karl, you say the sweetest things."

"Gregor, you have connections in the criminal world. If he's getting help there, I'm sure you can find out."

Gregor bowed his head slightly. "But of course."

"And you need me to look for him online," Zoe said.

Karl nodded. "You're the expert. If anyone can find a trace of him, it's you. And don't just check the web, but also police reports, traffic cameras, banking records, credit cards, passports…"

"Hey!" Zoe snapped. "I know my job."

"All right then," Karl said. He stood and gave the three a long look. "You all have my number. If anyone finds a trace, call the others *immediately*. This task is your only priority. Make it the focus of your every waking minute."

"What if someone else gets to him before we do?" Gregor asked.

Karl pursed his lips. "Nick would be very unhappy. And none of us want that."

TWENTY-FOUR

Steve slammed the door shut, but the short officer stuck his foot in the way.

Steve stomped on the intruding foot as hard as he could in his stocking feet and banged the door against the foot again and again with all his strength. The officer yelped and the foot withdrew. Steve slammed the door shut, hoping it would lock behind him.

Spinning around, he jumped down the few steps onto the basement floor. The boom of an impact against the door echoed through the basement.

"What the hell?" Hannah screamed as she rounded the corner, with Asia close behind.

Steve didn't respond. He raced past the locked elevator, grabbed Hannah's hand, and drew her with him into the dark recesses beyond.

A loud boom shook the basement. The door would not hold long.

Steve headed toward a far corner of the basement where a door was barely lit by a red "exit" sign. His stocking feet slipped on the concrete floor. His arms swung out wildly for a few seconds before Hannah helped him regain his balance.

Asia jumped past them and threw opened the door. An echoing bang sounded from the opposite end of the basement as the police crashed through the locked door.

A faint light flowed into the basement from the narrow stairway. Asia dashed up the stairs. Steve glanced at Hannah as they followed. Her frightened eyes reflected his own fears. This time, escape might be beyond their reach.

The heavy fire door slammed behind them, sounding too much like a prison cell door clanging shut.

Dim ceiling lights lit the windowless warehouse. Rows of pallets full of shoulder-high stacks of flat boxes held together with plastic binding filled the space with the smell of cardboard.

Asia darted into the maze of boxes.

"Where are we going?" Steve asked.

"Warehouse door's locked from both sides. Fire escape on the roof."

Steve had one moment to contemplate descending a flimsy, narrow metal fire escape ladder before Hannah shoved him after Asia. He floundered forward a few steps and crashed into an unyielding stack of boxes.

Pain shot from his knee, taking his breath away. Cardboard boxes shouldn't be that hard, he thought as he rubbed out the pain.

Hannah grabbed him and yanked him forward.

The noise of the officers' heavy boots echoed up the stairs.

Asia ducked behind one of the cardboard towers. Steve and Hannah took shelter beside her. Asia appeared calm, but Hannah's eyes were wide, and her breath came in short, shallow gasps... just like Steve's.

A deep voice rumbled through the warehouse. "Drop your weapons. Come out slowly with your hands up."

Steve looked to Asia, who glanced at him and then pointed to the open door of the freight elevator, more than twenty feet away.

"This is the Police. Put down your weapons and slide them down the aisle toward us."

Two sets of footsteps tapped along the wooden floor in the distance, but the high ceiling and stacks of boxes distorted the sounds so that Steve could not tell exactly where the men were. The two stopped, held a brief, low-voiced conversation, and then the deep voice announced, "We've called for backup. You can't escape. You'd better surrender."

Steve grabbed Hannah's arm and waited till her eyes looked into his. He gave her the best smile he could manage and pulled her to her feet before nodding to Asia. The three of them scurried, half crouching, toward the elevator.

A shot rang out. The three of them dived into the elevator.

Keeping as low as possible, Steve pushed the button for the top floor and yanked the ancient accordion door shut. The elevator jerked and began its ascent.

Through the gates, Steve watched the officers approach, jerking their guns from side to side as if they expected an army of presidential assassins to leap from behind a cardboard stack. Sirens sounded in the distance.

The bare bulb at the top of the elevator flickered, and the elevator screeched and shook, drawing the officers' attention. Steve backed away from the gate as a shot pinged off the wall nearby. Within seconds, it had risen beyond that floor.

Hannah grabbed a handful of Steve's shirt and shook him. "What the hell were you thinking? Answering the door?"

"I wasn't thinking!"

"Obviously!"

Steve willed the elevator to go faster, but it didn't respond. "By the time we get up there and down the fire escape, their backup will be here."

Asia waved her hands in the air. "If you've got a better idea, now's the time."

Hannah remained perfectly silent, body stiff and tense, angry eyes focused on Steve.

The elevator jerked to a stop in a small room not much larger than the elevator itself. A rusted bicycle covered in cobwebs sat on top of a cracked and moldy recliner propped against the wall. To the left, stairs descended to the factory. A metal door was about ten feet away. Instead of a handle, it had one of those bars in the center that you press to open.

Steve threw the grate open and jumped out of the elevator. As soon as Asia and Hannah exited, he grabbed the bicycle and jammed the elevator door open. He checked to make sure his fix would hold while Asia darted to the door and threw herself against the bar. Hannah followed her onto the roof. As Steve reached the doorway, footsteps sounded on the stairway.

The waning light of day was fading into the constant glow of New York City. Too bright to allow starlight to pierce the luminosity, the Manhattan skyline shone over the East River, illuminating the vicinity with an artificial moonlight, gray and unfriendly.

Ignoring the sharp pricks of the roof pebbles that poked through his socks, Steve ran to the edge of the building, leaned over the ledge, and peered down at Plymouth Street. The rickety fire escape on that side looked like the slightest added weight would pull it loose from the wall.

Hannah joined him at the ledge, and after a long look at the fire escape, grimaced. "I don't think so."

The sharp echo of footsteps pounding up the stairs grew louder.

When Asia looked at Steve and shook her head, he pointed to a sizable cylindrical wooden water storage unit on short, rickety legs that might have last been used during the Nixon administration. Nothing else on the rooftop offered a hiding spot.

Steve gave Hannah a shove toward the reservoir and hobbled across the pebbled roof in her wake. He dived behind the water tank, then crawled beneath, where Asia and Hannah already lay.

From his position, Steve could see most of the roof. He swallowed, hoping the shadows from the tank hid them.

"This is stupid," Hannah muttered. "They're going to find us."

"That fire escape could never hold all of us at once," Steve whispered.

Asia glared at him. "You should have gone down."

"I didn't want to leave you two."

"Don't get all heroic on us here—it's you they want. They might not have even seen us yet. If you had gone down, they would have followed you. They might not have even noticed us."

Steve closed his eyes for a second. "Too late now."

The two cops peered from the doorway, weapons held before them. They paused, which gave Steve a clear view of each. The tall one was a brawny Latino man with a crew cut. His partner was at least six inches shorter—a white man with a shaved head and a nose that looked like it had been broken more than once in the past.

Like men who had trained by watching scores of action movies, they slowly moved across the rooftop, with guns outstretched, pivoting left and right and occasionally pausing. The Latino maneuvered to the ledge, peered over, and then nodded to his partner, who raised his eyebrows but then tilted his head toward the tank. They held a brief, whispered conversation and then pointed their weapons toward the tank.

"Come on out," the Latino said. "We know you're back there."

Steve scooted forward. When Asia grabbed his arm, he tried to jerk free. "Let me go."

"Shh!" Asia stared at the two cops.

"What choice do we have?" Steve whispered.

Asia held up a hand to silence him.

"Don't make this hard, Edwards," the Latino said. "We'll shoot if we have to. Drop your weapons and walk out with your hands over your head."

Steve crawled forward. Once again, Asia's hand clamped his arm. "I have some martial arts training. Let me handle this."

"Are you crazy?" Steve whispered. "They'll shoot you!"

Asia stared at Steve. "Listen to me! Do not go out no matter what. Do you hear me? *Stay here.*"

The force of her will and the serious look in her eye took Steve aback. "Uh…" he said.

Asia wriggled forward and stood. She held her hands before her but did not raise them above her head.

"That's far enough!" the Latino officer said. He and his partner knelt down and trained their weapons on Asia. "Hands over your head!"

"I don't have a weapon," Asia said. "You don't want to shoot me."

"Damn right, sister, so hands over your head!"

Asia did not slow her advance. "I just want to talk to you."

The officers twitched.

"Maybe she has a bomb!" the smaller said.

Asia was only about a dozen feet away at that point. "Remain calm. I just want to talk."

Hannah wrapped her fingers around Steve's wrist. Her grasp aroused a pang of guilt. He should've gone out instead of letting Asia endanger herself. Why had he listened to her?

Asia took a step forward.

A shot rang out.

Asia fell to the rooftop, her hand clasped to her shoulder. Blood spurted from between her fingers.

TWENTY-FIVE

Meet the Press, *October 25*

GREGORY: We are very pleased to have with us this morning Presidential candidate Norman Mark, live via satellite from his home in New York city, where he is still recovering from an assassination attempt.

MARK: It's great to be here, David.

GREGORY: Mr. Mark, how are you doing?

MARK: Quite well. I have wonderful doctors. I should be on the campaign trail again very soon.

GREGORY: After the convention, your numbers rose slightly but then stagnated. They've risen since the assassination attempt. What do you plan on doing to attract more voters, other than get shot at again?

MARK: [*laughs*] My campaign didn't really kick into effect until just recently. People are still learning about my political views. All most people know of me is what they've seen in Greenphone commercials and news reports about the assassination attempt.

GREGORY: Many political analysts and Democratic advisers are, honestly, shocked at the things you are saying. Here's what Dan Hart wrote recently in the *Wall Street Journal*: "While liberals are pleased with Mark, they are also worried that his message is too far to the left for the majority of Americans. Democrats have been urging Mark to tone it down, but he has refused to do so, which illustrates his inexperience in national politics. Many Democrats are having second thoughts about Mark's nomination."

MARK: Well, that's what you'd expect politicians to say, since I refuse to play their games. I am *not* a politician, and I believe the American people are ready for someone who isn't part of that insider, back-slapping group. Americans want someone to get in there and shake things up. If they expect me to tone down my words, they're going to be disappointed. I will always speak my mind and tell the truth, and if that angers people, so be it.

GREGORY: The Finnegan campaign claims that, given your wealth and your New York City residence, you don't know what it's like in "Real America" and that you are too out of touch to be President.

MARK: Let's remember that John Finnegan wasn't born in a log cabin either. His father was governor, and he's spent his whole life in politics, learning all the tricks politicians know.

I have to say, David, that I object to the term "Real American." Whenever a politician says that—and it's always a conservative—they point to farmlands and small towns and discuss "the heartland." The implication is that if you live in a city, you're not a "Real" American.

Well, that may have been the case a hundred and fifty years ago, but most Americans don't live on farms anymore. The average American lives in a city or a suburb. How can "Real America" only include only a small portion of the people in it?

In the city, there are many religions, many races, many cultures all living together in relative peace and harmony. *That's* "Real America" to me! America is a land of immigrants, who come here to live together, complementing each other, each bringing something new to make the country greater.

Although I've lived in New York my entire adult life, I've traveled the country and I've learned that you find the greatest innovation and creativity where there's the greatest diversity. You seek out people with different ideas than you, and you listen to them. And that's what makes America great. We're *not* all alike. That's our *strength*.

I know what the American people want. I know it so well I've become tremendously rich off of it. So, to say I am out of touch is ridiculous.

GREGORY: Speaking of religion, in rallies across the country, Finnegan's running mate Gerald Proctor has accused you of being anti-religion because you spoke out years ago against placing the Ten Commandments in courthouses and public buildings…

MARK: The Supreme Court agreed with me on that one, as you know.

GREGORY: …and pointed out that there is no evidence that you have ever proclaimed a religion or have even gone to church. How do you respond?

MARK: I love America and I love our Constitution. Our Founding Fathers worried about the influence of religion on politics. That's why they made freedom of religion part of the First Amendment. That's why they made it unconstitutional to require any sort of religious test for public office. I love the fact that, here in America, we accept all religions and do not discriminate based on religious beliefs.

Proctor's insistence on inserting *his* religion into our laws would shock the Founding Fathers. Honestly, the things he is saying are un-American.

GREGORY: Strong words...

MARK: No stronger than his claiming that we are a "Christian nation" which needs "Christian laws" to prohibit gay marriage and make school districts teach creationism as if it were science.

GREGORY: But what about you? What do you believe?

MARK: That's none of your business.

GREGORY: That answer won't go over well with many voters.

MARK: I think Americans will respect my conviction that religion should be a private matter. If candidates want to discuss their beliefs, that's fine, and if they don't, well, that should be fine too. I believe in the Constitution.

GREGORY: But surely, people want to know this about someone they are electing.

MARK: I have provided all relevant information. I've answered every question about each political issue presented. My web page is full of position papers and facts about what I would do as President. I do not shy away from controversy. My biography is available for everyone to read.

But if people want to keep their religious beliefs private, they should. Religion doesn't belong in politics. No one should be voting for or against me because of my religious beliefs.

GREGORY: You think it's irrelevant?

MARK: And private. Would you ask a politician what his favorite sex position is?

GREGORY: Very well, we'll move on. You mentioned providing information about your political views and biography to the public, yet controversy about your early years continues. People still raise questions about your birth certificate.

MARK: I've made that available. The original is on file, and the Secretary of State of New York has confirmed it. But facts never satisfy some people.

Is there any doubt my parents were Americans? Then why does it matter where I was born? Even if I was born overseas—and I wasn't—children born to American parents are natural-born Americans no matter where the birth takes place. This whole dispute is ridiculous.

GREGORY: Well, the lack of school records and other information about your early years leads many to think that your parents may have adopted a foreign child and that you, therefore, were not a natural-born American as required by the Constitution.

MARK: My opponents are desperate to find anything they can to discredit me and are fooling gullible people with this nonsense. Seriously, David, all you have to do is look at a picture of my father. I'm told I look exactly like him.

These detractors are just scared of me. They're grasping at whatever straws they can find to keep me out of the White House, because they know when that happens, I'll disrupt the status quo. And I will. When I get into the White House, the people will once again run this country.

GREGORY: What about the vampire rumors?

MARK: As if the accusations against me can't get sillier, now there's this. I may have dressed up as one for Halloween when I was a kid, but no, I am not a vampire. Of course, that won't settle the matter with certain people, but that's okay. It's always nice to have some laughs on the campaign trail.

GREGORY: Are you looking forward to debating Mr. Finnegan?

MARK: Yes. My doctor assures me I will be healthy enough to participate. I only wish Finnegan had agreed to more than one. I wonder what he's afraid of?

GREGORY: And that's all the time we have now. I thank you, Mr. Mark, for a very frank interview.

MARK: That's the only kind I give.

TWENTY-SIX

Wrenching from Hannah's grasp, Steve scrambled out of hiding and raced toward Asia. He stopped short after two steps when Asia bounced to her feet and jumped toward the two cops.

She grabbed the white officer and tossed him aside as if he were weightless. As he crumpled to the ground, Asia's right fist connected with the Latino's chin. The tall man flew backwards, hit the parapet, and lay unconscious.

"I told you to stay back!" Asia roared when she saw Steve at her side. "I'm doing all this for *you*!"

Steve stared, wide-eyed, at the scarlet stain on her shoulder. "But you've been shot…"

She ignored him and her injury and knelt to examine the large Latino. When she rose, she gave Steve a hard, disapproving look.

"He seems okay," she said. "Keep an eye on him while I check the other one. Let me know if he wakes up."

Steve nodded numbly but Asia, who was already halfway to the white officer, never looked back.

Steve knelt beside the unconscious Latino. He had read something on the Cracked website about how life isn't like the movies—in real life, if an unconscious person doesn't wake up within a few minutes, there's probably permanent brain damage.

This guy didn't deserve that. He was just doing his job.

Steve set his fingers against the man's throat to check for a pulse. He felt nothing, but the officer's eyelids fluttered and he moaned softly.

"Should I try to wake him?" Steve asked without looking away.

The cop groaned again.

"All right, good. You're not going to die," Steve mumbled.

Hannah, who had emerged from hiding, crouched beside him. Steve backed away to give her room. As she examined the man's head and felt the bloody bump, Steve noticed the man's gun a few feet away.

He left Hannah to tend to the man and, wrapping his hand in a fold of his shirt, gingerly picked the weapon up by the handle, making sure to keep his finger away from the trigger. The gun was warm.

"Do you think he'll be okay?" Steve asked as he tossed the gun aside, far from the cop's reach.

"I don't—"

A mournful cry rose form the opposite side of the roof. Steve's gut clenched at the haunting sound. He glanced at Hannah. "Stay with him."

He raced to Asia, who seemed to have fallen atop the short white officer. Afraid that her wound must be more serious than she claimed, he grasped her shoulder and shook her.

"Asia? Are you okay? Asia?"

No reply.

Awash in dread, Steve clamped a hand on each of her shoulders and pulled. For a long moment he could not move her; then she abruptly backed to the side, raised a blood-drenched face, and stared at Steve with cloudy, reddened eyes.

Steve recoiled and stumbled backward onto his ass.

Blood trickled from the corner of Asia's mouth, dribbled down her chin, and dripped onto her red-stained blouse.

Steve glanced at the officer, at the bloody bite marks on his neck. His stomach wrenched.

Asia wiped her mouth on the back of her sleeve. "I told you to stay away."

Steve watched dumbly as Asia slapped the cop.

"Wake up!" she said.

The officer licked his lips and opened unfocused eyes. His head bobbled from side to side. "Hrm?"

Asia cupped a hand on each side of his head. "Look at me. And listen. Why did you come here?"

"Checking addresses… routine… for the FBI… vampire sites…" His voice was dry and rough, like he needed a couple dozen cough drops.

Asia gave Steve a quick, frustrated look, and then stared into the man's eyes again. "Right. You were mistaken in thinking you saw Edwards. There were just some drifter kids living in the dirty basement. You chased them to the roof, where your partner tripped, fell, and banged his head on the retaining wall. You checked the kids' IDs. They weren't who you wanted, so you gave them a warning and told them to get lost. Those are the facts. Anything else that pops into your mind is just your imagination. Understand?"

"Yes," the cop replied in a dazed voice.

Steve's heart kicked into overdrive when the sirens in the distance sounded closer. He gave a slight cough.

Asia ignored him. She stared hard into the cop's eyes for a few more agonizingly slow seconds. "Call dispatch now. Tell them to cancel the backup. You don't need it."

The cop reached to the communications device on his shoulder. "Johnston here. Call off the eighty-five. No further assistance needed. Ninety-one condition corrected."

"*What?*"

"Chased some kids to the roof. They're not who we're looking for. Just some hippies squatting here without paying."

The voice in the device crackled. "We'll be there in a minute. Hold them for us."

"Hold them for you?" The cop looked at Asia in confusion.

"Yeah, hold them for us. You deaf?"

Asia stood and turned to Steve. "You two take the fire escape and meet me on Bridge Street. And grab my phone!"

"Your phone? I—"

Asia's clothes collapsed to the rooftop. A small bat struggled from beneath the wet fabric, circled Steve's head twice, and darted into the sky. As he stared after it numbly, he felt sweat breaking out over his skin.

Hannah hustled to her feet. "Christ!"

Steve turned to Hannah. "Go! Down the fire escape!"

Hannah gaped at him a moment. Then the defiant glint returned to her eyes and she nodded.

As she headed for the fire escape, Steve forced himself to kneel and rummage through the damp, blood-stained clothes until he found the phone tucked into the pocket of the jeans. He jammed it into his own pocket, stood, and glanced around the rooftop.

The injured Latino still lay unconscious against the parapet. The shorter cop, who continued to argue with his superiors about the kids he had released, paid no attention to Steve as he raced to the fire escape.

He peered down. Hannah scuttled rung by rung but had only reached the third floor.

Steve cursed and grabbed onto the rusty ladder. Although he didn't trust the thing, he couldn't wait until Hannah reached the bottom. He began the descent, arm over arm, leg over leg. The fire escape creaked and groaned with the extra weight. Bits of reddish flakes scraped against his hand and flittered away on the wind.

The sirens grew louder.

As he stepped from the third-floor platform, the ladder shook violently. A large bolt ripped from the wall above and plummeted past Steve's head. He didn't even pause.

He reached the second-floor platform and looked down. Hannah stood on Plymouth Street, her pale, anxious face looking up at him. There was no ladder to the ground from here—it had fallen off or been destroyed long ago.

He sat in the absent ladder's opening, twisted around, grabbed the metal posts on each side, and lowered his body through the opening. He hung there, swinging, hesitating. The street was about six feet below his stocking toes, but Hannah had done it…

Steve let go. He landed hard on his feet. Stabbing pain shot up his left leg and he fell to his knees, clenching his mouth shut to hold back the scream.

"Come on!" Hannah urged, tugging at his arm to get him to stand.

"Bridge Street," he gasped though the agony. "She's meeting us on Bridge Street."

"Are you crazy? You're going to trust her? She's a fucking vampire!"

"What choice do we have?"

Sirens sounded increasingly louder. Steve watched emotions flickering one after another in Hannah's eyes. Her haunted eyes met his a moment before she ran toward the corner. Steve hobbled after her as quickly as he could, his leg still in pain.

The graffiti-covered garage door on a building on the opposite corner slowly opened. Steve peered in. A beautiful red Ferrari revved its engine. As soon as it had clearance, the car screeched onto the road.

"Get in!" Asia said. She wore a loose summer dress that fell from one shoulder.

Steve grabbed the handle and jumped into the cramped back seat. Hannah pulled into the front and before the door was shut, the Ferrari raced up Bridge Street.

"Oh, shit." Asia said, slowing the car. "Knew it couldn't be that easy."

Steve glanced through the front window. Police blockade.

Wishing he had a blanket or coat, he ducked and scrunched himself as well as he could into the tiny scrap of floor behind the seats. Empty plastic water bottles on the floor crackled beneath him and poked more discomfort into his abused body. He held his breath as the vehicle stopped, sure the tinted windows would not prevent his discovery.

The automatic window on the driver's side lowered. Asia's sultry, sweet voice said, "Hello there, officer. Is something wrong?"

"Sorry, ma'am, just looking for a person of interest."

"And you're not interested in me?" Asia's voice took on a sulky tone. "I think I'm insulted."

The cop gulped audibly. "Yes, ma'am. No, ma'am."

"Well, there's no point in searching my car then. There's no one in the back."

Steve cringed. Why had she said that?

"Yes, ma'am. No one in the back."

"So I can go?"

"Yes, ma'am. You can go."

"Thank you, officer. You have been most kind. And I'm sure you won't tell anyone that I've passed by here. It will be our little secret."

"Of course, ma'am."

"And you should tell your dispatcher that you see someone in the third-floor window of that building, don't you think?"

"Yes, ma'am."

Steve clenched his fists. *What the hell am I doing in the back seat of a Ferrari with a vampire who knows Jedi mind tricks?*

The officer's voice, dutifully reporting the sighting of the person-of-interest in a third-floor window, faded when Asia's window swished closed. As the car turned slowly onto York Street, Steve raised his head enough to see the officer—who stared right at him but did not seem to see him.

Breathing heavily, Steve plopped flat down on the back seat, determined to stay there. As the car picked up speed, he shifted around on his back until he achieved the least uncomfortable position. Sirens sang in the background, echoing off the tall buildings near the East River.

Steve gazed upward through the back window at the dingy walls and blank windows of the buildings that zipped past. The Ferrari made a few turns. Steve lost all sense of direction but could tell by the increasing traffic noise and the frequent slowing, weaving, and occasional stops that they had entered standard New York traffic.

Steve found himself trembling uncontrollably. His mind raced from the chase in the warehouse and the descent down the fire escape to Asia's bloody fangs—always to those bloody fangs!

An abrupt screeching halt slammed him into the back of the front seats hard. Honking horns and cursing sounded all around.

"Can you drive?" Asia asked.

"Um, I guess…" replied Hannah.

The car doors opened and the two women jumped out to exchange places. The cursing, yelling, and angry honking escalated until the slamming of the car doors muted the sounds. The Ferrari lurched forward as Hannah stepped on the gas.

Asia leaned over the back of her seat, stared down at Steve, and held out an imperative hand. "Phone!"

Steve dug into his pocket and pulled out Asia's greenphone. She grabbed it and dropped back into the passenger seat.

A helicopter's blades sounded overhead. Even though Steve knew he could not be seen from above, he pressed his back tightly against the seat.

"Where am I going?" Hannah asked.

"Follow the signs to the Brooklyn Bridge," Asia replied. "There. Take the lane to Manhattan."

"I've never driven in New York before…"

"Look, just go! I need to get this done!"

Steve could hear Asia clicking away at her phone.

Asia occasionally directed Hannah to turn left or right. With sirens passing by every few minutes, Steve's heart kept up a frantic beat. He didn't remember hearing so many sirens when he had worked in the city… or maybe he just had never paid attention to them before.

Steve gazed up at the stone or glass-covered, ritzy high-rises, places that seemed as far removed from his new reality as the moon. He wondered if the people in those buildings ever looked out, if they would care that the most wanted man in America passed beneath their windows. Once, this had been his world. No longer.

The Ferrari turned and descended. The sudden darkness brought Steve to full alert. The car slowed, drove through a dimly lit tunnel, and stopped.

The driver's window went down. Steve tried to make himself invisible as Asia leaned across Hannah and spoke.

"Good day, Wilson." Asia's voice had assumed a cultured quality Steve had never heard before. "I'm letting my friend drive the Ferrari today."

A friendly voice answered back. "Right you are, Ms. Nakazato!"

"I hope your wife is feeling better."

"Much better, thank you. I'll tell her you were asking."

"Give her my regards."

"I will, indeed." The man's voice became louder to be heard over the mechanical humming sound. "You take care, Ms. Nakazato."

"You too, Wilson."

The vehicle advanced cautiously into a more brightly lit area. As the driver's window inched up, Steve raised himself high enough to see through the rear window. The descending garage door cut off his view of the elderly man who sat in a glass-enclosed booth, staring at a sporting event on a small television.

Steve sat up all the way and glanced around. Rows of very expensive cars lined both sides of the underground parking garage. Asia—or was it Ms. Nakazato?—pointed, and Hannah pulled into an empty space.

"Quickly," Asia said. She grabbed a set of keys from the glove compartment, climbed out, and then pushed the passenger seat forward.

Steve wriggled through the small opening and stood on the cement floor, stretching muscles, trying to keep the weight off his hurt leg. Hannah came around the front of the car.

Asia trotted to an elevator marked "private." Hannah met Steve's eyes briefly before she raced after her. Steve hobbled behind her as fast as he could. They slid into the elevator just before Asia pressed the 'door close' button. She inserted a key into a slot and turned it. As the elevator rose, Asia typed away on her phone.

The elevator came to a stop and the doors opened.

Steve walked into a scene from *Lifestyles of the Rich and Famous*. Light streamed through the ten-foot tall, tinted windows which comprised the walls to the left and right. To his left was a fully stocked bar, backlit by the magnificent Manhattan skyline. A grand piano sat in the far corner just beyond the bar. Two brown leather sofas were arranged nearby for listening pleasure, a small coffee table situated between them. A massive plasma TV took up a large portion of the wall opposite the elevator. Two arched doorways flanked the TV, one leading to the kitchen and the other to a large dining room.

Steve stepped further into the room, reveling in the give of the plush carpet beneath his much-abused stocking feet. Expensive paintings hung on both sides of the elevator. Sculptures on ornate stands sat in two corners. Above the fireplace in the third corner hung an emblem showing two fighters in traditional Chinese garb posed for battle. The words in the ribbon surrounding the emblem read "The Society of Righteous and Harmonious Fists."

"I've got work to do. Make yourself at home," Asia said. "Bathroom's down the hall through that door. Bar's over there. Back soon."

When Asia opened a door near the elevator, Steve caught a glimpse of a disorganized office with the latest electronic equipment. A large poster of Mister Spock—Nimoy, not Quinto—adorned one wall, and a bookshelf contained what appeared to be dozens of miniature collectable toys acting as bookends to numerous paperbacks of varying sizes. Before he could see more, Asia firmly shut the door behind her.

"Well," Hannah said with a sigh. "Wasn't expecting this."

TWENTY-SEVEN

Steve stood at the window beside Hannah, staring down at the street below. A soft, misty rain distorted the view. Lights from the nearby windows twinkled reflections through the drops sliding down the glass.

Since he could see bits of Central Park through the fog, he guessed Upper East Side, somewhere in the 60s. This building beat the SunTrust Building, Richmond's tallest structure, by at least six stories, yet here in Manhattan, it squatted like a dwarf among giants.

His life seemed as fuzzy and dreamlike as the view through the rain-splattered window. What in the world had he gotten himself into?

But he had straightened a few things out in his mind. Although he could not foresee what the future might bring, he had made some decisions. He would take control of his life again.

"So what do we do now?" Hannah whispered.

Steve adjusted his glasses. "We could run for it while she's in the other room. You still have the car keys. But where would we go?"

Hannah frowned. "I don't trust her."

"Neither do I," Steve said, "but—"

He stopped mid-sentence when the door to the office opened. Asia slinked in, exuding a feminine sexuality no man could ignore. Not even the floppy, gray dolphin slippers dimmed the effect.

"Don't you want something to drink?" she asked. "After what you've been through today…"

She walked over to the bar, pulled a bottle of wine from the refrigerator, and poured herself a glass.

Steve hesitated for a second and then walked over to join her. He found some Bacardi, then searched for some Coca Cola.

Hannah crossed her arms and confronted Asia. "I need to know a few things."

"You need to know a huge number of things, actually," Asia said as she sauntered to the sofas near the piano. "Have a drink and let's sit down and talk. There's a coffee maker there, too—although now that I think about it, you probably need something to calm you down, not stir you up."

Hannah didn't budge.

"Oh, don't be silly, Hannah. I'm on your side. Mostly." Asia sat and gave a smile. "You're safer here than anywhere else right now, so take a deep breath and get a drink. You'll need it."

Hannah turned on her heel and marched to the bar where she began preparing the coffee maker. Steve could almost see the fumes rising off her, and deep inside, he applauded her silent reassertion of control over some small part of her life.

He carried his rum-and-coke into the main room and sat on the other sofa. As he sipped at his drink, he refused to make eye contact with Asia. That was how they controlled you, wasn't it? Or was that a fictional part of the myth?

He stared at the dark amber drink and swirled it slowly in the glass. Only when he smelled fresh coffee approaching did he look up. Hannah, holding a steaming Star Wars mug, nodded and joined him on the sofa.

"I didn't have to save you, you know," Asia said.

"You didn't have to lie to us, either," Hanna replied.

"I didn't lie. I didn't tell you I was a vampire, but I didn't specifically tell you I wasn't, either. Oh, come on now, look at me. If I wanted to do something to you—including killing you—I would have done so by now, wouldn't I?"

Steve glanced at Hannah before cautiously peeking at Asia. Totally at ease, she sat on the sofa like an elegant queen in her castle—so different from the nerdy girl in the dirty DUMBO basement.

Asia smiled. "I helped you. I'm not your enemy. Now let me try to answer the questions I know you have." She finished her wine, set the glass on a side table, and leaned forward.

"I've told you before that the strigoi are not much different from humans. We fight among ourselves, disagree often, fall in and out of love, and experience all the emotions you can expect among a large group of people."

Hannah snorted and mumbled "People?" under her breath.

Asia gave her a sideways glance. "We also have very good hearing. Like a bat."

Hannah stuck out her jaw.

"Humans, strigoi—we're all people." Asia tucked her legs under her. "The point is, if there is one thing strigoi all agree about, it's keeping our existence secret. You know as well as I do that revelation would lead to a huge witch hunt. Innocent people would be suspected, and many would die."

Hannah shifted restlessly beside him, but Steve kept his eyes on Asia.

She leaned forward. "Plus, since strigoi own or manage many large industries and banks, a witch hunt could also lead to world financial collapse and revolution—not to mention religious wars."

Steve narrowed his eyes.

"It's not what you think. There's no vast strigoi conspiracy to control the world—and we don't. Like I said, we don't all get along. For every one of us controlling some multi-national corporation, there's another operating a competing one, trying to put it out of business."

"You act like this is just about exposing a group that's being discriminated against," Steve said. "You want us to feel sorry for you, but vampires *kill* people, drink their blood, and force them to do what you want. There's no way you can make that sound noble or admirable."

Asia sighed and looked down for a few seconds. "I'll try to get to all of that, I promise. Let me finish my point first, though."

Steve waved his hand like a king giving speaking permission to an underling.

"Many strigoi are upset that Mark has become so prominent. When you're in the public eye as much as the President of the United States, it is tremendously hard to keep secrets. Clinton couldn't even keep a blow job private. Mark's secret will be exposed, and then not only will all the strigoi be in trouble, but—"

"Exposure is what you need," Steve interrupted. "You've been manipulating things behind the scenes too long."

"Don't be naïve. People with power have been manipulating things behind the scenes since the dawn of time. Rich people, politicians, generals—if you think that hasn't happened, you're ignorant."

Steve snorted. "That's not the same thing…"

"Yes, it *is*," Asia insisted. "Strigoi may be very persuasive, but so is anyone with a lot of money. So are armies. Strigoi don't always win. And there are many more humans with wealth and power than there are strigoi."

"Yes, but they're not killing people."

"Of course they are!" Asia said. "They kill people with their pollution, with their wars, with their slavery and poverty wages. They don't give a damn about people; they only care about money and power."

"And the people you kill are different?"

Asia crossed her arms. "I haven't killed anyone in many years, and those I killed always deserved it."

"So you *just* bite people and drink their blood?"

"Yes, I have to in order to survive. Like a mosquito. It doesn't kill anyone."

Hannah shook her head. "A mosquito? You compare yourself to a mosquito?"

"It's better than a mosquito," Asia said. "When one of us bites you, our saliva sterilizes the puncture wound and speeds the healing. You go unconscious for a short while and when you wake up, you don't even remember being bitten."

"Is this before or after you make your victims commit suicide?" Steve asked.

Asia threw up her arms. "Fine. You don't want my help? I'll escort you out. Hopefully, you can make it a few blocks before someone recognizes you and you're arrested. That is, unless Karl gets to you first."

Steve glanced at Hannah. She didn't look any happier about the situation than he was.

"Steve. Hannah. Listen to me. You know that I have the ability to make you two do whatever I want you to. The fact that you are arguing with me right here and now proves that I am not. I swear that I'm on your side."

Steve took the time to sort through his thoughts and choose his words before responding. "Asia, you have to understand that this is very difficult for us. We've grown up with bloody Dracula movies and horror novels and vampire monsters at Halloween. The thought of a benevolent vampire just doesn't... seem right."

"We're not that different from humans, like I said. Some of us are evil. Just like some humans are. But I'm not one of them," Asia said quietly. "I helped you escape. I even took a bullet for you."

"That healed quite quickly."

"It's not completely healed. But yes, we do heal quickly. Luckily, the bullet only hit my shoulder. If he had gotten my heart, I wouldn't have gotten up very fast and we would have never escaped. If the bullet had hit my head, well, that would probably be the end of me."

Steve wondered how much of that was actually true.

"I took a big risk for you, Steve. I could've flown out of there any time I wanted, but I didn't. I tried to convince the officer to not shoot, but that didn't work. I couldn't get close enough to use my... *abilities*."

"The more you talk about the risk you took, the more I wonder why. Why risk yourself for me? I mean, what use am I to you, Asia? And is Asia your real name?"

"No, it's Naoko. But you can call me Asia—I'm used to that just fine."

"You didn't answer my first question."

"I will, but there's a lot more you need to know before you'll understand my reasons."

Steve opened his mouth, paused, took a sip of his drink, and then placed it down on the table. "Maybe you should tell us a little about yourself first."

Asia clasped her hands in front of her and spoke much more slowly than she usually did. "I had a terrible childhood. I spent a lot of time in China before it became so corrupted that I had to move. After World War II, I helped establish an insurance company in Japan. It's now one of the largest. I've become very rich off it. I moved to New York about twenty years ago. That pretty much sums it up."

"But what about the Van Helsing Society?" Hannah said. "Did you establish that?"

"Me and a couple of other strigoi. Such organizations had already started to pop up all over the internet. We figured starting one on our own would be a good way to monitor what humans were saying about us and give us some control over it."

Hannah glared.

Asia shook her head. "No, Hannah. I don't mean it that way. We didn't start the organization because we want to control humans, but to have some control over the dissemination of information. We think that perhaps the time has come for our existence to be revealed to humans. While there will certainly be some short-term upheaval, eventually the revelation will be for the best. For humans and strigoi.

"But a direct disclosure would have severe consequences. So how do we make the revelation with the least negative repercussions? Through the

Van Helsing Society, we can plant the seeds of knowledge and see how humans react—as well as getting them more used to the idea—so we can judge how best to proceed."

"That doesn't make sense," Steve said. "The Van Helsing Society hates vampires. Some of the members have killed vampires."

Asia smiled. "Well, they think they have. Most of those vampires just took on new Names. And, after all, this isn't going to be a short-term project. The shift from hatred to acceptance will take time, but strigoi live a very long time."

"You're willing to be outed?" Hannah asked.

"Not me personally," Asia admitted. "Not yet, anyway. But sooner or later, humans need to know we exist. Once they know about us, they would gradually lose fear of us and accept us. Only then would it be safe for strigoi to admit who they are."

Steve furrowed his brow. "But yet *you* want to remain anonymous."

Asia shrugged. "You think I'm a coward. Fine. Maybe I am. I admit I've covered my tracks well enough that I won't be exposed when the truth comes out, but that's just being prudent. There's bound to be some violence at first and a lot of upheaval. It may take a hundred years, but eventually we'll be accepted. Then I can come out. I can wait—I'm still young."

Hannah pouted. "How young?"

"Compared to Mark, pretty young. Compared to you, pretty old."

"How do you know *we* won't expose you?" Steve asked.

Asia assumed a hurt expression. "I'm helping you. I'm your friend."

"I hardly know you."

"And you've known Hannah how long?"

Steve stood and paced the room. Again he chose his words carefully. "Asia... surely you understand that no one likes to be manipulated and controlled, but that's what you vampires do. And that makes us all uneasy, and it always will. It means that I can't ever really trust you, because for all I know you have already manipulated me in some way."

Asia nodded. "That's a healthy attitude, Steve. But *everyone* tries to manipulate you—lovers, friends, advertisers, businesspeople, politicians —*everyone*. Strigoi just happen to be very good at it. And many humans are almost as good."

"But we can resist human control. Are you saying we can fight your control?"

"To a degree. Some humans have more success than others."

Asia leaned back and stretched out her legs. Steve forced himself to look away.

"Here's a fact of life, you two—good-looking women achieve more than average-looking women. Tall, handsome men get promoted more often than short, plain men. Harvard studies have documented this. Charisma and looks play a large role in how far you can get in life. You both know it's true."

Hannah glanced at Steve. "You can't expect us to believe that vampires can manipulate people because they're exceptionally good-looking. That's crazy."

Asia leaned forward again. "That's part of it. Sex plays a part, too. People are much more likely to be swayed by someone they're attracted to. A girl in a low-cut blouse can get many more men to sign her petition than that same girl in a shapeless, heavy coat."

"Yes. Well," Hannah said, hands waving. "What are you saying—all vampires are sexy?"

Asia smiled. "Partly. We also exude pheromones and other scents that humans do not notice but which have a great effect on people. Eye contact is imperative, though. With eye contact, we can plant ideas in a person's mind. When we're done, the person will believe whatever we want." She sighed. "Of course, that works better on some than others. Most will eventually discard the false memories."

"Is that what you did to the cop on the roof?" Steve asked.

"He was too caught up in the moment to be influenced before I bit him," Asia said. "Usually it works, but usually people are not in a life-or-death situation when it happens. Or maybe he was gay. That always makes it more difficult."

Steve shook his head. "But you only bit one cop."

"We had to get out of there! I didn't have time to take care of his partner. I hope the older cop convinced his young friend that he was mistaken, that he imagined seeing you there. But I can't guarantee anything." Asia chewed on a fingernail. "They were both knocked out long enough that they could have hallucinated. At least, their conflicting stories should keep their bosses confused for a while."

She had begun talking fast again. A sign of nervousness… or defensiveness? Steve wasn't sure. He sat back down beside Hannah and studied Asia.

"I used my cell phone to wipe the critical information from the computers in the basement, and I double checked from the computers here. All the authorities will find now is innocuous data about the Society and some documents belonging to Asia. All the critical, secret files are secure, and there's nothing to lead them to this place, which I own under the Nakazato name. You're safe here."

He didn't feel safe. He wasn't sure if he'd ever feel safe again.

"My clothes!" Asia suddenly said.

"What?"

"Did you get my clothes off the roof? When you grabbed my phone?"

Steve gasped. "No! You just said 'phone.'"

"Well, shit," Asia said. "Shit shitshit. That's not good. The clothes are sure to attract attention and make them ask questions."

"I, uh, I didn't think of it. I've never been in this kind of situation before…"

"I'm sorry. It's not your fault. I should have said something. We did the best we could, I guess. I'll have to figure out some way to get them back; I don't want the cops examining my DNA." She stared at the floor. "Shit, damn, cunt, and piss."

Steve waited to see if she was going to recite any more curse words but she remained silent. "You still haven't explained why you're helping us."

"Why is it so hard for you to believe that I really am a nice person?" Asia replied, eyebrows raised. "You didn't do anything wrong, and I don't want you to be killed by Karl's goons or captured by the police."

"You said you would help us expose Mark."

"And I will."

Steve crossed his arms. "I'm listening."

"Here's what I fear: Mark gets into office and then something happens that brings the strigoi to the media's attention, something that can't be hidden or denied. There would be absolute turmoil! And someone would dig up the fact that Mark stole the election, that he was born long before the United States existed and is not an American citizen. Think about what that will mean."

"Well, he'd have to resign."

"No, Steve!" Asia spread her hands to the sides. "This is a lot bigger than that, and you know it. Think about what it would mean to the world! Everywhere people would wonder if the person sitting next to them was a vampire. No one would trust anyone. People would call their rivals and enemies vampires. Governments would collapse. Businesses would fall apart."

"Religious fanatics would have a field day," Steve mused.

"And terrorists," Asia agreed. "Not to mention what this would do to the international economy. There would be a worldwide collapse never before seen. I don't think either of you want that."

"No," Steve said, "but you're not making sense. If Mark's exposure would cause such a world catastrophe, how can you expect us to believe you want to help us expose him?"

"I'm getting to that! Just know that I do want us to be exposed eventually, so we can be accepted members of society—but I want that done on *our* terms." Without a pause in her words, Asia picked up her glass, walked to the bar, and returned with a full glass of wine. "If Mark becomes President, the truth will come out abruptly and there will be no controlling it—or the reaction. He can't keep this secret for four or eight years. Not with the media and Secret Service dogging his every step."

"Assuming he doesn't declare himself dictator or something," Hannah said.

Asia gracefully resumed her seat and took a sip of wine. "We need to prevent that from happening. We have to threaten Mark with exposure and be willing to back up that threat if he refuses to resign."

Steve pursed his lips. "Blackmail."

Asia nodded her head and touched her nose. "That's where you come in. If I went to Mark and threaten to expose him, he'd never believe I'd actually go through with it. You, on the other hand, have every reason to carry out that threat. If you had real, hard evidence, and the ability to get it published, he'd have no choice."

"And you'd be willing for me to carry out that threat if he doesn't drop out?"

"It's not what I'd prefer, but it will happen anyway if Mark becomes President. His hubris won't allow him to see that. It would be better to release the truth gradually, in a thoroughly planned and carefully executed campaign—the kind of thing we've begun with the Van Helsing

Society—but if it gets out, it gets out. The world will descend into turmoil for a few hundred years, but the strigoi will survive it."

Steve tilted his head. "If I try to blackmail Mark, what's to stop him from just killing me?"

"We'll make sure there are backups of the evidence, with a control trigger so that you have to be there to stop it from being published. We'll set it up so that at a specified time, the information will get emailed to all the major media outlets. If he does anything to you, then the trigger password won't get entered and the information will be sent. You'll have to reset the password every few days or so—that way he can't get rid of you later. And if you can't, for any reason, enter that password, the information gets released."

"That might work," Hannah said, "*if* he were dealing with a human who couldn't force him to reveal the password with little effort at all."

Asia's eyes became unfocused. "We have to set it up so that only you can do it. Maybe with voice and iris recognition."

"He could still control me and force me to enter the password."

"You might have to trust some other people with the information. People who would release it if they think you're being controlled." Asia put her feet flat on the floor and leaned forward on the sofa. "We can work out the details, if you're willing to go ahead with this."

Hannah gave Asia a searching look. "Really? You'd really set all that up?"

"We have to. Mark has to know Steve isn't bluffing. We're very good at telling if you're lying. Never play poker with a strigoi."

"You seem fairly confident for someone who not so long ago told me that they'd never find you in that basement," Steve said.

Asia frowned. "You have a point. I thought I had covered my tracks. Maybe the FBI got the information from Hillman's computer. Dammit! I told him not to have my address written anywhere. Or maybe they captured him and he talked."

"Not likely," Hannah said. "He always thought the vampires would come after him, so he had escape plans. And on the off chance that they did capture him, he'd rant and act the crazy old man, like he did when they came to the house."

"Well," Asia said, "however they found out, you're safe here. No one in the Van Helsing Society knows the identity I use for this place."

"So what do we do now?" Steve asked.

"We take our time. We plan it carefully. I have some friends who can help." Asia's speech had slipped into fast forward again. "Meanwhile, you two make yourselves comfortable here. You'll like it here. I have two spare bedrooms you can use. And get online and order some clothes. Go to the Macy's page; I have an account with them—I'll take care of the costs. And, hey—we never did get that pizza. Guess I'd better order one. I don't know about you, but I'm starving. And Steve, let me get the door this time."

Steve winced.

TWENTY-EIGHT

Agent Richard Walker glanced at the badge of the woman who stood in front of his desk. When his gaze returned to her face, he found her eyes so unnerving he focused on her lips instead. "Everything seems to be in order, Agent Cremer, but I must admit that I'm curious about why I've never heard of the FBI's Special Division on Assassinations before."

Agent Cremer smiled. "The existence of the division is on a need-to-know basis, and previously, you didn't need to know. We're specially trained, but usually work on other projects until we're needed. Sadly, there was a need."

"Still, I don't know what we can do to help you. You must have seen the reports. Hundreds of agents have worked on this for days." Walker found her full, expressive lips as distracting as her eyes. He shifted his gaze to her eyebrows instead.

"Oh, come now, Agent Walker, you know as well as I do that not everything is included in the official reports. I want your impressions, your gut feelings about this."

Walker had never before considered a woman's eyebrows sexy. He lowered his eyes to below her neck. But her creamy white skin… shouldn't a federal agent have a few more buttons on her shirt fastened?

He cleared his throat. "Very well, ma'am. I'll be happy to assist in any way I can."

When Cremer strolled to the door to shut it, he couldn't drag his eyes from the sway of her hips. The way her blonde hair swirled around her head as she turned mesmerized him. He stared openly as she wriggled that perfect body into the chair that faced his desk. She leaned forward to pull a laptop from her bag on the floor, and his breath stopped at the clear view of her magnificent cleavage.

He swallowed heavily and then reached for his bottle of water.

"You have been coordinating the efforts here in Richmond since the incident, correct?" she asked while opening the laptop, apparently unaware of her effect on him. Her smooth Southern accent rolled off her tongue like warm honey.

"Yes, ma'am, I—"

"Oh, you can call me Maribeth. If we're going to work together, we needn't be that formal."

"Oh, I, uh, I'm Richard. Or Dick. It doesn't matter." He blinked nervously.

"Dick. That's a very nice name." The way Maribeth said his name, with just a hint of meaning, made Walker's heart race. "Why don't you start by summarizing the evidence found in Edward's car and home?"

Walker struggled to focus on her request. He leaned back in his chair, found that his back-support pillow had moved, and rearranged it. That helped. "Nothing that's not in the reports. Bullets the same caliber as the rifle, weapon magazines, a couple handguns, and a hand-written diary ranting about vampires."

"Anything on his computer? Emails, links to vampire sites, that sort of thing?"

"No, but we didn't expect to find anything. The guy's a reporter. He knows his way around. And these paranoid types avoid putting anything on their computers because they're certain they're being constantly monitored, even when they're offline."

"Witnesses?"

"The guard stationed at the door to the box seats swears Edwards had the proper pass and went up to the booth alone. Unfortunately, there was some glitch with the cameras in the corridors outside the booth and we have no surveillance of the area."

"No others?"

"Maybe he had an accomplice. Doesn't exonerate him, though. And Edwards disappeared in the chaos right after the shooting. Left his car at the ballpark, which seems odd unless someone picked him up." Walker shrugged. "He must have had another means to get away. And he never returned home, as far as we can tell. No security vids at his apartment building."

"But his phone was found?"

"Yes, a good Samaritan found it on the ground and turned it in to the staff. We hoped we'd get some leads there, but that didn't pan out. And the calls that came in later were from his wife, his editor, his friends, his sources. Nothing out of the ordinary."

"Interviews with these people produced nothing?"

"They all insist that this is not like him, that he hated guns, wasn't superstitious, didn't believe in vampires… or God, for that matter…"

"Guess they didn't know him as well as they thought they did."

Walker spread his hands. "A divorced man living alone and under a cloud—he could easily develop personality traits he kept to himself."

"So everything fits."

"Except the clothes."

Maribeth raised an eyebrow. The sensual sloping arch of it and the smoldering glint in her eyes sent heat rushing to Walker's head and crotch. He shifted in his seat, thankful that the desk hid his unprofessional reaction.

"You… know," he said, trying to get his scattered thoughts in order. "You read the reports."

"But, Dick," Maribeth said with a smile, "I want to hear your interpretation of it."

Walker licked his lips. "It, uh, just doesn't make sense. Why would a guy change clothes before doing this? And then why would he leave his ID on top of those clothes? That's crazy, and no one who knows the man sees that kind of craziness in him. And then there's the fact that the clothes were all wet…"

Maribeth nodded slowly. "So there have been no sightings of him since that time?"

"There's the incident in Maryland."

"Ah, yes, Maryland. I have some theories about that, but I'd like to hear your thoughts."

"I don't have much to add, I'm afraid," Walker said. "Edwards got away from us, with help from Cohen and Hillman, members of that Batty group. He stole an agent's car, and the other two may still be with him. Cohen's vehicle and Hillman's are still at the site."

"Still no sign of the vehicle or the three of them?"

"Not yet," Walker said. There were those two false alarms, of course —although the one in New York might still produce some information once the officer who fell recovered—but Walker felt a strong embarrassment at admitting their lack of success and so did not mention them. He wanted so much to please and impress Maribeth.

"Y'all are going to continue keeping this out of the media?"

"Yes. Fortunately, Hillman's place is isolated and nobody's come poking around. We're hoping he'll feel safe enough to come back online someplace else. When we find him, we'll find the other two. Or he'll know where they are."

"Right," Maribeth said. "Then let's get to work. If you could please copy the surveillance vids from the Diamond for me." She reached into her bag, rummaged around a bit, and pulled out a jump drive. When she straightened and smiled up at him, he found it difficult to close his mouth.

Touching her skin scorched his fingers as he took the drive. He fumbled inserting it in the USB port. While the data copied, he kept his eyes on the computer screen and fidgeted, unable to find a comfortable position.

He took a deep breath when he removed the drive. As he handed it to her—taking care to avoid touching her again—he asked, "Is there anything else I can help you with?"

"Oh, yes, Dick, very much so," she replied, leaning across the desk with a sultry smile that melted everything inside him. "What I have to say to you now is very important, and I want your full attention, so don't look away…"

TWENTY-NINE

Zoe answered the phone, never taking her eyes off the computer screen. "Yeah?"

"Zoe? It's me, Candy."

"Oh, hi, Marge. What's up?"

There was a long pause on the other end. Zoe inhaled it like a pleasant perfume. The image of Marge fuming at not being called by that ridiculous new moniker delighted Zoe. She popped another cashew into her mouth.

"I take it you haven't found anything yet?" Candy asked.

Candy's smug tone grated like fingernails on a chalkboard. "The world is a huge place," she replied. "He could be hiding anywhere."

"That's too bad, Sugar," Candy purred. "Guess it's up to little old me to get somewhere in this."

"Hey look, sister, I've checked all the usual sources. The guy hasn't used his credit cards or phone; he hasn't checked his email or logged onto any of his bulletin boards. For all we know, he's already dead."

"Very well," Candy said cheerfully. "*You* can tell Karl that we don't need to look any more."

This time it was Zoe who remained silent. She wished Candy were in front of her now so she could scratch the beautiful bitch's face to shreds. Candy must have found something and would never let Zoe forget she found it first.

"I just sent you some files," Candy said. "Tale a look at the video marked '7A'. It shows the riot after the shooting."

Zoe checked her inbox. "Yeah, I see it. Give me a minute." She downloaded the file folder and opened it to look at the contents. Marge had definitely found something. There were dozens of document files and almost as many video clips. She opened the one labeled '7A.' As the images flashed across the screen, Zoe strained to catch a glimpse of Edwards. "Geez, this is terrible. What's this from, a ninety-nine-cent security camera?"

"Probably," Candy answered absently. "Go to three thirteen and pause it."

"All right. Got it."

"See that girl with the frizzy hair who's looking at Edwards?"

Zoe squinted. "The hippie?"

"Yeah, that's the one. Turns out her name is Hannah Cohen. She helped him escape. She and Edwards wound up at the house of a crazy old man named Hillman. The three of them outwitted a couple of FBI agents, stole their car, and took off. There are sub-files there on Cohen and Hillman, too."

Zoe grudgingly admitted—though only to herself—that Marge had done a good job. "That's the last anyone has heard of them?"

"Apparently. But I'm sure you can dig out something useful from the files I procured."

Zoe had taken all she could of Marge's condescending attitude. With difficulty, she swallowed a snippy retort and responded evenly, "I will. Thanks."

"I beg your pardon? What did you say?"

"Don't push your luck," Zoe sneered. Wishing she had one of those old-fashioned handsets you could slam down, Zoe ended the call.

Now, to work. Zoe popped another cashew into her mouth. Smiling, she opened up her tracking software.

THIRTY

Steve yanked the curtains open. Upper Manhattan glistened in the sunlight. He loved the magnificent view, but a disturbing dream of bats spying on him through the windows had awakened him in the middle of the night. Although he'd seen nothing flying outside the windows, the nightmare had left him so shaken that he had pulled all the curtains closed before returning to bed.

From the height of the sun, he knew he had slept late. He glanced at the alarm clock on the backboard of the bed. It was almost noon.

He stretched out his arms and legs and tried to get his sluggish mind into gear. At least he had gotten a somewhat more restful sleep. He hadn't slept in the same bed for four days now, but this one was far more comfortable than Hillman's sofa or the make-shift bed on the factory floor. The soft, queen-size mattress with flannel sheets had felt pretty close to heavenly on a cool autumn night.

The whole room radiated luxury. Kind of ironic that he, a fugitive from the law, would find himself in such a setting. A plasma TV took up a large chunk of the wall opposite the bed, its remote perfectly centered on the bedside table. On the wall above the bed hung a large, framed photo of a landscape with a full moon reflected in a lake.

Through the open door to the closet left of the bed, Steve caught a glimpse of the clothes Asia had insisted he needed. She hadn't stinted—Macy's had delivered the new suit, a dozen or so shirts, and half a dozen pants, three pairs of shoes, along with the underwear and socks that filled the dresser against the wall opposite the windows.

Steve walked to the door on the other side of the bed, which led to a private bathroom. Although he'd taken a shower the night before, he needed another to wash away his grogginess. He stood under the hot water for a very long time. When he finally emerged, he slowly dressed himself, pulled on thick socks, and left the room in his stocking feet.

Hannah sat on the sofa watching the TV news with the sound turned way down. Steve nodded to her without speaking. He walked to the bar and poured himself a Coke, then returned to the sofa.

"What's up?" he said as he sat next to her.

"Well," she replied, her eyes never leaving the screen, "we're being held in a luxury prison by a creature that could kill us instantly and drain our blood or, alternatively, could control our minds and make us do whatever she wants, like jump off a balcony."

"No, I mean, what's up on the news?"

"Oh. Finnegan's campaign manager just died."

Steve's eyes grew wide. "Lantz?"

"Was that his name? I can't remember." Hannah settled back into the comfortable sofa cushions and focused her attention on Steve. "Car crash. Drove off the road and hit a tree."

Steve gazed at the TV. "You know, a week ago, I would have thought that was a terrible accident."

Hannah nodded. "Hillman told you there'd be more deaths."

"Hope the old guy's okay." Steve propped his stocking feet up on the coffee table and gave a very long sigh. "Lately, I feel like I am in some sort of extended, very realistic dream—like all of this cannot possibly be happening."

"Want me to pinch you? I can do that, you know."

Steve turned to her. "How do you do it?"

"You take your fingers and—"

"No, how do you handle the stress?"

"Sarcasm, mostly." Hannah rubbed her hands together and took a long time before continuing. "Seriously, I'm scared shitless. Before this, learning about the vampires was just... an interesting hobby. I mean, I wasn't obsessed with it like some people are. It was just fun." She took a sip of coffee and stared at the television, but Steve felt that she didn't really see it. "Now I've got cops shooting at me, and the FBI looking for me—but I guess I shouldn't worry about that because the vampires will most likely kill me first."

Steve resisted the urge to hug her. "Well... I thank you for all you've done to help me."

Hannah gave a short, humorless laugh. "Had I known what would happen, I wouldn't have."

"Well, still, thanks."

Hannah waved her hand but didn't meet Steve's eyes.

Steve lowered his voice. "So what's our next step? We've rested, we have clothes, we can take her car—do we stay here and work with her? Can we trust Asia, or whatever her name is? You've known her longer than I have. What do you think?"

"The person I thought I knew doesn't exist," Hannah said. "The question is whether we can trust this... *thing*."

"Shh! Remember, she has exceptional hearing."

Hannah snorted. "Yeah, but she's a vampire. She's probably still sleeping. After all, it's daytime."

"You know that's just a legend. How could vampires control the business world if they had to sleep during business hours? And look at Mark."

"She was still working in her office when I went to sleep. I don't know when she got to bed," Hannah said in a hushed tone. "And maybe they don't need as much sleep as we do. I don't know what's the truth anymore."

"Well, she seems to be sincere. She did help us out when she could have left us to the cops." Hannah wanted to say something, but Steve hurried to make his point before she could interrupt. "And she didn't kill those officers."

"Right; she let them live because she cares sooooo much about humanity." Hannah crossed her arms. "Don't be ridiculous, Steve—if she had killed them, every cop in New York would be after us now, leaving no proverbial stone unturned. If they dug deep enough, they might even discover Asia's true identity. No, it makes perfect sense to me that she would brainwash the cops instead. She let them live because it was the smart thing to do, not because she cares whether they live or die."

Steve was silent for almost a minute. Finally he stood and faced Hannah. "Maybe that's so. Maybe her actions are entirely self-serving. That doesn't change anything. I've got to take this chance. We have no money, nowhere to go. If we leave here, I lose every chance I might have had to find some solid evidence against Mark, and Asia said she would help me. I'm sitting on the biggest story in the history of humankind, and I need to prove it so that I'm not sent to the gallows."

"Firing squad, probably," Hannah said. "Or an injection. They don't hang people anymore. Well, maybe in Texas."

"I'm serious. We need to come up with a plan to get to Mark somehow, so I can get some proof."

"So that you can blackmail him into resigning."

"Right."

Hannah gazed earnestly at him. "And this helps you prove your innocence because...?"

Steve blinked. "I... uh..."

"Asia is right about one thing—beautiful people can get you to buy anything." Hannah shook her head. "Think about it, Steve. Her plan is to get you to do her dirty work for her. She wants you to put yourself at risk to get Mark to resign. Her hope is that Mark will do so in exchange for your not releasing the evidence against him, right?"

Hannah leaned forward and placed her elbows on her legs. "And then what? You're still a wanted man, and the evidence to prove your innocence remains hidden. Yet if you release it, Mark will certainly take revenge on you."

"I could figure out some way to produce the evidence that proves my innocence without mentioning any of the information about Mark or vampires."

"Then how will you explain Karl's disappearance, leaving his clothes behind? Do you think they'll believe he took the time to change clothes after shooting the rifle?"

Steve sat back down. "I'm dead either way."

"Asia doesn't really want you to release this information, Steve. She'll probably offer to put it on her servers so that if you try to carry out the threat, she'll be able to stop you."

"Then why does she claim that she wants me to be able to carry out the threat?"

"Because *you* have to believe it, Steve." Hannah's pointing finger punctuated her words. "Think about it. The plan is for you to somehow get to Mark, let him know what you have against him, and then threaten to release it if he doesn't resign. You have to tell Mark that if he does anything to you, it will be released automatically. Mark may try to see if you are telling the truth. Therefore, you have to *believe* it's true and that it's really going to happen—even if Asia has no intention of letting it happen."

Steve furrowed his brow and scratched at his beard. "So, we need to figure out some way to make sure *we* have control over the information."

Hannah leaned back. "Easier said than done. Neither of us has a computer. Even if we create new accounts under code names, we'll be doing it on Asia's computer. My guess is that she's talented enough to hack into any accounts we create, no matter how we protect them."

Steve rose and walked slowly to the unlit fireplace. "Let me think about this."

"Sure. We've got all the time in the world."

THIRTY-ONE

The Colbert Report, *October 28*

COLBERT: Welcome back! Before we begin tonight's interview, I need to make some preparations. [reaches under the desk, mumbling; pulls out huge crucifix, places it around his neck; pulls out a necklace of garlic cloves, places it around neck; grabs a wooden stake and mallet] OK, ready. Ladies and Gentlemen, the Democratic nominee for President, Norman Mark! [runs to the interview area where Mark is waiting]

MARK: You don't need all that stuff, Stephen.

COLBERT: Better safe than sorry, I always say. Welcome, Sir! I am honored to have you as a guest. Why did you decide to appear on my show?

MARK: Well, for the Colbert Bump, of course.

COLBERT: [to camera] You hear that? Suck it, Stewart! [back to Mark] But let's discuss the campaign. The election is only a week away and you're still behind in the polls. What can you do to resurrect your campaign; to have it rise from the grave; to bring it back from the dead?

MARK: I'm not worried about the polls. But people should recognize that this election isn't about who you'd rather have as President; it's about where you want our country to go in the next four years. It's not about me—

COLBERT: With all due respect, Sir, we've all heard your stump speech...

MARK: You're the one who asked the question, Stephen.

COLBERT: Yes, but it's my show, and you're not President yet, so I can interrupt you. A month from now, the Secret Service will wrestle me to the ground for attacking you verbally. So let's ask the tough questions now, while we can. Why do you hate America so much?

MARK: I love America, Stephen. What are you talking about?

COLBERT: Oh, really? Then where is your flag lapel pin? But more importantly, how can you love America when you want to bring socialism here, just like Europe?

MARK: And Canada, and Japan, and every other civilized industrial country? Stephen, America is already a socialist country; it's just not as socialist as the rest of them.

COLBERT: Blasphemy!

MARK: Just look at the facts, Stephen. We have public schools for everyone; we provide fire services no matter what your income; we have medicare, medicaid, and social security; there are libraries, public parks, unemployment benefits...

COLBERT: You're listing just about everything government does, Sir. That's not fair.

MARK: But it's true. We're not a pure capitalist society—we have all sorts of services provided by the government, and all sorts of regulations on business. It's time people stopped being afraid of the word "socialism."

COLBERT: Aaaaah! [ducks]

MARK: Socialism?

COLBERT: Aaaaah! Stop saying that! Let me move on—you recently gave a speech before an Italian-American crowd and spoke perfect Italian.

MARK: Yes, I studied the language when I went to school in Switzerland, and my father sometimes spoke it around me.

COLBERT: But you also spoke to a French group in French, a Latino group in Spanish, and a gathering of German-Americans in their own language, too.

MARK: Most of my classes were in German. As you know, Stephen, Switzerland has four official national languages—German, French, Italian, and Rumantsch.

COLBERT: Wait a minute—Rumantsch? Isn't that what they speak in Romania? And isn't that where you find...Transylvania? [turns to camera, lightning and thunder effects go off]

MARK: No.

COLBERT: I'm afraid you'll find that Transylvania is indeed in Romania, sir.

MARK: But they don't speak Rumantsch. Romanians speak Romanian. Rumantsch is an offshoot of Latin, spoken mostly in Northern Italy and Southern Switzerland.

COLBERT: [long pause] I knew that. Still, you do speak a lot of languages. Is there something you're not telling us? Is this another one of your superpowers?

MARK: [laughs] No superpowers, Stephen. I just had a very good schooling—the type that I want all Americans to have.

COLBERT: All Americans don't have billionaire fathers who send them to private schools in Switzerland, sir.

MARK: Yes, but there is nothing magical about Switzerland. There's no reason our public schools can't be just as effective.

COLBERT: Well, we're running out of time, but there is one question I've been kind of hinting at but not directly asking. It's on everyone's mind. Everyone expects me to ask this, and so I have to.

MARK: All right, go ahead.

COLBERT: Okay, here goes. What I really want to know is this… [suddenly becomes all bubbly] Can I be in your cabinet?

MARK: [laughs] No, but I know this guy named Dr. Caligari who would put you in his cabinet…

COLBERT: I'm sure you do! Thank you very much for being here and being such a good sport. Good luck next week. Norman Mark, everybody! [applause]

THIRTY-TWO

Karl rubbed his eyes. Perhaps his lack of sleep was the problem. He stared at the laptop, as if by sheer force he could make it do his bidding.

A sliver of early morning sunlight peeked through the blinds and colored his office a dull orange. Yesterday's *Times* lay scattered across the table with the half-finished crossword page on top. Three cold, partially filled cups of coffee weighed down various sections of the paper.

Karl winced at the mess, lifted one of the cups, and placed it gently onto the coaster before turning his attention back to the computer.

He tried opening another window but all that popped up was a white screen. A talking paper clip appeared and asked if he needed help.

"Have you got it yet?" Zoe asked.

Karl frowned. "I can hear you, but I can't see anyone." He moved the cursor around randomly on the screen just in case that might do something.

"Good enough," Zoe said. "I'm not going to wait around forever for you to enter the twenty-first century."

"I don't have to see all of your pretty faces. Let's get on with this." Karl reached across the desktop and adjusted the pen holder, which was a few inches out of its regular spot.

"This technology has been around for years, Karl!" Gregor's voice said. "Get with it already, no?"

"I don't sit around in my room all day playing with goddamn electronic devices," Karl growled. "I actually work for a living and have people deal with that shit for me. Besides, this is still fairly new in the scheme of things. I remember when the printing press was a radical new idea—"

"Jesus Fucking Christ, here he goes!" Zoe said. "'*When I was your age, we had to fly fifty miles through hurricanes for breakfast each morning—and we* liked *it!*'"

Zoe, Gregor, and Candy laughed. Karl scratched his cheek prominently with his middle finger, just in case they could see him. "Right, children, let's get to business, shall we? What have we learned?"

"I found a girl who was with Edwards after the shooting," Candy said.

"And?" Karl asked.

"No, Karl," Candy said. "This is the part where you say 'Thank you, Candy, I don't know how we could have done this without you!'"

"Thank you, Candy. Now Nick won't have you killed."

He heard Candy give a decidedly unladylike snort, and then Zoe chimed in. "The woman is Hannah Cohen, age twenty-eight. Dropped out of a couple of colleges, married once, no children. Lives just outside of Richmond. Worked as a secretary a few times, in a health food store for a while, and as a waitress. Lives alone and is currently unemployed."

"How does she know Edwards?" Karl asked.

"I'm not sure. There doesn't seem to be any connection. But she's one of the Batties—she posts on the bulletin boards, especially one called 'Vampires Are Among Us.'"

"Ah!" said Gregor. "A fan!"

Karl crossed his arms. "Interesting, but how does this help us find Edwards?"

"Come now, Karl, it's *me*." Zoe said. Karl didn't need the computer screen; he could see her gloating expression in his mind. "They stayed at a house in Maryland and then stole an FBI vehicle. A car matching its description but having a license plate that belongs to a truck was towed from a spot in D.C.'s Chinatown this morning. It's sitting in a police lot now, waiting for someone to claim it. Apparently no one has thought to run the VIN."

Karl tapped his fingers on the desk. "So you're sure he went with her?"

"That's what the FBI records say. The Feds almost caught him in Maryland before they stole the car. And it looks like they have the homeowner—and old guy named Hillman—with them now, since he's disappeared, too."

Karl paused to think about this. He could hear Candy and Gregor laughing about something in the background.

"So the trail ends in Washington, then?" he asked. "We need to search there?"

"No nono!" Gregor said. "You give your team too little credit, Karl. As soon as Zoe told me about this, I contacted my friends in Washington, and especially those in Chinatown. They already have begun searching and have some brilliant suggestions. I will be heading there immediately."

"Me, too," Candy said. "I'm very good at getting information, you know."

"Bah!" Gregor replied. "Your skills will do you no good if you do not know who to ask! You do not just walk up to people on the street and say 'Hey! Have you seen this assassin guy?'"

"Having both of you there is a good idea," Karl said. He leaned back in his chair. "Sounds like we've made some progress here. Contact me immediately if you discover anything important; otherwise we'll have another conference call—"

"Skype," corrected Zoe.

"—tomorrow at the same time," Karl finished.

"Right," Zoe said. "And next time, put on a clean shirt, will you?"

THIRTY-THREE

When Steve returned to the living room a few hours later, Hannah still occupied the same spot on the sofa and stared at the news with the sound muted. A half-empty bag of potato chips and an open bottle of wine sat on the table in front of her. Most of the pillows from the back of the sofa had been arranged under her and around her, creating a soft cocoon of comfort. Her bare feet rested on another pillow perched on the edge of the coffee table.

"Welcome back to the land of the living," she said. "Oops, sorry. The land of the undead. My mistake."

"They're not undead," Steve mumbled.

"Are you finished thinking?" She raised her glass. "*I* have been celebrating. It's a major breakthrough when you think about it. I finally know for sure that vampires exist."

"Other than your own eyewitness account, you have no proof. You can't tell anybody."

"There is that."

Steve walked over to the bar. "I've been online."

"You didn't use your password, did you?"

"Not that stupid. Found a laptop and turned it on. She has wifi here, not surprisingly. I was reading up on the election." The cloudy day made that side of the room dark. Steve squinted at the bottles lined up on the shelves behind the bar. "Can't see a damn thing in here."

"There's a series of light switches just behind the bar," Hannah said.

Steve reached behind the bar and, after a few wrong guesses, found the right switch and flicked on the overhead track lighting. He grabbed a glass from the cupboard and rummaged in the refrigerator for the open two-liter bottle of Coca Cola. "Anyway, Mark has made an amazing recovery—almost like he's not even human."

"Shocked! Shocked I am!"

After filling his glass with ice, he poured in a generous amount of rum and coke. "He's picked up support, but mostly in the blue states where he already was ahead. He needs to get Florida and Pennsylvania, maybe Ohio and Virginia, and he's behind there."

Hannah waved her drink over her head dismissively as Steve walked toward the sofa. "You've apparently confused me with someone who pays attention to politics. Or cares."

"I guess it doesn't matter anyway, since he's probably going to steal the election in those states. A few switched votes in each precinct would hardly be suspicious, but add them up and you're in. And he doesn't need to do that in the red states, because he apparently plans on winning the electoral college and not the popular vote."

"You remind me of my uncle," Hannah said without meeting his eyes. "He had memorized every baseball statistic going back fifty years. He was also boring to talk to."

Steve rounded the sofa with his drink and sat on the other sofa, facing her. "This is important stuff, Hannah. Politics affects our lives every day."

"It doesn't seem to matter to most people."

"Which is why the wrong guys keep getting elected. If people would just pay attention and *vote*—"

"Are you going to lecture me now on my civic duty?" Hannah said, her voice rising. "I have freedoms, you know, which include the freedom not to give a shit."

Steve gave a long and heavy sigh. "I wish Mark wasn't a vampire."

"I'm not a genie."

Steve ignored her. "He'd make a great President. He has workable, sensible ideas for reform that impressed me a lot—until I learned that he's a murdering vampire. And Finnegan—he'll ruin us. Especially with that crazy running mate of his."

Hannah looked over at him with a bored expression. "I'm sorry, I wasn't paying attention. Please let me know if you plan on discussing things that do not cause normal people to fall asleep."

"The problem is Machiavellian, in a way."

"Machiavelli? I hate that perfume."

"Machiavelli created the phrase 'the ends justify the means.'"

Hannah gave Steve a stern look. "Just because I don't care about politics doesn't mean I'm ignorant of them."

"Does the end of having a really good President justify the means he took to get there?" Steve said, more to himself than her.

Hannah stared stubbornly at the TV.

Steve silently admitted defeat. He would never have the conversation he wanted with Hannah. He didn't understand people who cared nothing about government and politics but persisted in their *disinterest* as adamantly as he pursued his *interest*. If only there weren't so many of them in the country.

He grabbed his drink, stood, walked to the window, and looked down at the Manhattan streets. "Asia still not up?"

Hannah shrugged. "For all I know, she flew out the window hours ago."

"The windows don't open."

"There's a sliding glass door from the dining room to a terrace with a pool. A heavy awning covers the first ten feet or so. Easy enough to walk outside and 'change.' Keep it unlocked and you can return at any time. Do the old switcheroo under the awning and the neighbors won't see a thing."

"Clever."

"And speaking of the windows, have you noticed that they're all tinted? We're not getting any direct sunlight here."

Steve squinted at the descending sun. "What does sunlight do to them, anyway?"

"It certainly doesn't make them burst into flames or anything, like in the movies." She grinned. "*That* would make your job proving their existence a lot easier."

"Mark has attended outdoor events in the daytime."

Hannah made a dismissive noise. "Not really. The events may have been outdoors, but he always gave his speeches in huge tents and under tarps. Trust me, we've noticed. The few times he had to go into direct sunlight to get to the tents, they moved him along as quickly as possible. No stopping for hand shaking or kissing babies there."

Steve sipped his drink. "So what—it makes them uncomfortable?"

"Apparently. But it might be more than that. Maybe they can't concentrate and use their skills in the bright sunlight."

"Well, that could be useful to us if it's true."

Hannah pouted her lips. "I doubt it. The whole 'sunlight-harming' thing was created for the movies. In the original Stoker book, Dracula walks around in the daytime without any problem."

"But that's fiction."

She shook her head. "Maybe. Some of our members think Stoker knew the secret and based the novel on a true story. I've often wondered if old Vlad didn't fake his death and move to England…"

Steve strode back to the sofa, set his drink down, and perched on the edge, facing Hannah. "Well, in any event, I've been thinking about how to get the evidence we need and clear my name in the process—and help you and Hillman, too."

Hannah glanced at him from the corners of her eyes for a few seconds and then straightened, throwing off the mound of pillows. "Let's hear it."

Steve held up his index fingers about six inches apart and stared between them. "We need to think like investigative reporters. The media considers the vampire claims pure fiction, so no reporters have done any digging. Information is out there; it's up to us to find it."

"Spoken like a true reporter." Hannah's tone was only mildly sarcastic.

Steve stared at the ceiling. "The first step is to look for some evidence in Switzerland. Although the school he supposedly attended burned down along with all its records, the local papers should have some mention of his father, the famous, wealthy American."

"He *was* his father."

Steve grimaced. "You know what I mean. The point is that there will be *nothing* in those newspapers. He never went to college, but he knows five languages and is an expert in government and economics and a bunch of other things. His campaign propaganda claims he learned it all at that school. Surely some of that vast knowledge would have made the local news. Its absence will help us prove he never attended."

"The lack of information may be odd, but it's not proof." She crossed her arms. "And don't you think my group and others have already thought of that?"

"They don't have the resources we have, through Asia. Right now, the only searches are on the web, and you're not going to find school records online from a time before the internet even existed. But we might be able to find out names of students and teachers who were at the school at the time Mark supposedly attended. Asia can hire people in Switzerland to interview them and take statements. They could also interview locals who had dealings with the school. If we find enough people to verify that Mark did *not* attend the school, that's evidence."

Hannah nodded her head slowly. "All right. That's a start. What else you got?"

"Next, we research the birth records. Obviously, he has a fake birth certificate. If there is a way we can confirm that, it would help. Maybe the typeface or the paper is different from other certificates issued at the time. If we can find some discrepancy…"

"That one's been done over and over again already, Steve. No one has found anything."

"Yeah, but only by the Batties, and some of them are… well, not exactly reliable. No legitimate news network has devoted any time or energy to the search. Once the Batties mentioned vampires, all the other accusations against Mark seemed like more of the same conspiracy nonsense." He shook his head. "Mark probably even encouraged the vampire talk to make all the accusations against him seem absurd and ensure that few journalists would dare investigate even legitimate allegations for fear of being ridiculed."

Hannah pursed her lips. "Even if you find something, it wouldn't be enough. Original birth certificates can be lost and then replaced. Mark said in an interview that he was born in New York City. You need to look for newspaper birth announcements. Given Sal's wealth and status, some mention of the birth would be in the society pages. And we should check all the hospital records in the city for his birth date. All the lack of corroboration isn't proof positive, but it will add up."

Steve smiled at Hannah's sarcasm-free participation. "Good, you're on the right track. This is exactly the kind of stuff I need for my breakthrough story."

"But it's not enough."

"No… all that would prove was that he lied about his birth and schooling. It doesn't lead to the conclusion 'therefore he's a vampire.'"

Hannah switched off the TV. "Well, that's a moot point, anyway, because there's no time to do all that research in the four days left before the election."

Steve sighed. "I know…"

"Can't you just write the article anyway? Do we have to wait for the evidence? I mean, if they follow up on what you write, they'll see it's true."

"Well, that's not how journalism works, especially not for me. Not now," Steve said. "Look, I like to think I am an honest, decent person. I went overboard while trying to bring down a bad guy. The substance of what I wrote was completely true; some of the names were just made up. I shouldn't have done that, and I really have paid the price. I'm not going to do that again."

He sighed. "Besides, If I don't give quotes from real people or list the exact places I visited to research the story, no one will believe me. People will assume that Steve, the assassin who once fudged a source, is at it again."

Hannah placed her elbows on her knees and set her chin in her hands. "And what else can you tell me about the twentieth century, Old Man Steve?"

"I'm serious."

She leaned forward. "I admit those are strikes against you, but your ideas of modern journalism come straight from some ivory tower school. Look at the crap Fox News gets away with these days. Say a lie often enough and people will believe anything."

"Maybe. But not a lie from me. Because of my past history, I have to have definite evidence. I have to prove I have ethics."

"I'll be sure to put that on your gravestone after the vampires kill you. 'Here Lies Steve—he was stupid, but boy, did he have ethics.'" She pointed a finger at him. "This is *war*, Steve. Write your article. Your name alone will gather attention and give it more weight than if I or some other vampire watcher had written it."

"Yeah. And they'll read it and laugh. It will look like I'm just trying to get myself off the hook for shooting at Mark. Without evidence, who would believe it?"

"One of the reporters who knows you will believe it. One of them will investigate it. They'll do the checking for you. Everything you write will be *true*. Let them do the research and see for themselves."

"Not unless I give them more than suspicions. I need to give them *evidence*."

"Tell them about Karl."

Steve paused. For many long seconds, he stared at nothing while Hannah waited silently.

"Perhaps you're right," he said. "It will fit the facts. The FBI has to wonder about the pile of clothing left behind. And if they haven't already checked the rifle for fingerprints, this might spur them to do so and then they'll know the prints aren't mine." He sat back and glared at Hannah. "Wait a minute! Do vampires even *have* fingerprints?"

"I assume so. I suppose we could find some excuse to look at Asia's fingertips to make sure.... But, you know, if they didn't, someone would've noticed, and vampire hunters over the centuries would've checked suspected vampires for just that. That hasn't even appeared in the fictional vampire accounts. Besides, vampires look completely human in all other regards."

"Until they bite or change into a bat."

Hannah clasped her hands together and stared at her fingers. "This is something we've debated over and over again on the Board. Some members persist in believing that vampires are magical, undead servants of Satan—"

"Like Hillman."

"Yeah, like Hillman. But others have concluded that vampires are a distinct, humanlike creature, evolved alongside humankind—and maybe with a shared ancestor—which has developed some special abilities, including transformation into a bat and perhaps even a wolf or other animal..." She looked off into the distance.

Steve tilted his head. "And what do *you* think?"

"I don't know any more. Having seen it happen, I know it's true, but I can't explain it. It doesn't seem to obey the laws of science." She shuffled the pillows around and settled into the new arrangement. "Think about it—the mass has to go somewhere. Asia weighs—what?—maybe one hundred thirty pounds? And how much does a bat weigh? Asia didn't turn into a hundred-thirty-pound bat. A bat that heavy couldn't get off the ground... and would be a lot bigger than a real bat."

"I'm no scientist, but that makes sense. Unless Asia herself only weighs a few pounds." He grinned broadly until he noticed Hannah's thoughtful expression.

"You might be onto something there, Steve." Her brow furrowed for a few seconds, then smoothed. "What if vampires really could control their bodies—I mean, *really* control them? Their control enables them to heal quickly, right? And of course, they can change shape. What if they really did weigh very little but could concentrate that weight where they needed it? Like into their hands when you shake hands with them."

Steve adjusted his glasses. "I find that hard to believe."

"Right, because so far everything else we've learned has been so utterly believable. I don't hear you coming up with any explanations."

"Suppose you're right. What do they do, shift their molecules around? That's ridiculous." When he saw the storm brewing in Hannah's eyes, he added, "That theory creates more problems than it explains. If the mass shifts to their hands, why wouldn't their backs collapse inward?"

"All right. Well, how about this: the human body is sixty percent water or something, right?"

Steve paused. "I guess."

"What if they release water when they change? They'd get rid of a lot of mass right there."

"You've been thinking about this."

"Of course I've been thinking about this! What else have I got to do around here?" She stared into Steve's eyes. "Do you remember when Asia turned into a bat?"

"How could I forget?"

"Well, did you notice any water at the spot?"

Steve thought back. "Now that you mention it—when I rummaged through her clothes to find her phone, I noticed that they were wet with sweat—real wet, now that I think about it."

Hannah's eyebrows raised and she smiled in an "Aha!" manner. "You stood right next to her a second before she changed into a bat and her clothes weren't wet then, were they?"

"Damn. This is weird."

Hannah grinned. "That basically describes the last week or so, yes."

Steve finished his drink, placed the empty glass on the table, and stared at it. "It still isn't enough, though. Even with that much loss of water, the bat would be too big and heavy to fly."

"Yeah, I know. But it's all I can think of."

"And then what about when they want to change back? Do they have to fly into a bucket of water or something?"

"I don't know. Maybe they can pull water from the air or something. Maybe they need to live in humid places. Maybe there are no vampires in Arizona."

"Makes sense. Too much sun there, too." He crossed his arms and sat back.

For a few minutes, lost in thought, neither spoke.

Steve slowly rubbed his chin. Just how did vampires change? Why did they have abilities like no other animals on Earth? Hell, could it be possible that they had not originated on Earth? Hadn't Asia made some joke about that a while ago? If it was a joke...

Steve shook his head. They had more important things to worry about. "What were we talking about before?" he asked.

Hannah blinked. "Uh. Getting evidence against Mark, to prove he's a vampire."

"Right." He sat up straight. "It all boils down to two things. First, I have to prove that vampires exist, and then, I need to find proof that Mark is one. And I need hard proof, like a confession."

"And how are you going to get that?"

"The only idea I've come up with is for me to wear a hidden microphone and get to Mark somehow and get him to admit it. I'll wear a couple devices, hidden in different places. If he finds one, it won't matter. And we can send the signal to several locations, so if Mark sends his cronies to destroy one..."

"That's loony. I mean, how would you ever get near him? When you were a reporter you might have had a chance, but now? You'll be arrested as soon as someone recognizes you."

Steve scratched his head. "Well, that's the part I haven't quite figured out yet."

THIRTY-FOUR

Hannah looked up and beyond Steve, and he turned to see Asia walking into the room, yawning deeply. Her long hair was attractively pulled back from her face and secured with a pink bow. She wore a Babylon 5 tee shirt that stopped at her upper thighs—and apparently nothing else.

Steve took a deep breath and returned his gaze to Hannah. If all female vampires looked that beautiful, they would need no special powers to get men to do whatever they wanted.

"What haven't you figured out yet?" Asia asked as she walked to the bar.

"How to get to Mark," Steve replied. "Writing an article won't be enough. I need to get a recording of Mark admitting he's a vampire."

Asia opened a bag of coffee beans, poured them into a grinder, and turned it on. "Good idea," she said over the noise of the grinder. "What's your plan?"

"Did you just wake up?" Hannah said.

Asia raised her eyebrows. "You have a problem with that?"

Hannah crossed her arms and glared at Asia. "Did you go out last night?"

"You're not my mother," Asia replied, without making eye contact. She turned off the grinder and poured the ground coffee into the coffeemaker.

"We need to know what you've been doing," Hannah said.

Steve's eyes slid from one to the other. "That's enough. While we may not necessarily trust each other completely, we don't have time for this. We need to work together."

Asia glanced at Steve as she turned on the coffeemaker. "Not really. We don't need her at all. She's just another Batty—no one takes anything she says seriously. You're the one who has the power to get something accomplished."

Steve felt the weight of Hannah's glare. "Hannah's in this with me. If it hadn't been for her, I'd be dead or in prison now."

Asia shrugged and opened a cabinet to get a coffee cup. Steve took the opportunity to widen his eyes at Hannah to keep her quiet.

"I need to get Mark to admit he's a vampire," Steve said, trying to bring the subject back. "I need a way to get to him, and then, a way to record what he says."

Asia leaned against the bar. "The recording part is easy. We can use Mark's own technology against him. I like the irony of that. We can hide more than one of his little recording devices on you. Keep them always broadcasting. I can set up my computer to receive everything that's said."

Steve smiled. "I need it to go to my computer, actually. You've already been compromised once."

"Now, wait a minute," Asia said. "It was a fluke that they found me in DUMBO. There's nothing anywhere to connect this place to the Van Helsing Society or any other Batty group. My computers here are totally secure, but yours... yours is undoubtedly in the hands of the FBI right now. They've probably confiscated your work computer too."

"Well, then, my editor's computer."

"I thought we agreed not to release the information but only use it as a threat to get Mark to resign."

Steve exchanged a quick glance with Hannah and then spread his hands. "I need to control the evidence, Asia—not you. It's my life that is in jeopardy here."

"Can't you save it online somewhere?" Hannah asked. "On one of the storage websites?"

"Actually," Asia said, "we could. There are plenty of sites that will store documents and audio files. We can set it up to send the feed directly to one, or more than one, if you want."

"We're going to need visuals," Steve said. "A video of Mark confessing will carry a bigger punch. And no one could claim it's faked."

"Are you serious?" Hannah said. "You guys think you can play James Bond and get away with it?"

"I don't have a lot of choice. We can hide a nice simple recording device easily enough. I don't need all the bells and whistles. One that looks like a button would work."

"One on your glasses too," Asia suggested. "Maybe a couple others in case he searches you and finds one or two. I'll bear the cost."

"I could wear a ring or watch with a camera too."

Asia smiled. "Good. We'll set it up that all the devices feed directly to the storage engine you choose."

"But only I get the password," Steve said.

Asia straightened, tilted her head, and looked back and forth between her guests. "What in the world do I have to do to get you two to trust me?"

Steve's gaze met and held hers. "Letting me have my own password would be a good start."

Asia glanced at the coffee maker, which had not finished its task. "Not a good idea. Think it through, Steve. All Mark would have to do is charm you to give him the password. And if you were able to resist that, he'd just bite you, and you'd give him whatever he wants. Someone else has to have the information. Someone Mark can't get to."

"Hannah."

Asia looked at Hannah, who stared back defiantly.

Asia shook her head. "And if they got to Hannah too? They have to know that she helped you escape."

"The three of us will have duplicate storage sites," Steve said. "Each with its own password, known only to us. We'll need backups, too. The more places it's stored, the safer we are."

Asia considered. "You must make it clear to Mark that you'll release the information if he doesn't resign. And make sure he knows that the information will automatically become public if anything happens to you."

"Even if all this works, it still doesn't help me clear my name."

Asia checked the coffee maker again and clicked her tongue happily. She poured out two cups and handed one to Steve.

"Once Mark steps down, you can concentrate on gathering the evidence to prove your innocence. I'll help," she said as she stirred cream and honey into her cup. "Mostly it will be finding evidence to show that Karl was the shooter, so that shouldn't be too hard."

Holding her cup with both hands, Asia settled on the intact sofa, tucking her legs beneath her. She sipped her coffee and yawned. "But right now, we need to concentrate on Mark."

Steve glanced at the clock. It was almost eight P.M. Asia was certainly substantiating the vampire mythos—or reinforcing the stereotypes.

"So how do we get to Mark?" Hannah asked.

"I have some friends who might be able to help," Asia said. "Mark's election night party will be held at the Marquis Hotel in

Times Square—that's the only place we can be sure of getting to him."

"On election night?" Steve asked. "With a thousand people and the media there?"

"He'll be in his room with only a few advisers until he's declared the winner."

Steve mulled over the possibility. "They won't call the election until the polls close on the West Coast, and that won't be until eleven o'clock or so. And the hotel is here in Manhattan, which means I won't have to travel far, so my risk of being recognized is slim."

Hannah crossed her arms. "Are you two serious?"

Steve raised his eyebrows.

"That's the best you can do? Try to sneak into a hotel filled with police, hotel security, Secret Service agents, media, and every supporter who can squeeze inside?"

"You have a better idea?"

"No, but there must be some smaller rally where you can get to him. Maybe you can send him an email saying that you know his secret and ask for a private meeting…"

Steve started to speak but Hannah interrupted. "Yeah, I know. As soon as I said that, I realized it wouldn't work. He'd just have the Secret Service waiting for you."

"Or worse," Asia said, "His personal strigoi bodyguards and supporters."

"They might be with him already," Steve pointed out. "For all we know, his campaign manager and other advisers are vampires."

"Strigoi," Asia said.

"Right. Okay. Whatever the objections, it's the only plan we've got. Better than nothing."

"Definitely," Hannah said. "Your chance of success doubles with this brilliant plan—from one percent to two percent."

Steve turned to Asia. "You said you have friends who will help?"

She nodded. "Assuming we don't come upon other strigoi, we can get you past just about anyone."

Steve picked up his cup, took a swallow of coffee, and propped his feet on the coffee table. "You seem overly confident for someone whose plans went awry on the rooftop in Brooklyn."

Asia waved his concerns away. "I was alone, and they'd already called for backup. If we had more time, everything would have worked out fine. At the hotel, if we avoid the crowds, four or five of us can handle any people we run into."

Steve swallowed hard as it hit him that she meant four or five vampires. Maybe Hannah was right about the craziness of this plan. But what other choice did he have?

Asia held up a finger to forestall his response while she sipped her coffee. "We need to get to Mark's suite. The Secret Service will have guards stationed at various spots that we'll have to pass. You'll need to stay out of the way while my friends and I will take care of them. Then we'll move on until we come to the next bunch, and eventually we'll get to his rooms."

"Take care of them how?"

"Well, hopefully, just by convincing them we're harmless. We'll get some hotel worker IDs and slide right past some of the check points. Distract them." She smiled and fluttered her eyelashes. "I happen to look very good in a French maid's outfit."

Steve's mouth hung open for a few seconds. He closed it and stared into his coffee cup, but the seductive image remained burned into his mind. Unable to think of anything else, he felt immensely relieved when Hannah spoke up.

"Right!" she said. "Manhattan hotel workers always dress like French maids from a porno movie. It's brilliant—no one will ever suspect a thing."

"Oh, come now, Hannah, I'm kidding." Asia shook her head. "Well, I'm kidding about using that as a disguise. I wasn't kidding about looking good in—"

"Where are you going to get fake IDs?" Steve said quickly.

"I didn't say they'd be fake. Getting real IDs is easy enough. I'll stop by the hotel tonight and charm IDs off some workers. I have a friend who can replace the pictures easily enough."

"How does that work?" Hannah asked. "That *charming* thing? Can you get people to do anything?"

"Well, up to a point," Asia replied. "The ability varies among the strigoi, but most of us have no trouble convincing an unsuspecting person that whatever we suggest makes perfect sense—even jumping off a hotel balcony in Boston. If a person knows he's facing a strigoi, though, it's a lot more difficult because he can actively try to resist the charming. And it's hard to do long-term things."

"Such as?"

"I could easily put an idea in your mind and convince you it's your own, but once you're out of my reach, given time, you could learn new information, think about that idea, and change your mind. The closer the implanted idea is to your own, the longer you'll retain it, and the more likely you will adopt it as your own."

Hannah pouted and looked at the floor. "So, you can convince the Secret Service guys to let us go by?"

"Oh sure, that's easy, assuming they're human." Asia ran her fingers through her hair. "But I can't give them a completely false and absurd memory to replace it. I can be very persuasive, though, and convince them that they were mistaken about what they saw—like I did with the cop on the roof."

"Could you persuade them not to tell anyone they saw us?" Steve asked.

"Of course! I do that all the time. People remember seeing me-- but want very much to keep our secret."

"And the biting? That helps?"

Asia nodded. "It amplifies everything. No one can resist the suggestions of a strigoi who has bitten them—at least, not until the bite heals completely. But it's a highly personal thing."

"What do you mean, 'personal'?" Steve asked.

"If I bite you, the bite would help me charm you but would have no effect on Hannah. And it wouldn't help any other strigoi charm you," Asia explained. "The bite makes a connection between you and me, an *intimate* connection."

Steve licked his lips uncomfortably and fought to keep his mind focused. "So, if you bit me and another strigoi came in and tried to charm me, he couldn't?"

"Oh sure, he could—but the other strigoi wouldn't have the benefit of the bite; he would just be dealing with a normal, everyday charming."

Hannah let out a *huh* sound but didn't look at either Steve or Asia.

Steve had no comment. It would take him a while to think through all he'd learned about vampires—assuming that what Asia had told them was the truth.

Asia finished her coffee, set the cup aside, and stood. "Now that we've settled on a plan, it's time to get to work. Stand up, Steve."

Steve narrowed his eyes. "Why?"

Asia smiled evilly, showing very sharp teeth. "It's time for you to learn how to defend yourself against a vampire." Her eyes gleamed with a fierce glee as she took an aggressive stance.

Steve gulped.

THIRTY-FIVE

Jian's breath formed misty clouds that dissipated quickly in the cold October air. The overhead streetlight shone onto his clipboard, which he glanced at with dissatisfaction. Still fifteen seats left.

He lit another cigarette. The smoke mingled with his breath. Shivering slightly, he tucked the clipboard under his arm, and with his cigarette tightly clenched between his lips, zipped his jacket to its highest position. He'd wear his winter coat tomorrow night if it didn't warm up.

The clock in the storefront read 11:54. Another six minutes and the bus would leave. Jian could then go back inside and relax for a half an hour or so.

The sound of footsteps snagged his attention. He looked up. A white man and woman headed his way. He frowned. Not customers. Their elegant, expensive clothes looked out of place on a weeknight in this part of Chinatown. Jian wondered if they had gotten lost.

He got a good look at them when they passed under a street light. He couldn't take his eyes off them.

The man stood well over six feet tall and walked with the confident step of someone with authority and money—the kind of man who would not be pushed around. His face sprouted a dark, full beard, and he wore a navy blue suit with a red tie. A gray scarf hung useless around the shoulders of his long black wool coat, and when he reached up to scratch at his strong nose, numerous gem-coated rings glinted in the light.

His companion, a stunning blonde with a killer smile, clung to the man's arm. Her coat barely reached to her knees, revealing long, stocking-clad legs in red high heels. Despite the chill in the air, the top buttons of her coat hung open, showing the edge of a low-cut black dress and the necklace of oversize sparkling gems nestled between her breasts.

Jian's throat went dry. With difficulty, he raised his eyes when the man spoke.

"Good evening!" the man said with an obvious Slavic accent. "I wonder if you could help us."

Jian nodded, wanting nothing more at that moment than to help these two people.

"That is so kind of you," the woman said, parting bright red lips to reveal perfect white teeth. "We are trying to find out what happened to some friends of ours, and we've been told they may have been here." She held up a piece of paper. "Have you seen them in the last week?"

Jian forced his eyes to look at the paper in the woman's hands. He concentrated on the two pictures copied from a computer—a white man with glasses and a woman with curly dark hair.

"I think maybe," Jian said, speaking slowly. He understood English well, but still had trouble pronouncing everything clearly—and he really wanted to help these people. "Two like this take the bus to New York. About a week ago. I remember because they seem very nervous. Like they not used to bus full of Asians. But maybe no—the man had a little beard and light hair, not dark."

"New York, you say?" the man replied. "To Chinatown?"

Jian nodded. "Allen and Canal."

The couple beamed with happiness. Jian smiled broadly, pleased that he had been able to help them.

"Do you keep records of your passengers?" she asked. "Do you write down their names?"

Jian felt crushed that he would disappoint them. "No. I am very sorry. They pay like everyone else and they get on the bus. That is all. Very sorry."

"No matter. You have been most helpful!" the man said, holding out a hand.

Honored, Jian shook the man's hand.

"Thank you very much," the woman said. She leaned over and planted a kiss on Jian's cheek.

Warmth flushed Jian's face. He could not stop smiling as he watched the two walk away. It wasn't until his cigarette burned his fingers and he jumped that he realized the pair were no longer in sight.

THIRTY-SIX

With a groan, Steve dragged himself out of bed and trudged to the bathroom to empty his bladder. He'd left his glasses on the bedside table, but even with them, he doubted the scruffy, bearded guy with the dyed blond hair that he saw in the mirror would look more like a reporter than an aging beach bum.

With the collection of bruises, aches, and pains his body had become, he moved like an escapee from an old-age home as he gingerly stepped into the shower. He stood under the blessedly hot water and let the heat ease away the stiffness.

Learning how to defend oneself against a vampire, he had discovered, mostly meant getting out of the way. He had spent a large portion of the past few days learning to land without hurting himself too badly.

"It's like jujitsu," Asia explained, "where you must learn how to fall before you can fight. Except against a vampire, there will be no fighting—just falling."

A few minutes' workout against Asia convinced him she hadn't exaggerated.

"You have no chance at all in a battle against a strigoi unless you've got a gun to his head," Asia said, "and even then, your chances are next to nothing, because we're very fast."

She demonstrated by having Steve use a spoon as a gun and snatching it from his hand before he could raise his arm. Then, to really drive the point home, she had him hold the spoon against her head and try to say "bang" before she could disarm him. He failed. Twenty times.

"So now you see why if you're confronted by a strigoi, you run away as fast as you can and hope he doesn't care enough to follow."

"And if I run into more than one?" Steve asked.

"Then you better hope they don't want to kill you."

The lessons had driven home the extent of the danger he faced, and Steve fervently hoped he would never have need of them.

He wrapped a towel around his waist, walked back to the bedroom, and collapsed onto the bed, his mind a mix of emotions.

Asia had garnered the high-tech spy devices and other equipment they needed. She had even scrounged up a pair of thick-framed prescription sunglasses so he could better disguise himself. The fancy gadgets gave the whole escapade a kind of James Bond-ish aura, and despite the danger, Steve felt a thrill of excitement.

The alarm clock said 10:23 A.M. He sighed, rose, and dressed himself.

Hannah dominated her spot on the sofa, surrounded, as usual, by pillows. She stared in the direction of the television with the sound turned down, but gave him a quick once over as he entered.

"You look awful," she said.

"Thank you, thank you, you've been a wonderful crowd." He lowered himself gently and slowly onto the other sofa. "Be sure to tip your waitress."

Hannah crossed her arms. "So glad you've been training. You're in perfect shape to go up against some vampires now."

"The election's not until tomorrow. I might be better by then."

"Oh, right, of course." She gave him a glance. "Want some coffee?"

"I will owe you my soul."

"You already do." She emerged from her pillow nest and walked to the kitchen. "Have you had breakfast yet?"

"No, I just got up."

"There's some fruit. Oranges and apples."

Steve blanched. "Fruit's not breakfast. Donuts are breakfast. And bacon. Preferably bacon donuts."

"All I see is fruit." She leaned out the doorway and tossed him an orange. "You need to eat healthy. You're going to want to keep your blood clean for the vampires who will bite you tomorrow night."

Steve grunted. "Asia must be a fruit bat."

Hannah turned on the coffeemaker. "Too bad she isn't a bacon donut bat."

Steve began peeling the orange. "Why am I doing this?"

"Vitamin C?"

"No, why I am going to see Mark and possibly get killed?"

Hannah leaned her shoulder against the door frame. "It's the *brilliant* plan you've come up with to get Mark to back out of the race. If you tell

Mark about Karl, he'll know you're telling the truth. And if he's the person you think he is, he might even help you clear your name."

"But you're not too sure about that."

"He's a vampire. I don't trust any of them."

"If I tell him Karl did it, he'll probably send the vampire mafia after him or something."

Hannah pulled a cup out of the cabinet. "Look, if this works out the way you hope it will, just don't forget about me, okay? My name needs to be cleared too."

"You sound doubtful."

"Well, I am. It's a crazy scheme. And you're doubtful too, or we wouldn't be having this conversation."

"What choice do we have?" Steve sighed. "Maybe it is crazy. Maybe I should just not risk it. Maybe we should just ask Asia to get us new identities and go into hiding until I can gather enough evidence to clear my name."

"Why would she?"

Steve looked up from his orange.

"Steve," Hannah said as she walked toward the sofas carrying two cups of coffee. "Don't forget that Asia has her own agenda. Giving us new identities doesn't do one thing to advance *her* plan. She needs to have *you* go to Mark and blackmail him into dropping out of the race. She can't do that herself, not if she wants to survive in the vampire community for a normal lifespan. She has to remain anonymous behind the scenes. She can't let Mark know she's behind this. That's why she's helping you. That's the *only* reason she needs you." She put his cup on the coffee table and settled herself among her cushions. "Well, unless she gets hungry."

Steve popped an orange slice into his mouth. His mind suddenly reeled with the memory of his daughter. He would separate oranges into the individual pieces and then Gabby and he would place one in their mouths and flash orange smiles at each other. They'd laugh and dance around the living room…

Dammit. He missed her laugh more than anything.

Steve shook his head, as if the memory would disappear like lines on an etch-a-sketch. He may never see Gabby again.

He sighed and tried to concentrate on the matter at hand. "Forget I said that. Hiding wouldn't work, anyway. I couldn't stand living out my life as… as another person. No." He chewed another sweet slice, leaned forward, and continued in a lowered voice. "I really need to write this story, to get the truth out there and redeem myself. What happens then—who knows? Maybe they'll arrest Mark and Karl. If they do, then I'll have my life back. I might even make a fortune on the book."

"And Asia?"

"We don't have to mention that she's a vampire. Just Norman Mark and Karl."

Hannah frowned into her coffee. "The whole world will change."

Steve turned a doleful eye to her. "Exciting, isn't it?"

Hannah's cup clunked onto the tabletop. She ignored the coffee that sloshed over the edge. "There will be witch hunts. People will suspect everyone in power. Friends will turn on each other. No one will trust anyone."

Steve spoke slowly. "Sounds like you're having second thoughts about this."

"My opinion hasn't changed." She pulled the pillows around her again and sighed. "We deserve to know when someone is controlling us. Humanity needs to know the truth. But we're going to be living in a chaotic hell for a while. Innocent people are bound to get hurt."

Steve piled the orange peels on the table and picked up his coffee. As he inhaled the bracing aroma, he considered the picture Hannah had painted. He took a sip and gazed at Hannah. "I'll do everything I can to prevent the chaos, but the truth… the truth has to come out."

"It does," she agreed.

Steve strongly believed in the importance of truth. He always had. So why did the thought of revealing this truth fill him with misgivings?

The flashing images on the television screen caught his attention, and with relief, he changed the subject. "So, what's the news?"

"Mark did well in the debate the other night, but is still behind in the polls. It's close enough in a few states that he could pull it off. No one seems to have discovered that he owns the company that makes the voting machines."

"Something else I can add to my story."

"And atheists are supporting Mark, which has the religious right up in arms."

"That's probably one of the reasons Mark is behind in the polls. Believers always vote, and the fundamentalists think they're doing God's will by electing Republicans or something."

"Well, it's getting violent," Hannah said, pointing to the television. "There have been some fist fights, and people have come to some of the religious rallies wearing guns."

"Wonderful." He sighed. "That's one thing I hate about this—once I expose Mark, there's going to be quite a backlash against liberals too."

"The truth is always more important," Hannah replied, but she didn't sound as certain as she had before.

Steve took another sip and watched the screen. Wolf Blitzer stood in a computer-generated world, pointing to charts and graphs that showed the latest poll numbers in significant bellwether states.

It had been like that for a generation—the horse race grabbed more attention than the issues. Elections had become more of a popularity contest than anything else, with the more charismatic and taller man always winning. People chose Presidents based on which candidates looked more presidential, not on their experience or their policies.

By that standard, though, the polls should show the tall, handsome, athletic Mark, with his telegenic movie-star charm, way ahead of the short, pudgy, balding Finnegan, who was not an engaging speaker.

Steve actually felt a moment of optimism for politics. Despite his looks, Mark's liberal policies, far to the left of most Americans, kept him from leading in the polls. Maybe issues still mattered in America.

"I need to get to work," he said. "I have to finish writing my story and upload it, along with the evidence I've gathered so far."

"How is that going?" Hanna asked.

"Asia showed me how to set up the storage file. She said she can attach a program to it that will release the information automatically to the sites I want unless I enter the password every day."

"And you believe her?"

"Not necessarily. That's why you need to have a separate file. And maybe we should create some backup files with a couple others in the Van Helsing Society who you think we can trust. We can set something up so that their files will be released if ours are erased."

"You don't know how to do that," Hannah pointed out.

"Asia can show me."

"That might work. *If* we can trust her." Hannah picked up her coffee. "Make sure you use a strong password. Not something obvious, like 'swordfish.'"

Steve grinned at her. "Maybe I'll use the name of the Slightly Silly Party candidate."

Hannah tossed a pillow at him, but he easily dodged. All that practice with Asia was good for something, after all.

THIRTY-SEVEN

Karl smiled at the sound of the phone ringing. A phone. An actual phone. *Not* a fucking computer.

Leaning forward, he pushed Speaker and then Line One. "Hello?"

"Ah, Karl!" Gregor's voice boomed through the room. "So you do not want to see us, no?"

"I am perfectly happy with the old-fashioned way of having a conference call, Gregor. I don't need to see all of you to get work done."

"That's too bad, Karl," Gregor said with a laugh. "Last time—you couldn't tell—but Candy, she flashes her breasts at the camera, knowing you couldn't see. Quite a show, no?"

"Ah, Candy," Karl said. "Do you really think there is anyone on the East Coast who hasn't seen your tits yet?"

"Are the pleasantries done?" Zoe interrupted.

Karl heard the strain of suppressed excitement and anxiety in her voice. "What is it?"

"I've traced Edwards."

"Where?"

"Edwards and Cohen took a bus from D.C. to New York City—"

"Gregor and I discovered this," Candy interrupted.

"Yes, thanks to Marge and Gregor." Zoe's voice did not indicate pleasure at the interruption.

"So they're here in New York?" Karl's heartbeat quickened. How wonderful! And deliciously ironic for them to obligingly flee right to him.

"Looks like," Zoe responded. "No idea what happened to the old guy, though. We can look for him too, if you want."

"Don't bother. Edwards is the one Nick wants." Karl frowned at the silver and black plastic phone. "Have you had any luck tracing their movements in New York?"

"They evidently went to the headquarters of the website 'Vampires Are Among Us' dot com in a slum area of Brooklyn. The FBI has asked local police departments to check out homes and offices of people who post Batty stuff online, and I found a strange police report of an incident there."

"That's the web site that Heidi posted to, right?"

"*Hannah*. Yes. It looks like Edwards was there with Hannah, but they got away with the help of an oriental girl. The odd part is that the two cops wrote up entirely different accounts of the incident. One cop claims they found a bunch of teenagers illegally hanging out in the building's basement and chased them off."

She took an audible breath before continuing. "The other cop says they found Edwards and chased him and two females to the rooftop. He states that he shot the oriental girl but she kept coming and knocked him flat. He didn't see anything else until backup arrived."

"Are you implying…"

"No! No implying. The oriental girl is one of us. She has to be. The shot didn't stop her, and she obviously got to one cop but not the other."

"They like to be called 'Asian' now, Zoe," said Gregor.

Zoe's snort came through loud and clear.

"Who is she?" Karl asked.

"So glad you asked," Zoe said, and Karl smiled at the satisfaction in her voice. "It took a bit of work. She hid her trail well."

"But not so well that you could not find her," Karl prompted.

"The basement apartment is rented to a young oriental woman named Anastasia Collins, who has no past and no gainful employment—yet apparently is never late on the rent."

"Collins?" Candy said. "Like the vampire from that old TV show?"

"Not very subtle, huh?" Zoe said. "And it just so happens that a very wealthy Japanese insurance executive named Naoko Nakazato left her company in the hands of trusted subordinates and moved to New York City about twenty years ago. When I got into the motor vehicle records and checked out these ladies' photos—they are the same person."

"Neither of those names are familiar to me," Gregor said.

"That only proves she's an eccentric, wealthy woman," Karl commented.

"Ah, but I have more, Karl. I back-tracked Naoko Nakazato, who first appears in Japan just after World War II, when the chaos made it easy to hide one's background. In a time when few women were allowed into the business world—and not only in Japan—she built up a substantial insurance business in Tokyo. Few photos of her during that time still exist, but I found enough to confirm that she looks exactly the same now. She's strigoi."

"Anyone know her?" Karl asked.

"No," replied Gregor and Candy.

"I'm not finished yet," Zoe said, clearly enjoying her starring role.

Karl struggled to control his impatience. "Tell us the rest. Without the dramatic pauses, please."

"Her trail gets murkier before the war, but I think I've uncovered her original identity. If I'm not mistaken, she's from China. And her First Name is Mei Hongdeng."

"Now *that* name is familiar," Gregor said. "Where have I heard the name Hongdeng?"

Zoe chuckled. "If I mentioned 'The Society of Righteous and Harmonious Fists,' would that mean something to you?"

"But of course!" Gregor said. "The Boxers!"

"Well, y'all got me," Candy said. "She's a boxer?"

"The Boxer Rebellion of 1900," Gregor explained. "A Chinese rebellion against the Catholic Church and imperialist Western countries who were trying to carve niches in China and force their views and ways on the Chinese people. The rebellion was led by a secret organization known as The Society of Blah Blah Blah, like Zoe said. They also attacked the Cossacks. I was traveling and had not yet joined the Royal Court, but all of Russia knew of it."

"One of the leaders of the Society was a man named Zhu Hongdeng," Zoe said. "It happens that our friend Zhu had a daughter named Mei. He managed to smuggle her to Hong Kong, but he was killed—permanently—in the revolution. There's not much on her from Hong Kong, but I found one picture. Mei now lives in a penthouse in Manhattan."

"But what does all that history have to do with her connection to Edwards?" asked Gregor.

"Well, you've got me there," Zoe replied. "She obviously went into hiding so her Japanese colleagues wouldn't discover her secret. They probably think she's enjoying her retirement among the amenities of New York. She should've faked her death by now and taken on a new Name. You'd think she'd have returned to China to fight against injustice there or something."

Karl grunted. "That's not important to me at the moment. Why is she affiliated with a group dedicated to exposing the existence of vampires? And why is she helping Edwards?"

"Not sure, Karl. I should mention, however, that you show up on this website quite frequently."

"*Me?*" Karl stared at the phone, as if that would help him understand.

"Oh, yes. They keep close tabs on you. They know where you go all the time."

Karl sat back in his chair. This was not good at all. If the police monitored that website, they'd know of his presence in Virginia at the time of the assassination attempt. The sooner they got Edwards, the better. And that Asian girl, too. She had to go.

"But why would she join such a group? Why help them track her own kind?" Gregor asked.

"She was raised by a family of revolutionaries, remember," Zoe replied. "Fighting against oppression and authority, against those who tell you what to do and think and all that."

"Apparently," Candy added, "she sees the strigoi establishment as the current oppressive authority. She resents our society insisting that strigoi remain hidden and change our identities all the time. While I consider it a perk of being strigoi, some do not."

Karl's eyebrows raised. Candy's insightful explanation reminded him that the "dumb blonde" persona was just an act. "That makes sense. And if it's true, her assisting Edwards and the Batty woman is a major act of rebellion. Damn! She could actually *want* the world to know we exist."

"That would be bad," Gregor said. "Very bad. We have to stop her, no?"

"Well, fortunately, I have her address," Zoe replied.

"There's no time to waste," Karl said. "Where are you all now?"

"Gregor and I are still in Washington," Candy replied.

"I'm at my farm in Vermont," Zoe said.

"I need you all in New York as soon as possible. I'll arrange private transportation and hotel reservations and get back to you with the details. We'll meet in my office tomorrow."

THIRTY-EIGHT

Agent Richard Walker tried to identify the city below. Was that Atlantic City already? It seemed they had just left Reagan.

He glanced at his watch. The case had him so distracted that time had slipped by him. He stared down at the flat ginger ale the stewardess had provided earlier, picked up the glass, and downed it.

His gaze returned to the scene outside the window. Misty clouds drifted beneath the wings, obscuring the city in the same way the facts about Edwards obscured the case—too many things just didn't make sense about the man.

Going a bit crazy after being publicly humiliated and then losing his job and wife? Believable. Becoming paranoid, believing insane conspiracies, and joining a bunch of loonies? Believable. Trying to shoot a presidential candidate because, in your delusions, you think he's a vampire? Sadly, still believable.

But changing your clothes at the scene, then leaving them? *With* your ID? Even a crazy person wouldn't do that.

And why were the clothes soaked?

Walker realized his fingers were drumming on the tray. He set the empty plastic cup at his feet, pushed the tray back into the seat in front of him, and secured it in place. He hated being annoying—or noticed.

While Edwards was clearly involved in the assassination attempt, he could not have acted alone. The little inconsistencies in this case had kept Walker awake nights: no connection between Edwards and the weapon; no evidence that Edwards had ever used a shooting range or even owned a gun; the misspelling of words in the diary of a well-educated journalist; the absence of Edward's presence on the vampire conspiracy websites. There was too much Walker did not know, and Edwards alone could provide the answers.

Walker needed to collar Edwards as soon as possible. If there was one thing the profiles of similar crazies revealed, Edwards would try again, in another highly public manner—and this time he might be successful.

After all, if Edwards had managed to sneak a high-powered rifle past the Secret Service before, he could certainly do it again. He most likely had help from someone on the inside—perhaps a Secret Service agent or someone on Mark's staff.

Mark had mostly remained secluded since the attack, but he would have to appear at the election night party. Walker's gut told him that Edwards would not bypass the opportunity—which was the reason for this trip to New York.

Walker glanced at his watch again. The party would start in another six hours. He'd have plenty of time to check into his hotel, taxi to Times Square, and search the hotel for things the Secret Service might miss, either by careless mistake… or by purposeful omission.

And when he found Edwards, he had lots of questions. They would have a nice, long talk.

Unless he had to shoot first.

THIRTY-NINE

With a growing sense of dread and excitement, Steve reread his article for the fifth time, making changes here and there. He took a risk in writing this story, a risk greater than any other he had ever taken in his life—greater than most journalists had ever taken. As he stared at the screen, he felt his heartbeat quicken.

Unlike most of his articles, this one dispensed with the formalities of impartiality required in serious journalism. Instead, he had written in first person, giving all the details of the assassination attempt and how he had learned the truth. He made no mention of Hannah or Asia and gave no information about where he had hidden or who had helped him. The story, after all, wasn't about them or even about him—it was about the vampires.

He did one final read-through before taking a photo of himself with the webcam and attaching it to the bottom of the file to prove that he had written the article. Publication would blow his disguise, but that couldn't be helped. He posted the file, along with the other information he had gathered so far, to the primary storage space and backups. Hannah and Asia would have to do the same to their own storage spaces.

Steve leaned back and sighed. Everything was in place. If he didn't enter the "stop" command every twenty-four hours, his story would be distributed to newspapers, blogs, magazines, and reporters all over the world. Even if most of them ignored his article, enough would pay attention to get the word out—especially when they realized who had written it.

He stared at the story, the best piece of writing he had ever done.

Why wait? Why not send it now? Create the storm and topple the vampire candidate. Expose the truth and confirm a spot for himself in history.

His finger swiveled the mouse. One click. Just one click and he would make history.

"Shit."

He couldn't do it. More was at stake here than his place in history. And he still didn't have that final piece of evidence that would seal the deal and convince everyone. Once he attached the video to the file…

Voices wafted in from the next room. Asia had apparently returned with her vampire friends.

How odd that he felt not a bit of anxiety at the arrival of a group of vampires. Much had happened in the past few weeks. Much had changed.

Writing this expose was the kind of thing he had always dreamed of doing. The adrenalin pumping through his body as he pursued a *damned important* story—this was why he had become a reporter. Although he now lived with constant fear, danger, and uncertainty, he couldn't quite bring himself to wish it otherwise.

Steve glanced at his story on the laptop one last time, resisted one last impulse to distribute it immediately, and closed the file. After turning off the laptop, he walked into the living room.

He stopped just inside the doorway. Hannah, in her standard couch position, held a pillow tight against her chest, staring uneasily at Asia and the two newcomers.

Asia handed a glass of red wine to a large man with an equally large handlebar mustache. His eyes twinkled at her. Laugh lines etched his face, and though he appeared to be in his mid-fifties, he probably had lived well over four centuries. He wore an antique velvet coat and top hat like a character from an old Charles Dickens movie. People probably labeled him "eccentric," but Steve had seen stranger sights on the streets of Manhattan.

His companion, a trim, fit girl, also accepted a glass of wine from Asia. Short and cute, the girl had the kind of chubby-baby face that invited cheek kisses. Her close-cropped hair had blue-tinted ends spiking out, like she had rubbed gel into it and then forgot to comb it out. She wore jeans and a gray sweatshirt that said "Brooklyn," and her face and complexion proclaimed her Indian or Pakistani heritage.

Like all the vampires he had met, these two oozed charisma. Steve felt a strong urge to approach and get to know them better—and this, before they had even turned their attention on him. As he used the techniques Asia had taught him to fight the urge, he hoped he would have the strength to withstand a vampire deliberately trying to charm him.

"Steve! There you are." Asia held out her hand, inviting him further into the room. "Allow me to introduce Lord Martin Geer."

Steve stepped forward and shook hands with the man. "I'd say 'charmed,' but I'm afraid you'd take it literally."

Martin laughed and slapped Steve on the back.

"Sense of humor; that's good!" Martin boomed with a British accent that reminded Steve of Terry Thomas in those '60s comedy movies. "Please call me Marty."

"Marty here was a Lord in one of his previous Names," Asia said, "and we often call him that in a teasing way. He won't admit it, but he likes it."

"Consider it a longing for the old days," Marty said with a toothy grin. "Back before you colonies decided you didn't like tea."

"And this," Asia said, indicating the girl, "is Chandra Darwish."

Chandra grasped Steve's hand limply in a quick, perfunctory shake. "Hi."

"Chandra is young. Even younger than you. She really *is* only twenty five."

"That doesn't mean I'm a kid." Chandra pouted. "I'm tired of being treated like a child who doesn't know anything."

"Well, *I* appreciate your help," Steve said. "You might be young, but you can do lots more than I can."

She nodded but didn't change her expression. Steve hoped she wouldn't be a liability.

"Pardon my curiosity," Steve said to the three of them, "but I thought you guys aged differently... Like it took you ten times longer than humans."

"We mature at the same rate as humans until we hit our twenties," Asia explained. "Then we slow down. Can you imagine if we didn't? Having to breastfeed a baby and change its diapers for ten years?"

"Well, that would explain why there aren't that many of you," Steve offered.

Marty gave a hearty laugh and slapped Steve on the back again. "I like you, lad!"

"Right, then, let's get down to business," Asia said, motioning everyone to the seats around the coffee table, which—to Steve's delight—held a large tray of fruit, cheese and crackers, and an open bottle of red wine.

Steve filled a plate with cheese and crackers. When he had poured himself a half glass of wine, he sat on the sofa beside Hannah. Marty and

Chandra shared the other sofa, and Asia straddled the piano bench at the end of the coffee table.

"We don't have a lot of time to prepare," Asia said, "and we don't have anyone else we can depend on to help us, so we need to be ready for anything that could go wrong."

"Why couldn't you get more vamp—strigoi to help?" Steve asked.

After exchanging glances with Chandra and Marty, Asia swung her legs back and forth a few times and then looked at Steve. "Well, to be honest, although many of us want Mark removed from the public eye, there are two big obstacles. First, a good number of us think having Mark in the White House would be the greatest thing ever. Many strigoi business people believe Mark will channel government contracts their way. They have no fear of exposure because they haven't really thought this through."

"Simpletons," Marty added. "They're so used to always getting what they want that they can't imagine that their whole way of life could be in jeopardy."

"With all that socialist talk, the strigoi businesspeople support him?" Steve asked.

"The government is still going to have to buy things. It's good to have one of your own in power in those circumstances." Asia sipped at her wine. "Unfortunately, the bottom line is most important to them."

Steve crossed his arms, unconvinced. "What's the second reason?"

"Those who don't support him... well, I don't think they'd agree with our plan to blackmail him," Asia said.

"They'd rather take the risk that he gets exposed and then takes us all down with him," Chandra snarled, "than try to remove him quietly behind the scenes."

"Mark is bloody powerful," Marty added. "For years he's built alliances with other strigoi, invested in their businesses, and done favors for them. Many owe him. And many are afraid of him."

"He'd kill you?" Steve asked.

"Good lord, no! Strigoi rarely ever resort to something like that. We appreciate life too much. Any strigoi who murders another faces swift and severe punishment. No, no, lad—Mark would destroy us in other ways. Ruin our finances, our reputations, our lives. Make us start all over with nothing. Why, just ask Chandra."

Chandra glared at Marty. "My family is doing just fine. We don't need Mark's approval."

Steve broke the uncomfortable silence that followed. "So, Asia, does the fact that you think these strigoi wouldn't agree with our plan mean that you didn't even ask any of them for help?"

Asia shrugged. "I knew Marty and Chandra would help but couldn't be sure about anyone else. I didn't want to risk having one of them warn Mark. Better to stay safe."

"So it's just us?"

"It's just us."

Steve let out a deep sigh. The plan seemed more suicidal every minute.

He looked at Hannah, who stared at the pillow she held. She already knew her role in this endeavor. She would stay in the penthouse to monitor the feed from his cameras. She would know immediately if something went wrong—a frightening prospect—and would release the video, his article, and the information he'd gathered.

Marty cleared his throat. "We only have a few hours before people start gathering at the hotel. Let's go over the details."

Asia pulled out four hotel employee IDs and handed them out one by one. "Chandra, you and I are housekeepers. Marty, you're the night manager. Steve, you're the hotel electrician."

Steve glanced at his ID. Although they had made his photo dark and indistinct, no one would suspect that the ID had been altered. "What if the real Dennis Higgins shows up?" he asked.

"Dennis and the others will call in sick tonight."

"What did you do to them?" Steve asked, his voice tense.

"They're fine, Steve," Asia replied. "I just convinced them that they were feeling poorly and shouldn't go to work. Now pay attention; we don't have much time."

Steve crossed his arms and listened.

"I reserved a suite for us a few floors below Mark's. The entire hotel is booked so I had to pull a few strings to get it. Steve, you'll start off dressed as our limo driver."

Steve took a deep breath. "And for a disguise?"

"You'll be a limo driver," Asia repeated. "You'll have a hat and dark glasses. No one ever pays attention to the servants. Trust me, when we three make our entrance, all eyes will be on us. It will be the best disguise you could hope for."

Steve was not convinced.

"Once we're in our room, we change into our hotel uniforms. I've hidden weapons in the janitorial closet; we'd never be able to get them into the hotel tonight with all the Secret Service there."

She handed each of them a floor plan. "This is the layout of each of the top floors. The location of each security camera is marked. You'll notice that no cameras are trained on the service elevator, which is what we'll be using." Asia smiled and her eyes glinted with a reddish flash. "But, regardless, the security guard in the monitoring station tonight will ignore everything he sees on the cameras, *and* make sure the feed does not get to the Secret Service."

"You've been busy," Marty said.

"Yes, and I'm sated," Asia replied in a casual way that made Steve shiver.

"What about noise?" Chandra asked.

"One of the hotel's selling points is the soundproofing," Asia said. "Hopefully, we won't get into a fight."

"*Hopefully*, the soundproofing is as good as they say it is," said Marty.

Asia handed out a series of photographs. "These show the hallway, the door to the Presidential Suite, and the rooms in the suite. I have the maid's skeleton key so we can get in."

"Do they actually still make skeleton keys?" Steve asked.

"It's a goddamn piece of plastic with a magnetic code on it, all right? Now pay attention." Asia pointed to the pictures. "This is the forty-second floor, and here's the entrance to the suite."

"How did you get these pictures?" Steve asked.

"Downloaded them from the hotel's web page," Asia replied.

Steve ignored the impatience in her voice. "Won't there be guards at the door?"

"We'll get to that in a moment. Now shut up." Asia glared him into silence, then continued. "The suite has a second floor but there's no entrance to it from the forty-third floor. You can only get there using the elevator—or emergency stairs—inside the suite. Since the second level offers a great view of Times Square, that's where Mark will most likely wait. Here's where the stairs inside the suite are located…"

Steve's mind wandered as the three vampires hammered out the details. His part wouldn't come until the end.

The end. He mentally cringed. What chance did he have with a supporting force of three? Against dozens of hotel and private security, police, and Secret Service agents trained to take down a threat and ask questions later? And worse, against God-knows-how-many vampires loyal to Mark?

Steve took a healthy sip of wine and let it flow around his tongue. He might as well savor the small pleasure.

After all, this could be his last night alive.

FORTY

CBS Special News Report: Presidential Election Coverage, November 2

AXELROD: It's election night, and despite the fact that Norman Mark is behind in just about every poll, the supporters here at the Marquis are enthusiastic and confident of victory.

COURIC: Jim, are they seeing internal polls they are not sharing with the press?

AXELROD: That's possible. However, it is the network policy to not discuss exit results until after the polls have closed, so we cannot speculate at this time.

COURIC: What plans have they made for what they see as a celebration?

AXELROD: Well, Katie, the main hall at the Marquis can only hold so many people, and so invitations have been treasured. A number of famous movie stars and musicians are in there now mingling with all the campaign workers and invited guests. In fact, earlier we asked the candidate about the guest list.

[Cue clip]

MARK: *Usually, the invitations to such events go to the biggest contributors to the campaign. Since I did not accept campaign contributions, I instead invited a fair mix of celebrities and the campaign workers who usually never get to go to these things. I want to reward their devotion and hard work by giving them a chance to meet some movie and sports stars. I apologize to those I could not include due to the limited space, but that's why we are also having a huge party in Times Square.*

[end clip]

AXELROD: In fact, as you can see behind me, the party in Times Square has already begun. The jumbotron will show the latest results as soon as they come in, and Mark has paid for entertainers to keep the crowd happy. Many of the celebrities have also promised to come outside from time to time to shake hands and sign autographs. New York is prepared to cheer on its native son in this one.

COURIC: It's now seven o'clock here on the East Coast and voting has ended in some states. The first results are coming in. CBS News is now predicting that Norman Mark has won the states of Connecticut, Massachusetts, and Vermont. This is not unexpected, of course, since he has led in those reliable Democratic strongholds for most of the campaign. We also declare John Finnegan the winner in Alabama, North Carolina, South Carolina, and West Virginia. Other states still have their polls open or are too close to call…

FORTY-ONE

Hannah's eyes drifted from Wolf Blitzer, waltzing around in his CGI map, pointing at states and making them magically switch to red or blue, to the laptop on the coffee table in front of her. Asia would not turn on the cameras until Steve left the hotel room, which would not be for a while yet, but she just couldn't stop checking.

She hugged a pillow to her chest and pulled up her legs. They had left about a half an hour ago, and she hadn't relaxed since then. There was no way this would end as Steve wanted. The bad guys had too much power. Something would surely go wrong.

And then what would she do?

If Steve failed to get Mark to resign or was caught, she would release the information. She had promised to do that. And that information would exonerate Steve. Or, at least, throw doubt into many people's minds.

But how would that help *her*? The FBI had a warrant out on her too. Even if Steve were cleared of the assassination attempt, that wouldn't exonerate her. After all, she had helped to steal an FBI vehicle, hadn't she? And she and Hillman both had aided and abetted a known fugitive.

Maybe Hillman would let her live in one of his hideouts. It wouldn't be much of a life, but much preferable to prison.

She had never felt more confused and lost than at that moment—with no idea what to do or where to go.

Why had she stayed to help Steve? She should have run like everyone else after that assassination attempt.

But that's just the way she was. Or at least the way she used to be.

She frowned. Why had that thought popped into her mind? The way she *used* to be?

Hannah's mind raced to her earliest years in college—idealistic and optimistic, she had thrown herself into those years with gusto. Everything had seemed possible. She had fought for the rights of the underprivileged and downtrodden, maintained a vegetarian diet to avoid hurting animals, helped at a local food bank, volunteered at the hospital, and even worked on progressive political campaigns.

And then came Brian.

A man who shared her love of humanity and desire to bring change. A man willing to go the extra distance to make a difference in someone's life. A poet, a thinker, a musician. A lover of the world. Her soulmate.

Her parents had objected when they spoke of their desire to marry. She was still too young, and they were both still in college, with no reliable source of income. But she and Brian had known their love would always last, and secure in their euphoric bubble of happiness, they had run off to a justice of the peace.

Her parents had refused to speak to her, which disappointed but did not surprise her. She and Brian had rented a small apartment near Shockoe Slip, and for a few years, had lived in blissful semi-poverty. She had worked part time in a health food store while attending classes at night, while Brian finished his education to better support the two. They didn't see each other as often as they would have liked, but it didn't matter, because they had their whole lives ahead of them.

Or at least she had thought so at the time—until she had discovered that Brian loved more than the world in general. He literally believed in loving everyone. Individually. Physically. *The fucking asshole slept with every goddamned piece of sleazy ass that snuck into their house when she was away. And he saw* nothing *wrong with it—he expected her to accept his tomcat lifestyle or else she wasn't the open-minded, tolerant person he thought he had married, the goddamn fucking piece of...*

Damn it! Why did this still bother her?

Hannah jumped up and paced to the windows. Brian belonged in the past, not in her present, which was complicated enough... though the thought of a vampire feeding on the bastard appealed. Maybe, if everything worked out, she could prevail on Asia...

What *was* she thinking? This waiting was driving her crazy!

She stomped to the bar, opened a bottle of whiskey, took a quick gulp, and coughed. Damn it.

But the second gulp just felt warm. Smooth.

She leaned against the bar and glared at Wolf Blitzer. *Probably cheats on his wife, too. They all do.*

A humming noise drew her eyes to the far side of the room. The elevator?

She glanced at the laptop. Steve had not turned on the cameras. Had they finally realized the futility of their plan?

Still holding the whiskey bottle, she stepped toward the sofa to resume her usual position, but her steps slowed. Steve wouldn't have given up. Not at this point.

Something was wrong.

The humming became louder and changed pitch. Hannah frantically glanced around the room.

There was no other way out. Not for a human.

She flicked off the lights and ducked behind the bar just as the elevator doors opened with a shushing sound. She held her breath and listened.

At first, she heard nothing but Wolf Blitzer's droning. Which meant it wasn't Steve—or Asia, or her friends.

Hannah strained to hear over the pounding of her heart. Someone walked very slowly through the living room.

No. More than one person. Were they whispering to each other?

Hannah's fingers tightened on the neck of the whiskey bottle. Not an ideal weapon, but maybe good enough to gain her time to run to the elevator. She shifted her grip.

The footsteps came closer.

"There's someone here," a man whispered.

"Yes, I smell her, too," a woman responded at a normal level. "Not one of us."

"Come out, come out, wherever you are," a softer female voice with a southern accent said in a singsong tone. "Come on, sweetie. Might as well make it easier on yourself."

"We have no interest in you, my dear," said a second male voice—this one with a heavy Eastern European accent. "We only want Steve."

Four of them. Maybe more who hadn't spoken. Vampires. If she ran for the elevator, her chances of escape were slim. But if she remained behind the bar, she had no chance at all.

Hannah grasped the whiskey bottle tight, took a deep breath, and jumped from behind the bar. As she dashed into the living room, she threw the bottle at the first person she saw.

A young black woman calmly grabbed the bottle in mid-air.

Strong arms locked around Hannah's waist from behind. The wind left her as her captor lifted her feet off the floor. Hannah kicked and struggled to break free, but the constricting grip only tightened.

"Not a smart idea, Honey," the woman whispered in her ear. She tossed Hannah onto the sofa.

The bleached blonde wore her hair pulled back in a ponytail. A half-zipped, skin-tight jumpsuit clung to a body any woman would envy. The heavy eye makeup of an Egyptian concubine adorned her eyes, and her red lipstick would make a fire engine jealous.

"You're in the wrong place," Hannah said between gasping breaths. "The Catgirl tryouts are uptown."

"Feisty," the woman replied, raising one eyebrow. "You will make interesting prey."

"Look," Hannah said, doing her best to hide the shaking, "I accept that you caught me, but please—do I have to put up with the cliché villain dialog, too?"

A sharp, deep laugh rumbled behind Hannah's shoulder. A tall, dark, bearded man walked around the sofa to stand beside the woman. He too wore black—a turtleneck sweater and jeans. "I like you!" he said. "But Candy may not after that, no?"

"*Candy?*" Hannah said. "A vampire named 'Candy'?" She pointed at the man. "And what do they call you? Count Chocula?"

Candy's eyes flared but she showed no other reaction.

The man chuckled and gave a slight bow. "I am Gregor. You must be Heidi."

"Hannah," the other woman replied as she walked into view and tossed the bottle onto the sofa. Short but athletic, she too had dressed in black from head to foot—except for the array of electronic devices tucked into her belt.

"Yes, Hannah, of course. My apologies." Gregor indicated the new arrival with a flourish of his hand. "This is Zoe."

Zoe gave Hannah a brief glance before frowning at Gregor. "Do we have time for this shit?"

Standing side by side, the three had a powerful presence. Hannah sucked in her breath and tried to resist their charm. Avoid their eyes, Hillman had often said. On the other hand, Asia had claimed the ability also involved voice and smell and other things. Whatever its source,

Hannah did not intend to tamely give in. She needed to find out why they were here, and to delay them if possible.

"So," she said with as much calm as she could manage, "would you like some tea?"

"No, thank you," a fourth voice said. "We're in a rush."

Another man walked around the couch to stare at her. He wore black, of course. A black sports coat over a black shirt—which made him look more like a handsome gangster than a vampire.

"Karl Weaver," Hannah said in an almost normal tone, despite the tightness in her throat. "So nice to finally meet you."

Karl's fists clenched. His eyes darted to his companions.

"Told you they've been watching you," Zoe said with a broad grin.

Karl growled. He leaned in until he was inches from Hannah's face. "Where are they?"

"Who?" She got the word out, but her voice squeaked.

"Don't play stupid. I can tear the information out of you, if that's what you want. Then we will all get our fill of you and toss your body off the balcony." He took her chin in his fingers and lifted it toward his face. "But we have no real interest in you. Cooperate and we leave. And you live."

Hannah's whole body trembled, and she couldn't control it. Her eyes filled with tears, but she found the strength not to look into his. This vampire had tried to kill another of his own kind—something Marty said they just didn't do. Karl would have no qualms whatsoever about killing a mere human.

"So let's try this again," Karl said. "Where are they?"

Hannah closed her eyes and, for the first time since she was a little girl, she began to pray.

FORTY-TWO

Steve couldn't believe the traffic. "We're hardly moving. We'll never get there on time."

Asia gave a big sigh from the back seat of the limo. "It's because of Mark's party in Times Square. He's taken over the city. It's like New Years' Eve except the weather doesn't suck. We should have left earlier." She was speaking very fast again. Not a good sign.

"It will be all right," Marty said, and his voice calmed Steve tremendously... until he realized why it had placated him so easily.

Steve pulled his cap lower, hunched down, tightly clutched the steering wheel, and tried to still his rampant nervousness. Cars, taxis and buses inched past the Ed Sullivan Theatre.

Caught up in their own giddy excitement, a horde of pedestrians shoved their way toward their party Mecca in Times Square, jaywalking through the stalled traffic. Some carried Norman Mark signs; many wore campaign buttons. Only a few glanced into the limousine, hoping for the sight of a celebrity.

"Relax, Steve," Asia said. "Even if they could see through the tinted glass, none of them have the slightest interest in our chauffeur. Trust me, it's the perfect disguise."

The actions of the few who stared inside seemed to verify her assurance; they looked past him toward the passengers. Still, he kept a white-knuckled grip on the steering wheel as he inched along with the traffic. Only a block or so to go...

"They're making the traffic turn," Marty said.

Steve looked ahead. Armed officers ignored horns and curses and waved angry drivers off Broadway onto West 47th. Only one car separated the limo from the police.

"What do we do?" Steve said through a mouth suddenly gone dry. "There's still another block and a half to the hotel, and—"

"Drive up and open the back window," Asia said.

"The back window?"

"*My* window. Let me talk to the cop."

"Is this it?"

"No! That's the inside light. Turn that off!"

"Well, where is it?"

"It has to be there someplace!"

"The cop is here! He's knocking on my window!"

"Oh, for Christ's sake, look for something labeled 'window'!"

"There must be a control back there, too!"

"Oh, right. So there is."

In a moment, the officer, a weary-looking, rosy-cheeked man of obvious Irish ancestry, stepped toward the back of the limousine. Steve rolled his window down a crack and twisted in his seat to watch.

"I'm sorry, ma'am, but Times Square has been closed for the night…"

"I know that, officer," Asia said. "We just need to get to the Marquis. We're invited guests of Norman Mark himself, and we have luggage that needs to be taken in. Once we've unloaded, the valet service will whisk the limo to the parking garage and it won't be in anyone's way. I promise."

The poor man's posture showed he was already caving in. Glad the sweet persuasion in Asia's voice was not directed at him, Steve faced forward and kept his face down. He imagined the cop looking into the back seat at the elegantly dressed people invited to attend the private celebration for the new President-to-be. The combined charisma of those three vampires would melt the stiffest resistance.

"Well…" he heard the officer say. "All right, you can go through. But go slowly. And watch out for the pedestrians." He raised his voice. "The limo needs to get through, Vinnie!"

"Thank you so much, officer!" Asia gushed. "You are so very kind."

Steve could imagine the cop's cheeks turning redder as his partner cursed and cleared the way before them.

"Go on, James," Asia said in a magnificently imperative tone.

"Yes, ma'am," Steve said.

As he heard Asia's window closing and raised his own, Steve pulled in a deep breath and edged the limo forward, pausing now and again for heedless partying pedestrians.

His passengers had settled into silence. He couldn't tell if that made him more nervous, or less.

The limo crept across West 48th. A glass tower covered in advertising, the Marquis blended into the area so perfectly that casual visitors did not even realize it was a hotel. The place filled the block, and an entire lane of Broadway—precious real estate in Times Square—had been set aside for the taxis and other vehicles.

Steve guided the limo into this lane and pulled as close to the entrance as he could get.

"Leave the engine running," Asia said. "Go around and open the door for us."

"Better be a tip in this for me," Steve mumbled as he stepped out of the driver's side.

The crowd ignored him, just as Asia had predicted. They stood behind wooden barriers, anxiously awaiting the arrival of celebrities. Keeping the crowd in order fully occupied the police and hotel security. Still, Steve kept his head low as he circled the limo. He opened the car door and stood back.

Chandra stepped out first, sparking an explosion of camera flashes and noise. She glanced at the crowd haughtily and tapped her foot as she waited for the others.

Marty emerged next, providing an impressive sight with his ivory walking stick and expensive three-piece suit. He turned toward the car and held out a hand for Asia, who made sure to reveal an eye-catching view of her shapely legs as she slid out.

As she took Marty's proffered arm, Asia waved a hand at Steve and ordered, "Get the bags, James."

"Yes, ma'am," Steve replied.

He kept his head down as he walked to the back and opened the trunk, unloaded the luggage, and placed the bags on the sidewalk. A bellhop arrived with a rolling cart and helped Steve pile the luggage atop it.

Asia sauntered over and gave the young bellhop a sultry smile as she tucked a wad of money in his pocket. "Thank you, sweetie. James will take the bags to our room for us."

The bellhop blushed and walked away, looking like his every wish had been granted.

When a valet drove the limo away from the curb, Steve felt suddenly alone and vulnerable. He swallowed hard, put his hands on the bars of the cart, and pushed it behind the three vampires as they strolled toward the entrance.

"I say! What a beautiful night!" Marty remarked in a loud voice, hamming it up for the crowd. "Lovely weather for November. Smashing! Perfect for a party."

Asia headed toward the check-in counters while Marty and Chandra lingered about ten feet away, talking loudly with passersby, drawing attention away from Steve. To the right of a large central garden, red velvet ropes herded the guests for the Presidential party toward a metal detector and waiting security personnel.

Steve leaned against the luggage cart and did his best to look inconspicuous. As he waited, the jostling people, the police, all the pandemonium… and the last ten years… faded away.

A palette of tans and yellows made the hotel's interior warm and inviting. Flecks in the black marble floor reflected the overhead lights like a billion stars shining in a dark night sky. From every floor, a balcony jutted into the spacious atrium, allowing guests to stare up into the heavens or down into the abyss, where the long counter on the main floor overflowed with smiling employees to assure that no lines would delay the business or pleasure of their guests.

He had brought Linda to the theater district for their first date, to see a new production of *A Funny Thing Happened on the Way to the Forum*. She had worn that amazing red dress, the one with the small bow in back. A blanket of snow greeted them when they emerged from the theater, and traffic barely budged in the raging storm. So they had sought shelter in the hotel bar, which remained warm and dry. Too many drinks later—with the largesse of a recently cashed bonus check in the bank from his first big story at the *Times*—the two tipsy friends decided it was easier to just get a room than take the subway or hail a cab. They giggled like school kids as they called in sick to work the next day and then relaxed with a room service delivered breakfast.

The memories distracted Steve, so he didn't notice the man with a limp purposefully heading his way with one hand reaching for the weapon strapped to his side.

FORTY-THREE

CNN Election Coverage, *November 2*

BLITZER: And at this point, the totals show Mark with one hundred and forty-three electoral votes and Finnegan with one hundred and thirty-two. Anderson, what do you make of the races we've called so far?

COOPER: Well, Wolf, Mark was always strongest on the coasts, so you would expect him to be ahead at this point. Once the Midwest numbers start coming in, this race will become much closer. He has carried all of New England except for New Hampshire.

Pennsylvania and Ohio are still too close to call. We've already declared Finnegan the victor in Virginia and Florida. The consensus is that you must win at least two of those four states in order to win the election, and so far, Mark has won none of them.

BLITZER: It's going to be a long night.

FORTY-FOUR

Instinct honed by training had drawn Walker's eye to the scruffy-looking chauffeur with the blonde hair and dark beard.

Edwards. Walker was certain of it, despite the oversized sunglasses and chauffeur's cap.

He started forward, keeping his gaze trained on Edwards, who stared into the distance, oblivious to his immediate surroundings. Was the man lost in thought… or searching out the location of his accomplice? Walker had scoffed at Galanti's conspiracy theory, but perhaps he had been mistaken.

Walker's heart pounded. He had to stop Edwards now. The man could have anything in those cases. Rifles. Grenades. A bomb…

As he marched forward, Walker's hand unsnapped the holster on his hip. He slowly pulled the gun from its cradle—

"Leave the weapon where it is, friend," a voice said in a deep, commanding tone. "You don't want to start a panic."

Walker blinked, startled to find an amiable-looking man in an expensive suit standing in his way. He felt a momentary confusion, and his steps slowed.

"Indeed, it would be best if you kept your gun in its holster," said the stunning young woman who had appeared at his side. With difficulty, he dragged his gaze from her face and refocused on his goal.

"Out of the way!" he said as he attempted to push between them. "FBI. I need to—"

"No, put the gun away," the man said, placing a strong grip on Walker's shoulder. "You don't want to do that."

"What do you…" Walker looked up at the fellow, who smiled back pleasantly. Colors swirled like rainbow whirlpools in the man's dark eyes. Walker barely felt the light touch of the woman as she placed her hands on his arm to ease his gun back into place.

The woman leaned to his side and murmured in his ear. "Drawing your gun could frighten the guests."

Walker struggled to concentrate. "Yes... he could start shooting..."

"Who, our chauffeur?" the man said. "James has never shot a gun in his life. All he knows is cars."

"That's not a chauffeur..." Walker protested weakly.

"James is our chauffeur," the woman insisted. "He's been with us for years."

"But..." Walker forgot what he was about to say as the woman ran her hand up and down his arm.

"You have mistaken him for someone else, that's all," she whispered.

Walker felt certain she was right. Maybe he had become so fixated on finding Edwards that he saw him everywhere.

"You should look elsewhere," the man suggested. "The man you seek in not in this area."

Walker nodded. Indeed, he felt foolish to have mistaken the driver for Edwards. The man probably stared around the hotel lobby because of boredom or bemusement at the commotion caused by the surging crowd. Who could blame him?

"Perhaps I should look elsewhere," Walker said to the couple.

"Yes," the man said with a smile that beamed warm approval. "You should check out the ballroom."

"The ballroom," Walker repeated. Yes. That made sense.

What a pleasant couple, Walker thought as he hurried to the ballroom.

FORTY-FIVE

"Let's go," Asia said in a quiet but commanding tone.

Steve looked around. Asia stood a couple feet from the luggage cart, appearing to take no notice of him. A man limped away from Marty and Chandra, who walked toward and past the luggage cart when Asia beckoned. The three of them headed toward the elevator, ignoring Steve completely.

Steve adjusted the garment bag over his shoulder and pushed the luggage cart forward.

So far, so good—no hitches. Asia had been right. No one had recognized him. This might work after all.

The three vampires displayed none of the queasiness Steve felt as the glass elevator rose through the atrium, providing a dizzying view of the floor falling away. Steve leaned back against the elevator wall and stared at the floor light indicator. He let out his breath when it reached thirty-three, and plunged from the confining booth before the others stirred.

Once inside their room, Steve dropped the luggage and threw himself onto one of the couches. "How much time do we have left?"

Marty reached into a vest pocket and pulled out a pocket watch. "It's 8:36."

Steve rubbed his forehead. "The earliest they'll announce the winner is at eleven, when all the polls close on the West Coast."

Asia opened the suitcase. "Then we'd better get moving." She handed Steve a plastic bag and pointed him toward the bathroom.

A few minutes later, he adjusted his coveralls and admired his reflection in the mirror. He tilted his head to view his face from different angles. The ID badge clipped to his jacket proclaimed him as "Maintenance: Dennis Higgins." With his scruffy beard, blonde hair, and dark glasses, maybe no one would associate him with the assassin they've seen on TV.

He peered at the tiny recording devices hidden in his ID badge, his belt buckle, and left coverall button. They looked like just what they were supposed to be. He put on his dark glasses and checked his reflection one last time.

"You're sure these are recording?" he asked Asia as he walked out of the bathroom.

Asia finished tying her shoe and stood up. She had slicked her hair back into a tight bun confined in a hairnet, and the shapeless light blue maid's uniform hid her figure. Yet, even in this disguise, she exuded something that made her hard to resist. Damn vampires.

She pulled out her phone and moved her finger around the screen. "Yes. Have a look."

She handed him the phone. The screen, divided into quarters, showed an image from each camera.

"And it's saving these, of course?" he asked.

"Just waiting for your password to release it."

Marty, dressed in a perfectly fitting suit bearing a "Manager" ID tag, patted him on the back. "So far so good, eh, Steve?"

"I suppose," he replied. "I'm worried that people might not believe you three are mere hotel employees."

Chandra folded her arms across her oversized maid's uniform. "Why wouldn't they?"

Steve shrugged. "It's the good looks. It's the charm. Even if you dressed like homeless bums, it comes across."

Asia gave a slight smile. "And that just might save your sorry ass, Mr. Reporter. By the time anyone realizes that we don't look like your typical hotel workers, we'll be close enough to do our thing."

"And if the guards happen also to be vam—strigoi?"

"Marty has considerable expertise; Chandra, the agility of youth. And I think you'll find that I have fighting skills over and above those of my fellow strigoi."

"The Society of Righteous and Harmonious Fists?"

Asia paused. "How do you know about—"

"It's on your mantle."

She gave him a long look.

Marty coughed politely. "Time is running out, my dear friends."

"Right!" Asia said, as if breaking from a trance. She walked to the hotel door and stood there for a few seconds. "I don't smell anyone in the hallway," she announced. She opened the door and walked out.

Marty followed and held the door for Chandra. He turned to look back at Steve. "Are you coming?"

Steve took a deep breath, grabbed the toolbox, and then stepped into the hallway.

Halfway down the hall, Asia entered a door next to the ice machine. A few seconds later, she emerged with a maid's cart covered in towels and little shampoo bottles.

Steve trailed the others as they followed Asia to a door at the end of the hallway marked "Employees Only." Marty held the door for her, and Asia pushed the cart down a back hallway, past a door marked "Stairs: Emergency Exit," to a large freight elevator.

Their footsteps sounded over-loud on the uncarpeted, unfinished floor, but there was no one to hear them. Asia took out a key ring and inserted a key into the panel. The elevator hummed in response.

"Where did you get that?" Steve asked.

Asia gave him an exasperated look and didn't answer.

No one spoke. The vampires looked completely at ease, but Steve felt a growing tension in his throat, which bounded up another notch at the familiar ding of the elevator.

The doors opened.

Two well-dressed people stood inside—a man and a woman. Not a single muscle in their faces showed a reaction, and sunglasses hid their eyes. Both wore prominent earplugs with curly wires disappearing into their jackets. The woman held a greenpad.

Secret Service. Damn. Steve shifted to a position behind Marty and kept his head averted.

"Good evening!" Marty said. "I assume you are here to protect Mr. Mark, are you not? Can't take a step around here tonight without bumping into one of you."

"Your names, please."

"Of course!" Marty said, radiating charm. "I am Third Assistant Night Manager Albert Brown." He pointed to Chandra and Asia. "May I introduce Kate Jendral and May Washington, and that's Dennis Higgins."

Steve pretended to examine his fingernails as the woman scanned the greenpad for their names. The other agent stood still and kept his focus on the group.

"We need to stay on our schedule," Asia said, using a Japanese accent.

"We appreciate that, ma'am, but we have to follow procedure," the man said.

"Oh, I do hope Mark wins!" Marty said in a hearty voice. "He's such a nice man!"

The male agent smiled, caught himself, and resumed his stoic expression. "Yes, sir."

"I wonder if you both could do us a great favor," Marty said in a warm, mesmerizing tone. "It would make things so much easier for us as we go about our duties."

The two agents looked up. Asia and Chandra stepped forward to flank Marty, but the two agents merely stared at Marty as he continued to speak. "It seems we have a problem. Yes, a most inconvenient problem. We sincerely need you to exit the lift and come closer so I can explain it better."

As the two agents looked at each other, shrugged, and left the elevator, Steve marveled that he felt so little surprise at their response. Had he become that used to working with vampires in such a short time? Being wanted by the police for an assassination attempt certainly changed a man's perspective.

"Ah!" Marty said. "Excellent! You see, it is necessary for you to perform your duties from this very spot and not in the lift. Any people who want to harm Mr. Mark will surely be coming past here, and thus it is imperative that you do not move."

The two agents nodded.

"This plan requires you to *pretend* you are still in the lift, though. Can you do that?"

"Of course, sir," said the male, and his partner nodded emphatically.

"Brilliant! One final thing. To make sure this all works out, if anyone asks, you must say you never saw us. You will keep that secret, won't you?"

"Yes, sir," the woman said. "We can do that."

"I thank you most sincerely, Agents…"

"Agent Christine Norris. And this is Agent William Freeman."

"Excellent. Now we will leave you to your task as we get back to ours." Marty gave a slight bow. "Keep alert, Agents Norris and Freeman."

"Yes, sir!" they said in unison.

Without looking back, Marty walked into the elevator, waited for Steve, Asia and Chandra to enter, and then pushed the button for the forty-second floor.

The doors closed and the elevator hummed into action.

"That was amazing!" Steve said.

Marty smiled and shrugged.

"You could go into a store, take whatever you wanted, and convince them to let you have it for free, couldn't you?"

"Of course not!" Marty said, looking down his nose at Steve. "That would be wrong."

FORTY-SIX

Fox News Report: Presidential Election, *November 2*

HUME: And what's the mood like at Mark's headquarters?
KELLY: Still celebratory. Even after losing Ohio, Florida, and Virginia, the Mark supporters are refusing to show any sign of worry. As you can see, outside in Times Square, they're partying like it's New Year's Eve, and here in the hotel, they're now dancing to the music of—believe it or not—Vampire Weekend.
HUME: Someone there has a sense of humor.

FORTY-SEVEN

The elevator doors opened into a utility room so similar to the one they had left that only the absence of the two agents convinced Steve they had stopped at a different floor. Asia pushed her cart out with such determination that Steve followed without question. When everyone had exited, Asia reached into the elevator and clicked a button, locking the elevator doors open.

The three vampires looked at each other, as if to assure themselves that they were ready. Steve wondered if some sort of mental communication passed between them and frowned at his odd feeling of exclusion.

Asia pushed the maid's cart forward through the large doors and into the forty-second floor hallway.

"Hey! Stop!"

The hallway echoed with the rumble of booted feet as four heavily armed Secret Service agents raced toward them. Hoping not to be seen, Steve kept his head low and shuffled behind Marty's bulky form.

"My word!" Marty said. "Is there a problem, officers?"

"What are you doing here? No one is allowed on this floor," a stern male voice said.

"I assure you we have clearance, good sir," Marty said. "Your colleagues on the elevator already checked with FBI Agent Walker, who is currently patrolling the ballroom."

Marty gave a slight bow and continued before the agents could answer. "I am Albert Brown, the night manager. The rooms have to be cleaned, you know. This is a five-star hotel, after all! And maintenance needs to repair an electrical problem in 4204. I will make sure the work is done as quickly and unobtrusively as possible, I assure you."

Steve stared at his feet. He watched the polished shoes of the agents move around them until they were completely surrounded. If these agents checked with *anyone*, their plan was dead. Even if they disabled these agents, others would thunder onto the scene in minutes.

"Graveyard 417, where are you?" the male voice said, apparently talking into his collar radio device. A few seconds later, he said to his companions, "They're still in the elevator."

Steve swallowed. He had no options. Even with the training Asia had given him, he wouldn't make more than a step or two past these agents if he tried to flee. He felt like a trapped rabbit looking into the eyes of a pack of hungry wolves.

"See? Everything is fine," Marty said. "They checked our identifications and let us by."

After a slight pause, the male voice said "Graveyard 417, did you clear four hotel employees to the forty-second floor?"

Steve's squeezed his fingers around the grip of his toolbox to keep his hands from shaking. What had sounded like a great idea a short time ago now seemed incredibly stupid.

"They have cleared no one," the agent reported. "They haven't even seen any hotel employees." His words were pronounced in an ominous tone, like a funeral director reciting the names of victims of a great disaster. "Each of you, hold your hands out from your body and slowly step away from this device."

"It's my maid's cart," said Asia in her Japanese accent.

"Ma'am, please step away."

Steve slowly and carefully placed the electrician's toolbox he had been carrying on the carpet and held his hands up. If they came any closer and saw his face…

"Well done, gentlemen!" Marty said in voice free of any hint of a British accent. "You did not fall for the trick."

"Sir, if you—"

"I am Agent Lavelle." Marty whipped out an ID, flashed it quickly, and pocketed it again. "The Agency set this up to test your readiness, and your responses were perfect, although, for a second, I feared you would not try to verify my story."

"I—I am not certain I understand, sir."

"This was a security check. Agents Freeman and Norris—as well as any agents you might have contacted on the main floor—were instructed to give you contradictory evidence so that we could ensure that you would react according to instructions, and you did. You all did an excellent job. You should be proud of yourselves."

"This is—"

"What is your name again?"

"Agent Douglas, but—"

When Marty strode up to Agent Douglas, Steve raised his head enough to take a glance. Asia and Chandra stood very close to Marty, each keeping their eyes on individual agents. No one was looking at Steve.

"Agent Douglas, we received a tip, which sounds legitimate, that assassins will make an attempt on Mr. Mark's life from the stairwell." Marty looked into the eyes of each agent in turn. "You four are to stand guard inside the stairwell and keep an eye out for anyone suspicious. Do you understand?"

"But sir—"

"*Do you understand?*"

"Yes, sir."

"Very good. It is imperative that you remain there until notified by another agent. We think they have hacked into our radio system, so you must only obey a command given in person. Furthermore, if anyone contacts you on the radio, you must not reveal that you are anywhere other than here in this hallway. Clear?"

"Yes, sir."

"Your assignment is crucial. You must protect the stairwell while the four of us, in these disguises, patrol the hallway. We will meet up with the other agents on this floor—let's see, that would be Agents…"

"Agents Kondrak and Muth are guarding the door to the Presidential suite," Agent Douglas said. "Batman is in the suite with five of his campaign staff."

Steve bit his lip. Batman? Of all the Secret Service code names, they had chosen Batman?

"Right, right," Marty said. "I had forgotten about Muth. Very good. You understand your orders?"

All four responded in unison. "Yes, sir!"

"Carry on then. This is an important, secret assignment. Be alert! Do not tell anyone that I have asked you to do this, and if anyone inquires about us, all you know is that we are hotel employees who have been cleared for room cleaning and maintenance."

"Yes, sir!"

The four agents trotted to the door marked "stairs." Agent Douglas cautiously opened the door, peeked into the stairwell, and then motioned for the others to follow him. They entered like trained a well-trained SWAT team, one going left, one right, one high, one crouched low. Steve heard calls of "Clear!" as the door closed behind the four.

"Two more to go," Asia said.

"Indeed," Marty said in his normal voice. "But we should be wary. I suspect that Mark has found some way to get strigoi guards."

"How could he get them trained so fast?" Steve asked.

Marty looked puzzled. "What do you mean?"

"It takes years of training to be an agent."

"Oh, Steve," Asia said. "You just watched Marty convince well-trained agents that we are undercover agents ourselves. Don't you think Mark could do the same to get some of his strigoi friends installed as guards?"

"For that matter," Marty said, "since he's obviously planned this thing for years, he could easily have had hand-picked strigoi apply and go through the years of training. After all, what are a few years to one of us?"

Steve licked his lips nervously.

FORTY-EIGHT

ABC Report: Presidential Election Coverage, *November 2*

STEPHANOPOULOS: Let's go to our interactive map. You can watch the numbers grow when I turn the states blue or red. As you know, we just called Pennsylvania for Mark, and Ohio for Finnegan. Finnegan is still ahead at this point.

SAWYER: What does Mark need to pull an upset?

STEPHANOPOULOS: If Mark wins Illinois, Wisconsin, Minnesota, Hawaii and the West Coast—states that are usually reliably Democratic—he'll have two hundred and fifty-five electoral votes, and that's fifteen shy of winning the election. However, every poll in the last two weeks has shown him behind in every other state. Unless he can get Texas—very unlikely, as it is a pretty reliable red state—he'll have to pull out a victory in at least two other states, such as Colorado, Nevada, or New Mexico.

SAWYER: So, if he had won another big state like Ohio, he would be the front-runner right now?

STEPHANOPOULOS: Yes, or if he had won Florida or Virginia. But instead, he's got an uphill battle.

SAWYER: This certainly makes for suspense-filled election.

FORTY-NINE

As he reached the corner, Marty paused and held up his hand. Chandra stopped by his left side, and Asia halted the cart just shy of the corner. Steve waited at her side while Marty cocked his head, as if listening to something only he could hear. Steve held his breath.

Finally, Marty gave them a thumbs up and motioned Asia to go first with her cart.

Their footsteps made no sound on the plush dark blue carpeting of the hallway. Expensive paintings lined the walls, spotlighted by small directional lights in the ceiling. After about fifty feet, the hallway opened into a wider alcove about twelve feet wide and more than twenty feet long.

Steve briefly noted the large potted cacti—live, not artificial on this prestige floor—situated in each corner to the right beside the massive plate-glass window, which offered a stunning vista of brightly lit Times Square forty-two floors below. Then his eyes centered on the end of the passageway, on the dark wood double doors with the ornate golden doorknobs, and—more importantly—on the two solidly built, unsmiling agents standing guard with arms crossed. Though neither twitched a muscle, Steve felt the force of their unwavering attention.

Marty reached out and placed his hand on Asia's shoulders to halt the procession about twenty feet from the guarded doors.

Steve could almost feel the seconds ticking away as the two groups stared at each other. No one moved.

At length, one of the guards reached up and slowly removed his sunglasses, folded them, and slid them into an inside pocket. He patted his jacket to make sure they were secured and then smiled, showing an intimidating array of teeth. "Hello, Marty."

"I didn't expect to meet you here, Ivan," Marty replied.

"It's Agent Jake Muth now. And this is Agent Deidre Kondrak."

The other agent also removed her sunglasses and placed them in her inner pocket. "Nice to meet you," she said without a hint of emotion.

Marty strolled to the front of the cart. "So you're working for him now, are you?"

"He'll accomplish great things," Ivan replied. "Why do you want to stop him?"

"Stop him? What makes you think we want to stop him?"

Ivan grinned. It was not pleasant. "Because I know you, Marty. I know your opinion about one of us gaining too much public attention. I know why you're here. Don't try to convince me you disguised yourselves as hotel staff because you're fans wanting to meet the next President."

"It never works," Asia said, abandoning her fake accent. "Whenever any of us gets that kind of power, it goes to our heads, and then the rest of us have to step in before they expose us all."

"Mark's different," Ivan said. "He's not like that. He knows what he's doing. He's had this planned out for years. You're not going to stop him."

"We just want to talk to him," Marty said. "If you could—"

"Who is *that*?" Deidre—or whatever her real name was—pointed toward Steve, and he felt the onslaught of the guards' sudden attention like physical blows. "He's not one of us."

Steve checked his urge to flee and hoped his recording devices were working properly.

"This is someone who needs to see him," Marty said. "Someone who obviously knows our secret."

"No one is going to see him tonight." Ivan grinned. "He's kind of busy."

Steve took a deep breath and stepped forward. "Just let him know that Steven Edwards is here—"

"Edwards?" Ivan's eyebrows rose. "The assassin? The person everyone is looking for?"

"I'm not an assassin. If you'd just—"

Ivan gleamed. "My career is made! And the publicity Mark will get from this... Perfect!"

Marty took a step. Asia pushed Steve behind the maid's cart and moved into position beside Chandra. All three took a fighting stance.

"There are three of us and two of you," Marty said. "The wiser choice would be the peaceful one I suggested."

Ivan looked at each of his opponents in turn, taking his time. "You do have us outnumbered," he said. "There's something you're forgetting, though." He and Deidre reached inside their jackets. "We've got guns."

Asia whipped the cover off the maid's cart. The white fabric swirled into the air, momentarily blocking Steve's view of the two agents. By the time the cloth settled, Asia, Chandra, and Marty had grabbed their weapons from the cart and whirled to meet their opponents in the center of the alcove.

Asia, a long Japanese sword clutched with both hands, slashed down on Ivan's gun arm. Ivan growled in response. Though blood stained the slit in his clothing, the wound closed as Steve watched.

Before Asia could strike again, Ivan swung his gun at her head. She blocked the blow with her sword, carving another blood-spurting gash on his arm, which splattered the nearby wall with crimson spots. This wound closed as quickly as the first.

Chandra slashed at the other agent with two long knives, but Deidre—smiling smugly at Chandra's obvious inexperience—easily dodged the blows, which brought her right into Marty's range. With a sweeping arc, the baseball bat in his hands smashed into Deidre's back.

The gun flew from Deidre's hands as she fell forward. She tucked her legs, rolled once, and bounced to her feet.

Steve dived for the gun. As he slid across the floor, the rug burned his cheek and hands. He stopped five feet away from his target, feeling foolish.

Chandra grabbed the gun and tossed it over Steve's head far down the hallway. In a lightning move, she leaped to Steve's side, yanked him to his feet, and gave him a look that made it clear he was not to get involved.

Steve jumped behind the cart, cursing at his helplessness. Asia had instructed him to hide during a fight with a strigoi, but it ate away at him. He hated just watching. He had to *do* something.

Eyes locked, Asia and Ivan circled each other. Ivan darted in and swung his gun hand at her head. Asia ducked, fell to one arm, and swept her legs in an arc toward his feet. Ivan jumped, avoiding contact.

Asia bounced back to her feet, her sword before her. She licked her lips and threw herself forward. The sword slashed a line across Ivan's chest. More blood splattered across Asia as Ivan's back hit the wall. He edged his shoulder against the wall and twisted himself to face Asia. The bleeding from his chest had already stopped.

Facing two opponents, Deidre did not fare as well. She easily dodged Marty's unfocused, frantic swings, but this allowed Chandra to slowly slice up her back. Blood covered Chandra's knives. While Deidre's wounds healed quickly, the repeated cutting slowed her.

Steve's attention jolted back to Asia when she slammed back against the cart, pushing it into him. Her sword flew from her grip and tumbled to the floor. She grabbed the bulky cart, lifted it as if it were weightless, and heaved it at Ivan. A trail of travel toiletries and cleaning supplies marked its passage.

Ivan took the force of the plastic and iron cart on one shoulder, then shoved it aside. It landed heavily and rolled slowly toward the other combatants. The distraction gave Asia time to retrieve her sword. Before Ivan recovered himself enough to dodge, she cleanly sliced his calves. As Ivan fell to the floor, he hurled his weapon at Asia. The gun struck her hard against the temple, and she staggered backward.

With his protective cover gone, Steve set his back against the wall. He gazed beyond the fighting toward the door to the Presidential Suite. Was the suite soundproof? Or would Mark send reinforcements?

Deidre jumped. She landed on top of the cart, balanced like a cat, and smirked at the height advantage it gave her.

Marty and Chandra split to circle the cart. Marty swung at Deidre's legs. As Deidre jumped from the cart to avoid him, she kicked Chandra's chest. The younger woman smashed into the wall with the wind knocked out of her.

Steve started to move toward the Suite door. Getting him inside was the whole point of this enterprise. If the door wasn't locked and he could just slip past the others while the battle raged...

Deidre tugged a thick bed sheet off the cart. Whipping it like a towel at a bathhouse, she grabbed both ends and whirled it into a twist. When Marty swung his bat at her, she snapped the sheet and it wrapped around the bat. She gave a yank and the movement of the bat twisted Marty's arms painfully, but he did not let go.

Deidre growled. She tightened her hold on the sheet as she whirled to meet Chandra's lunge. Arching her back, she kicked forward. Her foot cracked into Chandra's face. Chandra's knives went flying as the young strigoi hit the floor hard.

Steve rushed to Chandra's side. Blood gushed from her nose and she lay with eyes closed, unmoving. But her chest rose and fell steadily.

The situation did not look good. Chandra didn't have much experience, but could Marty overcome Deidre without help?

Deidre yanked the sheet and the bat jerked in Marty's hands. He tugged but could not free it.

"Your weapon doesn't seem to be of much use, my lord," Deidre taunted.

Deidre gave the sheet another pull, and the two engaged in a tug-of-war. She adjusted her stance and then abruptly stepped forward. With the tension released, the bat flew backwards and bashed Marty in the shoulder. He laughed off the blow and, holding the bat like a jouster's lance, charged straight at her. When she leaped aside, he sailed past her and slammed into the wall not far from the suite's door.

The impact freed the bat. Marty grinned and swept the bat towards Deirdre's legs. She recovered her balance and jumped. The bat passed harmlessly beneath her.

Steve threw himself forward, grabbed the handles of the cart, and shoved it as hard as he could. Taken by surprise, Deidre landed unsteadily on the moving cart, catapulted backwards over the top, and slammed hard on the floor inches from Steve as the cart zoomed down the hallway, spraying small plastic shampoo bottles everywhere.

As Steve backed away from the mess, a part of his mind hoped that his cameras clearly recorded the gut-wrenching battle between strigoi. This alone would provide undeniable proof of their existence. No humans could live through such punishment.

He knelt beside Chandra. When she moaned but did not rouse, he turned so that the cameras could record the continuing conflict. He wondered what Hannah was making of all this.

As Deidre clambered to her feet, she scooped up a double handful of shampoo bottles and tossed them in Marty's face. Startled, he stumbled back a few steps.

Ivan struggled to his feet. Blood pooled on the carpet beneath him. As unsteady as he looked, he still dodged most of Asia's blows, but her relentless attack drove him back step by step.

Steve's eyes could barely follow the vampires' swift movements.

Asia's whirling blade flashed reflections of the lights from Times Square. Like a ballerina toying with an elderly elephant, she danced around Ivan, avoiding his attempts to hit her with his gun, while occasionally breaking through his guard to slash shallow, quick-healing gashes in his arms. With each renewed onslaught, Ivan retreated toward the suite.

To avoid Marty's blows, Deidre sidled behind the overturned cart. She dodged some blows and blocked others with her arms, but she winced with pain at each block. She could not continue this for long.

Steve felt so useless. With Chandra out of the fight, he longed to do something. On his hands and knees he scuttled past Chandra, scattering the travel-size bottles. Maybe he could provide a distraction by tossing some of them. He'd always had a decent throwing arm.

Steve hurled a shampoo bottle at Deidre, and it hit the side of her head with a solid thump. As she glanced toward Steve, she barely avoided Marty's bat. Grinning, Steve lobbed a cream conditioner at her head.

Deidre edged sideways but only managed two steps. Her foot came down hard on a plastic bottle that slid and burst open, spraying yellow shampoo across the carpet. Deidre's eyes widened and her arms flailed as her feet flew out from under her. She hit the ground hard, smacking her back and head on the gooey carpet.

Smiling like a successful predator, Marty advanced on his fallen opponent.

Steve turned his attention to Ivan. He palmed a shower gel bottle and shot it at Ivan's head. At the unexpected attack, Ivan glanced around, then ran for the corner.

That wasn't going to help him, Steve thought as he readied another missile.

Ivan grabbed a large potted cactus and hurled it, container and all, at Asia. Although she ducked the pot, the cactus spines scraped her face, leaving red streaks across her cheeks.

The pot smashed into the wall, and clay shards skittered across the floor. Asia scooped up a few and threw them at Ivan's head one after the other like a blizzard of Frisbees. He whipped his gun back and forth, shattering each as it reached him.

Steve joined in the assault. He gathered a handful of bottles and, when Asia hurled her last missile, he sent the handful at full force toward Ivan.

The distraction was all Asia needed. She grabbed her sword and closed the distance in a single leap. As Ivan flinched beneath Steve's barrage, she plunged her sword into his heart.

Blood spurted from Ivan's mouth. His gun dropped from limp fingers.

Asia set her foot against his chest and shoved. Ivan slid backward off the blade and collapsed to the floor, his hands pressed against his chest.

Deidre scrambled to her feet as Marty rounded the cart, wielding the bat with its its end aimed toward the center of her chest. Holding her hands in a defensive position, she eyed him warily.

In a lightning movement, Marty charged. He rammed the bat into Deidre's stomach. The blow sent her body backward, but her feet slid forward on the shampoo-slick carpet. As her arms flew to the sides, the points of two blades burst through her chest. Spreading red stains framed the blades. Deidre's eyes glazed and she toppled to the side.

Steve released Chandra's knives as Deidre fell. Blood streamed around the two knife handles that protruded from her back.

Steve rubbed his palms down his pants and glanced from Asia to Marty, breathing heavily.

"Are you all right?" Marty asked.

Steve swallowed. "A bat? You're a vampire and you fought with a bat?"

Marty grinned. "I thought it would be funny."

Steve trembled uncontrollably.

Chandra moaned, and the three came to her side. Asia knelt, gently felt Chandra's skull, and checked her eyes. "Head wound," she said as she rose. "She'll recover."

"What about them?" Steve asked, indicating Deidre and then Ivan with his hand. The two still lay on the floor, gasping and bleeding all over the very expensive carpet. "Will they die?"

"Good Lord, no," Marty said. "They'll be fine in a few hours."

"We need to move," Asia said. "Not much time left before Mark goes down to the party or someone else shows up. We can't wait for Chandra to fully heal."

"And there still are some advisers with Mark," Marty said. "Hopefully, they'll be human."

"I don't think it will be that easy," said a voice down the hallway.

Steve half-turned. A man dressed all in black sauntered toward them. In his left hand, he held the gun that had been tossed away earlier.

But Steve barely noticed the gun. All his attention focused on the familiar, smirking face.

"Karl Weaver," he whispered.

FIFTY

MSNBC Election Night Coverage, *November 2*

MATTHEWS: We're back. As you can see from the video of the Marquis in Times Square, the crowd is celebrating even though Mark remains behind in the early returns. Mark himself is up in the Presidential Suite on the forty-second floor waiting for definitive results before coming down to make either a victory speech or a concession speech.

TODD: And so far, it looks like it will be a concession speech. Finnegan is carrying all of the Midwestern states we have called so far, including the traditional Republican states of Texas and Oklahoma.

MADDOW: No surprise there.

MATTHEWS: The question will be whether Mark can take Colorado—which has become bluer and bluer over the years—and then one other state, such as New Mexico. If that's the case, he'll squeak by, assuming he doesn't lose California, Oregon, Washington, and Hawaii, which isn't likely.

TODD: The fact that he couldn't take a more reliable blue state like Virginia is troubling.

MADDOW: Yes, but Virginia has become more and more purple over the years, whereas Colorado and New Mexico have trended toward blue.

MATTHEWS: I feel like we're discussing art instead of politics! Red and blue and purple! Hah!

MADDOW: I will step out on a limb here and predict that Mark will actually carry it off.

MATTHEWS: Your prediction is sure to be well received by the Mark campaign, which is certainly watching. I'll bet there is a lot of excitement on the forty-second floor right now!

FIFTY-ONE

Asia casually raised her sword. "Karl. What are you doing here?"
Karl tilted his head slightly. "Have we met? I don't believe so. You must be that Chinese woman whose father was the revolutionary." He bowed slightly. "So very pleased to meet you."

Asia ignored his sarcasm. "I can't believe you're working for Mark."

Karl grinned. "I am not working for him. I only work for myself. Sometimes I make alliances when it's in my favor."

"Then what do you want?"

"Steve," Karl replied. "Hand him over and I'll go."

"Don't be ridiculous," Asia said. "You're outnumbered here."

"But I have the gun."

"You won't use it," Steve said. "I've learned that much."

Karl raised an eyebrow.

"You didn't kill Mark. With the rifle you had and the clear shot, you easily could've." Steve waved his hand toward the downed guards. "And they should've used their guns to stop us, but they didn't. You all value the lives of other strigoi too much to kill each other. You fight to disable, not to kill. Maybe you value life more because you live so long. Or maybe because there are so few of you. Whatever the reason, you're not going to shoot and take a chance that you might accidentally kill one of your own in a scuffle."

Karl gave a slow, appreciative nod. "You've learned a lot about us in the past week or so," he said. "But not everything."

Two loud pops echoed in the hallway. Asia's sword thumped onto the floor. Her hands pressed against the hole in her neck. Blood streamed through her fingers. With a strangled cry, Marty fell forward, fingers groping at the center of the blooming red spot on his chest. He toppled to the floor a moment before Asia collapsed.

"Damn," Karl said. "I missed."

Steve's heart pounded so hard he was certain it could be heard in Times Square. He gulped. His mouth worked and then closed. He stared at Asia and Marty on the floor, then raised his horrified gaze to Karl.

"I don't plan to kill *you*, Steve," Karl said. "I need you alive and healthy. But there are more bullets here. A few more to those two and they won't be coming back. So I suggest you cooperate."

As he glared at the blood-slicked floor, Steve's numb mind started working again. His gut clenched.

He flexed his fingers, inhaled a deep breath, and picked up Asia's sword, which he discovered to be surprisingly heavy.

Karl laughed. "Don't be stupid. You have a sword you can hardly hold, I have a gun, and I'm a fucking vampire. Put down the sword and come to me. Nick wants to see you."

"Who's Nick?"

"The man who arranged the assassination. For some reason, he wants to speak to you."

"I'm busy."

"So you refuse?" Karl shook his head and frowned with mock regret. "That's too bad. I was hoping I could avoid doing this."

Keeping the gun trained on Steve, Karl stepped to the side of the hallway, half-turned, and nodded.

Expecting an attack from unseen foes, Steve tensed.

Four figures rounded the corner and walked toward them. Three of them—two women and a heavily bearded man—wore unrelieved black like Karl. The fourth figure, a woman in jeans and a familiar tan shirt, walked unsteadily, supported by the other two women.

"Hannah!"

Karl pointed the gun at Hannah's head. "While you may not believe that I will kill another strigoi, you are well aware that I have no qualms about killing a human."

Hannah had stirred when Steve spoke her name. Her head tilted to the side, exposing the bite marks in her neck. Steve's heart ached. He hadn't foreseen this.

If Karl and his allies had snatched Hannah from Asia's apartment, he wondered if they could have somehow disrupted the video feed. He knew too little to guess if that could be done, but if they had done so, his whole plan lay in shambles. And at that moment, looking at Hannah, he didn't care.

Fuming, he stared at his feet. Hannah had given up so much of her life to help him, a man she hadn't even known.

"Will you let her go if I do?"

Karl beamed. "You're negotiating! Quite brave of you." He tapped a finger against his lips. "I won't need her after Nick speaks with you, so, yes, I agree to your terms. If you cooperate, I'll let her go."

"I have no choice."

"That's right," Karl said. "Now put down that sword and come here."

As Steve slowly set the sword on the floor, escape scenarios played through his mind. None of them would work. All of them would result in Hannah's death.

Karl stepped forward, kicked the sword aside, and grabbed Steve's arm. "Excellent. Zoe, Gregor—get the others."

Steve growled. "That wasn't part of the deal!"

"Which means there are no prohibitions against me taking them."

"But—"

"Your negotiating powers are rather weak right now." Karl smirked. "Nick may want to speak to them, too."

The dark-haired strigoi—Zoe—released Hannah but the blond held her easily alone. Gregor joined Zoe, and they stepped carefully around the mess on the floor.

Both paused and took defensive stances as Chandra rose slowly, unsteadily. Her hair stuck out like wind-tossed hay and blood still dripped from her nose. She grabbed Asia under one arm and Marty under the other and glared at Zoe and Gregor.

Without a word, Chandra started towards them with her burden, then turned at the last second, and dashed at the window. As she threw the combined weight of the three of them against the glass, it shattered, spraying fragments upon the crowd forty-two stories below. Chandra, Asia, and Marty tumbled through the splinters of glass into the open air and vanished from sight.

Steve jerked in Karl's hold and gasped.

"Didn't see that coming," Gregor mumbled.

"You moved too slowly!" Karl spat. "You idiots!"

"Yes, I remember you warning us that we should move fast in case someone suddenly rose up and crashed through the window," Zoe sneered.

Karl's fingers tightened around Steve's arm.

"We do not need them, no?" said Gregor.

Karl snorted, but his grip did not relax. "Let's get on with this."

"Now?" asked the blond strigoi, handing Hannah off to Zoe.

"Now, Candy," Karl agreed.

Karl twisted Steve's arms behind him and held Steve like a vise. Candy leaped toward him, tilted her head, and sank her teeth into his neck.

A sharp pain shot from the puncture but disappeared almost instantly. Steve's eyes blurred. His mind spun like a whirlpool. His limbs felt numb. Energy died within him.

He fought to remain conscious… tried to speak… but no sound came. Then all was darkness.

FIFTY-TWO

Steve became aware of a sound. A muffled sound, like a radio buried under blankets. He turned his head slightly and strained to listen.

"Steve?"

That voice came through clearly—Hannah.

Hannah was alive. And with him. What had happened?

He stirred, tried to open his eyes but failed.

"Can you hear me?"

He struggled to answer but only a strange gurgling sound came from his throat.

"Don't try to talk," Hannah said in a loud whisper. "Just listen. I know it's all kind of hazy right now, but it will come back quickly. That blond bitch bit you. She bit me too."

Anger drove out a little of the haziness. Steve growled and fought to open his eyes.

"I'm all right. You'll be able to open your eyes in a few minutes. Once you start to wake up, you come back to yourself pretty quickly."

Hannah sighed noisily. "I guess there's no point in whispering. They probably have cameras on us. I'm not sure where we are. I was still out of it when they put us here. And I'm not sure how long it's been."

Steve listened to her voice. Although for his sake, she spoke in a soothing, reassuring tone, underneath the fake calm was a very scared Hannah. Steve felt an urge to hug her tightly.

"You'll be getting the feeling back in your arms and legs soon too. They have our arms tied to chairs that have cushioned seats and backs, so it's not too uncomfortable."

Steve blinked and some light filtered in.

"The curtains are closed so I can't tell if it's day or night, but there are lights on in the room. It's a nice big room, too, like the person who owns it is rich."

Steve tried to nod but his muscles didn't obey his wishes.

"There are two other reclining chairs like the ones we're in. They're all set around an oblong glass table. Behind us is a king-size bed with two nighttables, a mirrored dresser, and a highboy that take up maybe half the room.

"There's a big plasma TV on the wall showing the election results, but the sound is turned off. Somebody picked some really ugly artwork for the walls. I see one closet, off to your right.

"They put a couple floor lamps near the door, so it's hard to see the other side of the room clearly in the glare, but the place looks spotless, like nobody ever actually sleeps here...."

"Thank you... for talking... to me," Steve finally managed to say.

"It was as much for myself as you," she admitted.

Steve smiled. Hannah's unfailing frankness brought a breath of normality to this surreal situation. They were alive. Hannah was Hannah. Perhaps he could hope.

He finally forced his eyes open and squinted against the bright light as he waited for his vision to adjust. A glance around the room confirmed the accuracy of Hannah's description.

"I wasn't sure it was you at first," Steve said. "The absence of sarcasm confused me."

Hannah allowed a slight smile but didn't speak.

"I want to thank you again for saving me that day," Steve said. "It's been... quite an adventure."

"You say that like it's over."

"Well, it might be. Nobody knows where we are. When they're done questioning us, they could easily keep us quiet—permanently—with no one the wiser."

Hannah's lips quivered but she remained silent. Regretting that he'd upset her further, Steve changed the subject. "How did they capture you?"

"They walked right into Asia's apartment. Probably got the key from that security guard in the parking garage."

"Hope he's okay."

"Why wouldn't he be? No reason to leave a body or injured man behind when you can convince a person to do whatever you want and forget about it afterwards."

That truth drove a steel spike into Steve's already half-deflated balloon of confidence. Despite the training Asia had given him, he could not hold out long against strigoi pressure. Not even a second if they threatened

Hannah's life again—something they knew well and that accounted for her presence here. His fault. His stupidity.

He would do what he could to get her ought of it, to convince this Nick to let her go.

Nick. Who the hell was Nick? Nick must be one damned powerful vampire if Karl did his bidding.

Steve didn't want to face Nick tied to a chair. He tested the bonds on his wrists and wriggled. Then he stilled. "I have the same clothes on."

He gave Hannah a meaningful look, but she didn't notice.

"So do I," she said. "Odd. You'd think our captors would have prepared a closet's worth of the latest fashions for us to choose from, wouldn't you? Ah well, you'll just have to put up with the blood stains."

He glanced around the room. It might not be bugged, but he didn't want to risk speaking the words outright. "The *same clothes*, Hannah."

For a moment Hannah regarded him like he'd grown a second head. Then her face brightened and, after a quick glance around the room, she nodded. "Um… yes… so do I." She cleared her throat. "Your turn now. How did they capture you?"

"I surrendered."

She stared at him.

"They had a gun to your head."

She bit her lip and fastened her gaze on a hideous pastoral painting on the opposite side of the room. "So what happened?"

Steve gave a brief account of the battle, ending with Chandra's dive through the window.

"Ah, good," Hannah said, returning her gaze to him. "Then they got away."

Steve gaped at her. "I don't think there's a ledge out there for them to land on, Hannah."

She gave him an incredulous look. "Steve. They're *vampires*. They transformed almost as soon as they got outside. Even an injured bat should be able to land someplace and heal up. They're fine, I'm sure."

Steve considered. Was that true? They seemed seriously hurt. He hoped it was true…

"The good thing about all of this is that at least if they do—" His voice caught. "If they do something to me, the plan still worked. There should be enough…"

The door opened and Karl peeked in. "Ah, thought I heard you." He leaned back but kept the door open a crack. "Tell Nick they're awake."

Karl, drink in hand, sauntered into the room and settled himself in one of the seats opposite Hannah and Steve. He swirled the glass around and watched the sloshing of the liquid inside. "Nick will be right in."

"What does he want with me?" Steve asked.

Karl sipped his drink. "Don't know, don't care."

The door opened and two sturdy-looking men walked in. Trained professionals, probably strigoi. One of the men took a position by the door and crossed his arms. The other circled the room and wandered over to Karl's chair. He glanced at Steve and Hannah, frowned, and glared at Karl.

"Nick isn't going to like this. Untie them."

Karl shrugged and placed his drink on the table. He loosened Hannah's restraints first, and then moved over to Steve.

The door opened again as Steve rubbed the soreness from his wrists, but Karl and the guard stood between Steve and the newcomer.

"How are my guests?"

The voice sounded vaguely familiar. Steve shifted but could not see the man. "Are you Nick?"

"You can call me that, I suppose."

When Karl plopped himself down in his seat and the guard walked toward the door, Steve and Hannah finally got a good look at the newcomer.

They both gasped.

Hannah recovered her ability to speak first. "You're... Norman Mark!"

He gave a slight bow. "That is my current Name, yes. My First Name was Nick, though."

"Your First Name?" Steve asked.

"The name I was born with." Mark took the remaining seat and smiled. "Karl and I go way back, and he and some of my old pals still call me Nick. Old habits die hard, I guess."

"What should I call you?" Steve said.

"In about half an hour," Mark said, looking at his watch, "you can call me Mr. President-Elect."

Steve and Hannah exchanged glances.

"Meanwhile, we have some things to settle," Mark said. "Hannah, your kidnapping was none of my doing, and I intend to make it up to you. I've opened an account in your name. One of my assistants will give you the debit card that grants access to it. My staff has already had all charges against you dropped, and I hope that with the money, which is a tidy sum, you can return home to Virginia, pay off all your debts, and live comfortably."

"Are you attempting to buy my silence?"

Mark looked hurt. "No, not at all. It's intended as a thank you for rescuing Steve and as an apology for all that you've been through. I sincerely want to make things right. There are no strings attached. You're free to go. If you want to talk about me being a vampire, I won't stop you. You've been doing it on that web page of yours for years, and it hasn't affected me much. I'm not sure why anyone would take you seriously now when they never did before."

Mark's words must have stunned Hannah as much as they did Steve. She drew in a hitching breath and clasped her fingers together in her lap.

"Karl, Zoe has the card," Mark said. "Would you take Hannah to see her?" He turned back to Hannah. "I took the liberty of arranging for a room at the hotel for you on another floor. I thought that would be more comfortable for you than staying here in my suite. It's a small room, but that was all I was able to arrange on such a short notice."

Hannah glared at Mark. "I'm staying right here. I'm not leaving unless Steve is free to leave, too."

"Come now," Mark said. "Steve can't go anywhere. As soon as he tries to leave, the Secret Service will grab him. He's safe here."

"Safe? *Here*?"

"I assure you no harm will come to him. But you should leave now before you become further involved in all this."

Hannah's jaw dropped. "Further involved? I think it's a bit too late for that now."

"Hannah," Mark said, "I am telling you this for your own good. I suggest you have no further association with Steve. There's no need for this misplaced heroism."

When Hannah crossed her arms and scowled defiantly, Mark left his chair and crossed to hers. Hannah cringed but maintained her resistance. Mark crouched in front of her, touched her hand, and looked into her eyes.

"No!" Steve yelled, but Mark and Hannah ignore him.

"You agree, don't you, Hannah?" Mark said. "You know it's in your best interest."

"Perhaps you're right," Hannah said in a dazed tone.

"Hannah, no!" Steve shouted.

Mark helped Hannah to her feet. "Karl will take you to Zoe."

"Thank you."

"Hannah!"

As she took Karl's arm, Hannah turned to Steve and smiled. "Goodbye."

Mark's powerful hand against Steve's chest prevented him from grabbing at Hannah, and he had to watch helplessly as Hannah blithely left the room with the smarmy Karl.

Steve glared at Mark. "What did you do that for?"

"It's for her own good, Steve."

"She should have been able to make up her own mind about that, not have that decision forced on her."

"People don't always make decisions that are in their own best interest," Mark replied. "Under other circumstances, I would have allowed her to make her own choice, but time is short, and you and I need to talk privately."

"You need to answer some questions first, and then we'll talk," Steve said, thrilled with the possibility of adding an actual admission from Mark's lips to the data he already had. If even one of the recording devices still worked, the truth would come out.

Mark blinked. Then his expression changed immediately, and he smiled as if there was nothing else in the world he would rather do at that moment. "Of course," he said with a wave of the hand. He sat and made himself comfortable. "Ask away."

Steve sat in the chair directly across from him to bring Mark in direct view of the camera. "First of all, what about Hillman?"

"The old guy? No one can find him. But I'll make sure the FBI is called off his tail."

Steve didn't believe that but hoped that Hillman was indeed still in hiding. He pressed on. "Why did you plot your own assassination?"

"Fake assassination."

"Fake?"

"Fake blood, illusion, and props, just like in the movies. Karl just shot a few people near me to make it all seem real. I wasn't going to risk being hit myself, of course."

"But why—"

"Did you see my poll numbers after that? I couldn't buy better publicity. Finnegan even stopped campaigning for a week while I was 'recovering.'" He paused. "I thought for sure it would have gotten me Virginia, though…"

Steve interrupted to pose the question that haunted him the most. "But why did you frame me for it?"

"Don't take it personally. We just needed a scapegoat."

Steve's mouth hung open for a few seconds. "Don't take it personally? Are you fucking kidding me? I could have been killed!"

"That would have been regrettable. Now that I've learned more about you, I find you quite impressive. You've come a long way under difficult circumstances and gained staunch, important allies along the way."

Steve snorted. "So, it might bother you to kill me, but it wouldn't have bothered you if you had picked another scapegoat, would it? Why should it? You killed a Governor, so why balk at killing a nobody? Or a score of nobodies? Do you really think we should have a murderer as our President?"

"You think all your Presidents have been squeaky clean, Steve? That none of them ever did anything wrong? Do you know how many of them cheated on their wives, lied to the American public, stole elections, took bribes, ignored the Constitution?"

"That's not the same thing as murder."

"They murdered innocent soldiers by sending them off to needless wars in order to push their approval ratings up a few points."

"Damn it, just because past presidents did some shady things doesn't mean we shouldn't aim at having an honest president!" Steve said.

"Honesty isn't the most important thing in a President. Think about Carter—he was probably the most honest, ethical President in your lifetime. And he was also one of the least effective. He could hardly get anything through Congress, and that was when it was full of Democrats."

"None of that justifies what you've done…"

Mark put his elbows on the armrests and tented his fingers. "Good intentions alone are not enough, Steve. Good intentions don't get things accomplished. You have to look at things in perspective." He stared off into the distance. "I have lived a very long time. A *very* long time. The United States didn't even exist when I was born. Over the years, human friends I made died much too quickly. I've even loved quite a few, and I mean real love, not just sexual love. But after enough heartbreaks, you learn not to get too attached to individual humans. You instead learn to love all humans—as a species."

Steve crossed his arms, realized he might be blocking the video feed from his button camera, and nonchalantly settled back in his chair.

"I cannot tell you how much evil I have seen over the years, Steve. Wars, genocide—"

"Murder," Steve added.

Mark continued as if he hadn't heard. "—and I have learned, from watching brave humans, that sometimes people have to die in order to achieve a greater good. One person's death can have a meaning for the entire human race that may not be obvious to that one person."

"And you being President is a greater good so that it doesn't matter who has to die for you to accomplish it?" Steve asked. "What kind of ego do you have, anyway?"

"I'm a realist," Mark replied. "I know that having me as President will move our country—and the world—forward by leaps and bounds."

Mark leaned toward Steve. "Think about what I can do, Steve. I can be *very* persuasive. I can root out corruption because I can get people to tell the truth when they don't want to. I can persuade Congress to stop funding wasteful projects, to balance the budget, and to pass progressive legislation that initiates major reforms. The United States can once again take its place as a world leader."

Invigorated by the possibilities, Mark sprang to his feet and paced back and forth in front of Steve. "Imagine what I can accomplish in foreign relations! I can convince countries to make peace with each other, talk dictators into resigning, and help bring human rights and democracy to every section of the globe."

He gave Steve a serious look. "We are on the eve of a New Enlightenment—the next great movement to finally bring this planet out of the dark ages."

Steve snorted. "If you can do all that, why did you need to kill Governor Brunswick? Why didn't you just 'convince' him to resign? The man didn't deserve to die, in any event. And even if he did, you have no right to play God and make that decision."

Mark sat back down. "I can be very persuasive but there *are* limitations. Some people are more resistant than others, and the effectiveness of my influence depends on how much my suggestions vary from the person's natural inclinations and beliefs. I can convince a person of anything, but once he is out of my presence... Well, if a person believes something strongly enough, he will gradually return to his original way of thinking."

He waved a hand in the air. "I could convince someone to choose the swordfish over the salmon with just a suggestion, but if I tried to get a happily married man stop loving his wife, it would be much more difficult—and then later he'd probably fall in love with her all over again."

"You've made your point," Steve said, "and that only makes it worse. I know Brunswick had a strong desire to be President, which would have made persuading him to drop out difficult. But the effect didn't have to last long—only long enough for him to announce he was dropping out. You didn't even try to convince him, did you? You just had him murdered."

"Steve, what if I showed you proof that Brunswick was cheating on his taxes and his wife? That he took bribes from the oil companies? What if I told you that he was a racist and a homophobe who pretended to be liberal in order to get votes, and that he had ordered the murder of one of his opponents years ago when he was young? That he would have ruined this country if he'd become President, and never be brought to justice for any of his crimes?"

Stunned to silence, Steve stared at his hands. He'd heard rumors of Brunswick's infidelity, and there had been some comments that were borderline racist... he had a feeling Mark could produce evidence to support all he claimed.

"Well, then Brunswick should've been charged and arrested."

"Steve, Steve! A man of Brunswick's wealth and connections would never have been charged, would never have faced a judge or jury."

"That still doesn't give any one person the right to take justice into his own hands."

"Let me ask you this. If you could go back in time and kill Hitler when he was young, would you do it in order to prevent all the harm he would cause?"

Steve gave Mark a hard look.

"It's easy to say no to a hypothetical question. But if it were possible, you would do so. Anyone would," Mark said. "Sometimes 'evil'—or at least *illegal*—things need to be performed for the greater good."

"No. Wrong is wrong."

Mark laughed. "So simple your philosophy! I suppose, then, that you believe it would be wrong to, say, combine some quotes in order to bring down an evil politician…"

"Wait a minute—"

"… or steal a car to escape capture by the police."

"That's different."

"Not in the slightest. You did what was needed to expose the truth and prevent a greater injustice—being found guilty of a serious crime you didn't commit. The ends can sometimes justify the means."

"Don't get all Machiavellian on me," Steve said.

Mark laughed again. "What do you know about Machiavelli?"

"I studied him in college."

"Did you read the book that phrase came from?" Mark asked.

Steve leaned back. "No, but I know it's from *The Prince*, the book he wrote giving advice to a nobleman about how to use power."

Mark shook his head. "*The Prince* was a satire. On the surface, a book to advise nobles on how to fool the populace and get away with it, but in truth, intended to expose the terrible way aristocrats treated the commoners."

"Oh, really? And you're some expert on Machiavelli, then?"

"Trust me," Mark said with a smug grin. "There is no greater expert in the world on Machiavelli than I."

"Now you're going to tell me that you knew him or something."

Impish delight lit Mark's face. "I venture to say no one knew him better."

For just a second, Steve looked into Mark's amused eyes. All the pieces fell into place, and he gasped. "Wait! I—you—*you're Machiavelli?*"

Mark gave a slight bow. "Niccolo Machiavelli, at your service. But my friends call me Nick."

Steve found no words.

"I wrote other books too, you know—books that clearly advocated things completely contrary to what's in *The Prince*," Mark said. "I discussed republicanism and checks and balances. I wrote about how those in power used religion to control those beneath them. Yet stupid political science professors continue to ignore the contradictions." He chuckled. "Really—what logic is there in publishing for all to read a book that supposedly gives 'secret' advice to a prince—especially to one who had broken both my arms because of things I had previously written? It never occurs to them that *The Prince* is a satire."

Steve shook his head, trying to take all this in.

"My books proved to be very popular among the American philosophers, such as Jefferson and Franklin," Mark continued. "They used my ideas about republicanism when founding the United States. It's very gratifying that hundreds of years after they were written, my words remained influential."

He gave a very contented sigh. "Think of the beauty of it, Steve! Things have come full circle. In a few months I will take the Oath of Office to obey the Constitution of the United States, a document based on my own writings."

Karl's return spared Steve's dazed mind from trying to formulate a response. With a brief nod at Mark, Karl resumed his seat, picked up his unfinished drink, and took a sip.

Mark continued to watch Steve but his question was aimed at Karl. "Hannah is settled into her room?"

"Zoe took her to the room. She has the debit card and the hotel room key."

Mark nodded. "I'm sure she'll be fine. She's obviously a very resourceful woman."

Anger cleared Steve's mind. He glared at Mark. "You expect me to believe this? How do I know she's even alive?"

"Karl would not lie to me, Steve. He knows the consequences of doing so would be severe." Mark frowned. "As for Hannah, what reason would I have to kill her? She's no threat to the country or to humanity."

"So your killing is purely altruistic? You kill only to help humanity?"

Mark nodded. "Yes. That's what I've been trying to explain. Individuals are important, but the people as a whole are more important."

"Now you're sounding like a communist. Or a fascist."

"Or a Vulcan?" Mark grinned and shook his head. "You know it's true. Even democracies believe that the greater good is more important than the individual. That's why soldiers fight wars. It's why Secret Service agents will die to protect the President." He leaned forward again. "And even you were about to say it could be all right to kill Hitler—or even Brunswick—for the greater good."

"I never said that!"

"But you cannot deny that the world would have been better off with both of them dead."

"Hitler was a mass murderer and Brunswick… I admit that such a man would have made a terrible President, given what you told me about him."

"None of it was true. Brunswick was clean as could be. Completely uncorrupted."

"What?"

Mark smiled. "I was just proving a point."

"But you said—"

"Think a moment, Steve. If one of Hitler's associates had succeeded in killing him, you would not have condemned that man, would you? No, everyone would have proclaimed him a hero. And, while you might not have lifted a weapon against Brunswick, after I gave you a long list of misdeeds, you condemned him as well and even felt relief at his death. The point is that you acknowledge that there are times when the sacrifice of one life is necessary for the greater good."

Steve glared at Mark. Out of the corner of his eye, he could see Karl smirking. "Maybe sometimes a person's death is necessary for the common good. And maybe I've discovered that I am willing to die for my country."

"Just as I said," Mark commented.

"But playing God is wrong. Nobody has that right, not even you." He pointed to his button. "This button is a recording device, and I have others on me. Everything that's been said, everything that's happened, has been streaming to secure sites for the past few hours."

Mark showed no shock, not even hint of surprise or anger. He reached into his pocket, pulled out his greenphone, and began moving his fingers over the screen.

"You can't stop it." Steve smiled triumphantly, though Mark's lack of reaction made him uneasy. "The feed has gone to several sites and back-up sites. Unless I enter the password only I know, everything will be released to the press tomorrow. Your secret will be revealed, along with everything you've done. The whole world will know that vampires exist and that you are one."

Mark continued to look at his phone. "I suppose Asia put you up to this?"

Steve's body tensed. "She helped me, yes," he said slowly.

"She's never liked me, ever since I helped to fund the Europeans against her father," Mark said, eyes still on his phone. "The Europeans were no great lovers of freedom, but compared to the Chinese, they were saints. Asia didn't see it that way, and she can really hold a grudge. I don't think she really wants to expose us so much as she just can't stand the thought of me getting what I want. Ah! Here we go."

He stretched his arm toward Steve and turned his phone for Steve to see.

A video played. With growing dismay, Steve watched Asia slashing at Ivan with her sword in front of the Presidential Suite. Mark turned the phone, tapped it briefly, and swiveled it to face Steve again. This time Marty and Deidre struggled with the bat wrapped in the bed sheet.

"Is this the video you refer to?" Mark asked, settling back into his seat. "The one you made using my operating system? The one you sent to a number of sites where you must input a password every day or the information will be released? Although I wonder about your password choice…" He squinted at the screen. "Kevinphillipsbong?"

Steve wilted in his chair.

"I've been building computers and phones for years, Steve," Mark said. "I know *everything*. I see *everything*. I monitor *everything*. Nothing is secret from me."

"That's—that's illegal."

"No, it isn't. We have a clause in all of our contracts that allows us to monitor usage for customer service and quality. The clause is in that legal release that goes on for pages on your screen which no one ever reads because it would take time away from installing the program."

Steve shook his head and looked down at his feet. All the energy drained from him, as if he had been bitten again and all his lifeblood sucked out. He slowly looked up at Mark. "So what happens to me now?"

"Now you join my administration."

"*What?*"

"I'm quite impressed with you, and I need a human adviser who knows the truth about me. The other humans who work for me don't know my secret, and my strigoi advisers cannot really give me the human point of view."

Steve found his voice. "Are you nuts? I don't want to help you! You're a murdering vampire!"

"I am going to be your next President. My internal polls in Colorado and New Mexico show that."

"Thanks to the fixed voting machines."

Mark frowned. "There are no fixed voting machines. I won this election fair and square. Trust me, if I had fixed the machines, I would not have lost Virginia, Ohio, and Florida. It is far better to enter the White House with a mandate instead of squeaking by on electoral votes like I'm about to do."

Steve blinked. "Well, that's beside the point…"

"Yes, it is," Mark agreed. "I will be President, with or without you. I'd like to have you by my side. I need your advice."

"Why?"

"Because I can trust you to give me your true opinion and to tell me when you think I'm doing something wrong," Mark said. "I am going to do great things, Steve. I've read your blog. I know you support the programs I intend to pursue. Before you found out I'm a vampire, I had your full support, didn't I?"

Steve swallowed. "Well…"

"You've worked with Asia. You've gotten to know us. We're not the evil monsters portrayed in fiction. You know that." He leaned forward. "Work with me. Work for your country."

Steve's resistance was crumbling. Mark had demolished every objection he had raised. He stared at Mark, wondering if he retained his free will or if Mark had exercised some subtle form of persuasion.

"This is a decision you must make," Mark said, as if he could read Steve's mind. "Do not let unreasoning prejudice and inaccurate stereotypes cloud your decision. I could easily use my powers to convince you to join, but then you would be useless to me. I need your real, untainted thoughts. I want you to criticize me when I need it. I have no use for yes men."

"You're forgetting that I'm a wanted assassin."

Mark waved his hand. "That's easy enough to solve. Some of the investigators already question your guilt. We merely have to give them another suspect."

Karl groaned. "You mean we have to find another scapegoat?"

"Oh, no, Karl," Mark replied. "We'll give them the real assassin."

Karl's face reflected utter disbelief.

"It's a simple solution, really," Mark said. "After conducting a long and exciting chase fraught with danger, investigative journalist Steve Edwards discovered that evil, rich executive Karl Weaver tried to kill Norman Mark because he hated Mark's environmental policies."

"You can't do this!" Karl shouted.

Mark continued as if he had not heard. "A quick test of the gun will reveal Karl's fingerprints. Karl will be arrested and will make a full confession, explaining how he planted evidence in Steve's apartment to implicate him."

"Nick!"

"Steve will be proclaimed a hero and I will offer him a position in my administration. He will then write a best-selling book about his adventures and tour the talk show circuit, becoming a celebrity."

"Damn it, Nick! I could sit in jail for decades. I could get the death penalty!"

"I am against the death penalty," Mark said. "And to prove my compassion, I will commute your death sentence. You'll sit in jail for ten years or so and then have a heart attack and die. We'll wheel you out, exchange bodies, and you can create a new Name and start over."

"But my company—!"

"A small price to pay for your failure." Mark leaned back in his chair. "And you were right—I am going to do everything I can to shut down your company for its gross violations of environmental laws. You will lose it anyway."

Karl shook uncontrollably. "Nick, this was your idea. You can't do this to me..."

Mark shook his head. "Don't embarrass yourself, Karl. Go back to your office and wait for the police, will you?"

With jerky movements, Karl pulled himself to his feet. The shaking of his hands splashed his drink down his pants, but he seemed unaware of it. His face frozen in a stricken expression, he shambled from the room.

Mark rose and turned up the sound on the television to reveal music and cheering. Red, white, and blue balloons drifted onto the crowd in the ballroom below. The camera switched to the scene outside. Car horns blared as Times Square erupted in celebration.

"Looks like I'll be giving that victory speech in a few minutes, Steve," Mark said quietly.

Steve stared at the pandemonium on the screen.

"I know your type, Steve. You want to reform the world. That's why you chose the career you love. By joining my team, you can make a real difference. Work with me, Steve."

Steve stood, faced President Norman Mark, and smiled.

ABOUT THE AUTHOR

Michael A. Ventrella writes witty adventure novels like *Big Stick* and the Terin Ostler fantasy series. His short stories have appeared in various magazines and anthologies, including the *Heroes in Hell* series and *The Ministry of Peculiar Occurrences Archives*.

He's edited over a dozen story anthologies, including *Release the Virgins*, *Three Time Travelers Walk Into…*, the *Baker Street Irregulars* series (with *New York Times* Bestselling author Jonathan Maberry), and *Across the Universe* (with Randee Dawn).

His nonfiction books include *How to Argue the Constitution with a Conservative* (with artwork by Pulitzer-Prize-winning cartoonist Darrin Bell), *The Beatles on the Charts*, and two books about The Monkees (cowritten with Mark Arnold).

On his web page (www.MichaelAVentrella.com), he interviews authors and editors and discussing writing while providing samples from all his books and stories.

He lives in the beautiful Pocono Mountains of Pennsylvania with his wife, award-winning dryer lint artist Heidi Hooper, and four spoiled cats.

In his spare time, he is a lawyer.